HAVE YC
Amazon Bestseller!

Glory was nominated for the Best Popular Paperback for Young Adults List by the American Library Association.

"A fantasy on the shoulders of a strong willed girl, *Glory* is not to be missed. 5-stars!" -*Midwest Book Review*

"*Glory* is a well-written, fast-paced novel that sets the stage for other stories in the same universe. O'Branagan introduces supernatural archetypes that slightly twist the usual take on the paranormal, making for an engaging read. Glory's ability to drive her own narrative is reminiscent of *Hunger Games*' Katniss. I would recommend *Glory* to YA readers who crave a little more out of the traditional heroine. Its premise is unique, its world intriguing, and Glory herself has many stories left to tell." -*The Universal Mirror*

"I absolutely loved this book! From the moment I started to read, I was hooked and was not able to put it down until I was finished. The wild ride you are taken on with *Glory* is an exciting one. With a lot of thrills, government conspiracy and a little bit of romance you will finish the book excited for the next installment. I for one cannot wait to get my hands on it." -*YA Novel Reader*

Also by Devin O'Branagan

Glory

Red Hot Property

Red Hot Liberty

Show Dog Sings the Blues

Threshold

With Brave Wings She Flies

Witch Hunt

Witch Hunt: Of the Blood

Of The Blood of Witches

Enjoy!

PRETTY SACRIFICES

Devin O'Branagan

Devin O'Branagan

Cornucopia Creations, Ltd.

Copyright © 2012 by Devin O'Branagan

All rights reserved. No part of this book shall be reproduced or transmitted in any form or by any means: electronic, mechanical, magnetic, photographic, including photocopying, recording, or by any information storage and retrieval system, or otherwise be copied for public or private use without prior written permission.

This book is a work of fiction. Names, characters, places, and incidents are products of the author's imagination or are used fictitiously. Any resemblance to actual events or locales, or any person, living or dead, is entirely coincidental.

ISBN-13: 978-1477497807

ISBN-10: 1477497803

Published by:

Cornucopia Creations, Ltd.

To author J.A. Campbell, who has been such an amazing, supportive friend.

And to all those who continue to fight the good fight against evil. The battle is real.

GLORY

The Templeton Farm – Union, Colorado

I was six years old when my sister, America, was kidnapped. Memories of the last few minutes spent with her still bubble up from the shadows of my subconscious. We shared joy in those final moments, even though I admit to being a total brat.

Perched together in our tree house, I sang "God Bless America" just to bug her. She hated her name, but Dad had a patriotic spirit and it spilled over onto all of us. I was named after the use of glory in "The Battle Hymn of the Republic," and I didn't mind when people sang "*Glory, glory, hallelujah*" to me, but Erica—as she preferred to be called—really did get irritated when teased.

She tossed her head. "You're not bothering me, Glory."

Despite her protestations, the gold flecks in her brown eyes always glowed when she became upset, and they were lit up like fireflies. I never did understand why her eyes did that, but it was a dead giveaway. My own eyes didn't have those cool flecks, nor did my hair shimmer with natural, golden highlights, and my lips never pouted as perfectly as hers. She was special.

"I like being America," she insisted. "It's an important

name and I'm a very important girl, you know."

I knew that. Erica was only a year older than me, but way smarter, more grown up, and everyone liked her better—even our parents. However, I didn't resent her because—truth be told—she was my favorite person too.

Despite my fondness for my sister, I did enjoy watching those golden flecks in her eyes come to life, and so I sang another verse of "God Bless America."

Erica pursed her pretty lips. "I'll show you just how much that doesn't bother me." She climbed down the ladder from the tree house, ran to the tool shed, and ducked inside. A few minutes later she came out wrapped in Dad's new American flag.

Uh, oh. Dad was really going to be mad. He took his flags very seriously.

Erica's right hand clutched a lighted flashlight, and her left hand held one of Dad's car repair manuals. She ran out into the middle of the driveway, posing as the Statue of Liberty with the flashlight raised high and "tablet of law" by her side. "Okay, Glory, sing to me now!"

I stood on the ledge of the tree house, placed my right hand over my heart, and belted out another chorus. I was so intent on my performance that I didn't hear the approaching car until it was upon us. The big black sedan sped up our long dirt driveway in a cloud of dust. I saw Erica's look of panic as she tried to dodge it, but her legs got all tangled in the big flag and she tripped. The car swerved to avoid hitting her, slowed down, doors flew open, men in suits scrambled to pull her into the car, doors slammed shut, the car whipped a sharp U-turn, and when the dust settled, America was gone.

KAIA

The Moonstone Covenstead – Crestone, Colorado

Kaia Moonstone and her family were witches. When Kaia was ten years old, her family bought a rugged one hundred eighty acre spread located in the foothills of the *Sangre de Cristo* mountain range, where they established their covenstead and called it MOONSTONE.

Kaia loved MOONSTONE. Time and space were different here. Similar in feel to where she had lived before in northern Arizona, the world seemed to breathe, and sing, and dance. It was like living in a river of ever-shifting light. Her parents spoke of ley lines and power matrixes, but at ten years of age Kaia didn't know anything about those things. To her, the land was simply alive with consciousness. The breath of the Goddess blew through the pine, aspen, and cottonwood trees whispering endearments, and abundant wildlife engaged Kaia in lively conversation.

The summer afternoon was lazy when Kaia delivered a bowl of red raspberries and blueberries to the albino bear she had befriended. They met in a dream the night before and the bear told her where in the magical forest to meet, adding that she had better not come without treats. Animals were always very clear and unapologetic in their thoughts, and that's why Kaia preferred her psychic interaction with animals to that with people. People's thoughts were anything but simple. She had liked animals more than people from the day that Topaz, a new family cat, conveyed the idea, *I'll consider loving you, but first I have a mouse to kill.* You always knew right where you stood with an animal, be it a cat, or a dog, and now an albino bear who wanted berries.

The bear was huge. If it had its genetically correct coloring, it would have appeared ferocious. However, after it dove into the basketful of berries Kaia placed on a nearby tree stump, it was now a colorfully polka-dotted creature with pink eyes. She couldn't help giggling at the sight of it.

"Did you call me here just for treats, Mr. Berry Bear?" Kaia stood a few feet away, rocking back and forth on her heels, struggling to contain her excitement. She had never been this close to a polka-dot bear.

The bear's gaze shifted from the empty berry basket to meet Kaia's expectant green eyes. When their eyes met, Kaia uttered a little gasp of recognition. "Oh, you're Mr. White Bear's familiar, aren't you?" Mr. White Bear was a Navajo medicine man the family had known in Arizona.

Totem. The word flashed across the clear sky of the bear's mind and Kaia accepted the correction. Of course, a Native American's familiar spirit was a totem.

Why would a medicine man's totem animal seek her out? A sense of unease percolated up through Kaia's excitement. She scanned the woods looking for her parents—she could sense them nearby.

White lightning split the sky, black thunder roared, and Kaia's fear took cover beneath the courage she did her best to summon. Thrusting her chin out defiantly, she said, "If you're trying to frighten me, you'll have to do better than that. My parents are demon hunters and I'm a demon hunter in training. We're tough, we are." She stamped her foot for emphasis, but fear pushed through her boldness. Why would Mr. White Bear's familiar, um, totem, be mean? Mr. White Bear was a *good* medicine man.

The bear stood up on two legs and slowly walked toward Kaia, his movements punctuated by huffing sounds. She didn't sense any ill intent and so stood as still as she could manage, in spite of trembling like a newborn foal. When he was a few inches from her, he leaned down and blew in her face, his breath sweet like berries. Then she noticed sadness in the pink eyes.

"Without the warriors of light, the world would be swallowed by shadows. Never waver in your commitment, no matter what the cost." The words transmitted in Mr. White Bear's voice through Mr. Berry Bear's mind and into Kaia's soul. His thoughts seared her like the lightning, which chose that moment to strike a nearby tree.

As thunder shook the forest, Deirdre Moonstone appeared, racing toward them while shrieking and flailing her arms about frantically. "Get away from my little girl!"

Mr. Berry Bear reached out and caressed Kaia's cheek before he turned away and the forest swallowed him.

Deirdre raced to Kaia's side and crouched to examine her face. "You're bleeding."

Kaia reached up and rubbed her cheek, then sniffed her fingers. "No. It's berry juice. He was a friend."

Kaia's father, Kevin, reached their side. "You're too trusting. Not all animals are good animals."

"What the hell was it?" Deirdre asked.

"It was Mr. White Bear's totem. He wanted to tell me something, but I'm not sure what his thoughts meant. He was real sad." Kaia didn't know how to put into words the underlying warning she had sensed. It was like how sometimes the forest whispered, but she couldn't quite hear the words.

"White Bear? Our friend from the Navajo curio shop in Sedona?" Kevin asked.

Kaia nodded, her red curls bobbing.

Kevin's bushy eyebrows furrowed. "White Bear's a powerful man. I wonder why he came to you instead of us."

"Well, I can talk to animals and you can't," Kaia said, a touch of haughty in her voice. Despite many lectures on the virtue of humility, she was proud that she possessed so many more magical talents than anyone else she knew.

Deirdre dissolved into uncontrollable giggles in a way that made Kaia feel much more mature. Sometimes her mother was downright silly.

"With power comes responsibility," Kevin said, making a mighty effort to stifle his own amusement. "You're a little too impressed with yourself, young lady. We've had this talk before."

Kaia ignored his chiding and accepted the hand that each parent offered. Linked together, the three of them headed back toward their little village. Kevin towered above the trio as the tall, dark, and handsome prince Kaia believed him to be. Deirdre, a tiny pixie-like beauty, was the fairy queen. Since Kaia resembled her mother, she grew up pretending she was a fairy princess. Of course, all those whimsical flights of fancy were grounded by serious discussions about the unique DNA of witches and the commitment their family had made to fight the good fight against evil.

"Speaking of your powers, we need you to stall the storm until after our ceremony tonight," Kevin said.

Kaia smiled. "I love controlling the weather." She liked talking to animals best, then controlling the weather, and finally using her clairvoyance and other psychic abilities. What she didn't like at all was the demon-hunting gift she had inherited. "If I make the storm go away, do I still have to come to the demon hunt tonight?"

Her mother squeezed her hand. "It's important to your training. We'll do the work, but you have to watch and learn."

Tonight they were going to summon and attempt to vanquish the demoness Nyx, who had recently been attacking Moonstone's sister coven, Starlight. Nyx killed that coven's psychic, Bridget, and tried to kill Bridget's infant daughter, Rory.

"Nyx has to be stopped," Kevin said.

Nyx was the most powerful demon her parents had ever hunted and fear traveled from their hearts, down their arms, through their hands, and lodged in Kaia's stomach. Kaia glanced at her parents' wrists. Each wore tattoos of the exquisite Celtic dragon that was the symbol of their magical tradition. Soon Kaia would receive one on her own wrist. The ties that bound them went far beyond blood—their connections were ancient and mysterious and involved an oath to protect the Goddess and Her Creation.

Deirdre pointed to high branches of a towering oak tree. "Oh, look at the mistletoe." She giggled and threw Kevin a provocative glance. "Catch me if you can."

Her parents released Kaia's hands and raced to the tree

that held the sacred mistletoe. Deirdre allowed Kevin to catch her under it and even climbed up on a foot-high outcropping of gnarled roots so that he didn't have to bend too far to capture her lips.

"I love you so much," Kevin murmured between eager kisses.

"I love you more," Deirdre said. Then her silliness quickly surrendered to Kevin's romantic mastery.

Kaia sighed.

The treetops sighed.

Kaia heard a mountain lion perched in a nearby tree sigh.

Everyone in and around Moonstone was getting used to the unabashed passions of Kevin and Deirdre Moonstone, but Kaia thought it was wildly inappropriate. Well, at the very least embarrassing in that special way parents had of mortifying their children. Kaia looked up to study the sky and take her mind off her parents' open display of affection. She hoped someday to be in love like they were, but was determined to restrain herself a bit better than they did. At least in public and especially around her children. Parents. You just couldn't take them anywhere.

As Kaia shifted attention from them and focused more on the incoming summer storm, something about it didn't feel right. She tried to tune into Mother Earth and Father Sky, and there seemed to be a disconnect. She had always understood the wild dance of lightning striking the earth and the passionate moans of thunder to be a form of lovemaking between the earth and the sky. Their very public, wild passion was natural and stimulated the electro-magnetic force field that helped create and sustain life. However, today the interaction felt off. The moans were not of pleasure, but of pain. Something was very wrong.

"Mom? Dad?"

Rolling thunder crushed the sound of Kaia's voice and her parents didn't respond. She took a step in their direction, but a tremendous gust of wind pushed her backwards.

"Mom! Dad!"

Kaia could practically see the words sucked from her mouth and sent skyward. However, she clearly heard the words her father whispered to her mother.

"We're rocking the world, honey. That's how powerful our love is."

"Mom! Da—"

A dazzling young woman appeared at Kaia's side, seemingly manifested from a dust devil the wind had invoked. Flowing hair that shimmered like black satin framed exotic features, and her hypnotic eyes morphed from amber, to gray, then coal black, and back again. Her blood-red lips matched the long cape that whipped around her. She leaned down and the words spoken into Kaia's ear carried on breath that smelled of spiced wine. "I am Nyx."

A scream rose in Kaia, but stuck in her throat.

"I detest being summoned, so I'm here *now*."

Kaia forced the scream, and it cut through the wind to reach her parents.

Deirdre's panic was instant. "Kaia!"

As Kevin and Deirdre turned to rush to her aid, branches of the tree reached out to encircle and imprison them.

"Oh, Kaia." Kevin wrestled in vain against his restraints.

In an instant, the wind died.

Nyx's laugh was throaty. "Funny thing about mistletoe, it's actually a destructive little parasite that eventually kills its host. Much like love itself."

"Run, Kaia." Deirdre said, the terror in her voice thick.

Kaia tried to move, but invisible branches of Nyx's evil had enveloped and rendered her helpless. A fear unlike any she had ever known filled her blood with ice.

"Very nice covenstead you've established here," Nyx said. "However, planning a vanquishing before erecting protective wards was a bit reckless."

"Let our daughter go," Kevin said. "This doesn't concern her."

Nyx reached out and wrapped one of Kaia's curls around her finger. "Oh, this concerns her intimately. I understand that she was born to be a demon hunter too."

"Please?" Deirdre begged.

Nyx yanked hard on Kaia's hair before releasing it. As Kaia winced, Nyx cocked her head. "Oh, that maternal bond is such a mystery to me. Tell you what, Momma Moonstone, let's see whom you really love more. I'll give you a choice. I will let you and your daughter live, but banish your husband to one of my special little hells of endless torment, or you and your husband will die together and I'll send you both to that happy afterlife realm you so quaintly call Summerland. Your daughter will be a sad little orphan, and I promise to never let her rest in peace. Which will it be, Momma Moonstone?"

A cry of anguish escaped Deirdre.

Kaia thought fast—she didn't want her father to suffer. "Aunt Brennan will take care of me, and I'll grow up to be the best demon fighter in the whole world. I'll vanquish Nyx someday. I promise."

Nyx regarded Kaia with a look of amusement, then returned her attention to Deirdre. "You've got thirty seconds to make your choice: your husband or your daughter? Whom do you love more?"

Deirdre stared at Kaia, her face pale as moonlight.

"Tick tock." Nyx's voice was smooth. "You choose, or I'll make the choice for you."

"Send us to Summerland," Deirdre whispered. "I'm so sorry, Kaia. I love you more than you'll ever know."

Kaia broke free of Nyx's invisible grasp and raced toward her parents. The albino bear magically appeared and tackled her moments before an enormous bolt of lightning slammed into the tree that held her parents captive.

Berry Bear tried to cover Kaia's face so she wouldn't witness the execution, but she bit his paw, he jerked it away, and she saw it all. The roar of thunder drowned out her shrieks. She kicked, pummeled, and bit Berry Bear until she was able to squirm out from beneath him. Trembling, she managed to stand tall and proud and face the enemy. "I *will* vanquish you, Nyx."

A slow grin crossed Nyx's face. "Our day will come, little spitfire."

Kaia's hatred exploded and she charged Nyx, but Berry Bear intercepted her. He scooped Kaia up in his arms and raced toward the village.

"I'll vanquish her," she whispered through choking sobs. "If it's the last thing I do."

"Love is everything it's cracked up to be. It really is worth fighting for, being brave for, risking everything for." - Erica Jong

CHAPTER ONE

GLORY

In September, the schools reopened and I enrolled for my senior year. It wasn't the beginning of a new semester, but life itself starting over—at least for those who had survived the pandemic plague.

When the pan-plague had erupted worldwide the previous spring, living stopped and everyone waited to die. Public gatherings ceased, and schools, churches, and most businesses immediately shut their doors. With the nightmare now over, survivors picked up the pieces of a shattered world.

Very few people in my immediate circle knew that my blood had contained the cure for the pan-plague. My mother did, because she injected me with it. The local Catholic priest Father Michael also knew, and he helped me after my mother was kidnapped. He contacted the mysterious Caretakers of the World who assigned a witch, an angel, and a vampire to guard me from the evil forces that tried to kill me. When it was all over and a cure had been manufactured from elements in my blood, I wanted to tell my two best friends Jesse and Carmela about my adventure, but it was so surreal that I was certain they wouldn't believe me anyway. Therefore, I kept my secrets.

Later, it was a decision I regretted more than any other in my life.

* * *

Union was an unremarkable farming community located by an impressive river east of the foothills in northern Colorado. The powerful waters that rushed through Union nourished the land and created an oasis of fertility in the high desert that gave birth to the town. Sometimes, due to the suspended reddish silt in the river, the water looked like blood, so the locals began calling it the Blood Mother River. The river evoked images of a fertile Mother Earth, and New Agers flocked to make Union their home. They began organic farms and created a local tradition of offering the first fruits of their crops to the river. The ritual sacrifice would fill the river with all manner of produce that the local wildlife would snatch up as best they could and presumably wonder at the idiocy of human beings.

Built next to the Blood Mother River was Union High School, an old red brick building that used to be a cannery. It was an ugly giant covered with creeping vines of ivy. When green, the vines gave it character, but when dead, the spindly, barren fingers clutching the building appeared monstrous. The vines had made it through the plague unscathed—somehow surviving without human intervention—and when I arrived for the first day of fall semester, Union High was a welcome sight.

Jesse was waiting for me near the front door, sitting on the landing of the concrete steps. He wore his signature James Dean-style clothes: form-fitting white tee shirt, classic blue jeans, and black boots. The day was too warm for his usual black leather jacket, so he had on the other coat the 1950's movie star had made famous in *Rebel Without a Cause*—a red windbreaker with the collar popped. Jesse, like Jimmy, was a rebel.

I greeted him the way I always used to, by messing up his perfect pompadour hairstyle.

He greeted me like he never before had—he stood, grabbed me in a fierce hug, and wouldn't let go. "God, I've missed you so much." His voice was raw with emotion.

I surrendered to his grasp and tried not to surrender to my tears. "I'm sorry I wasn't up to seeing you sooner," I whispered. "I needed time alone." My dad had died in the pandemic, my mom had melted down, and my mind was blown by the supernatural realities I discovered.

He hugged me even tighter. "I love you, Glory."

I knew he didn't mean it in a romantic sense; we honestly just loved each other. "I love you too, Jesse."

Under normal circumstances, in the old world, the kids swirling around us would have whistled, giggled, and teased. In this new world, a lot of us were hanging on to each other for dear life.

Carmela appeared out of the crowd. "Can I join the lovefest?" She had lost her mother, baby brother, and grandparents in the great tragedy.

Jesse and I each reached out and drew her into our healing embrace.

Our personal homecoming lasted until the bell—a voice that had been silent far too long—summoned us inside to a memorial assembly.

* * *

Union High was haunted and I could feel the souls of the lost hovering around me. Over half of the original students and most of the teachers perished in the pan-plague. We sat in the sparsely populated auditorium and listened to Principal Sanchez—Carmela's father—slowly read aloud the names of the dead. My mind struggled to comprehend the incalculable loss, and I was transported to some other realm where realities overlapped. I saw Emily Jackson, the queen of popularity, her crown melted in the fire of a raging fever. I saw geeky computer whiz Peter Becker's brilliant mind exploded into stardust. Fat and jolly Mrs. McFadden's joy burned out like a star gone nova. With each name spoken, my mind's vision was too vivid to bear. I clutched Jesse's hand, and his strength kept me from becoming lost in the netherworld. On the other side of me, Carmela sobbed and I reached out to her, but uncharacteristically she pushed me away and huddled down in her seat as if trying to hide from the horror of it all.

I wondered why the mortality rates were so high in Colorado, as compared with the rest of the world. My next thought made the connection that the pharmaceutical company that had bioengineered the virus was local. I tried not to think of my mom's unwitting involvement in those events, because her guilt had enveloped us in a death shroud. Squeezing Jesse's hand more tightly, I wanted to tune Principal Sanchez out, to think of other things, but each person who perished deserved my attention, my honor, my prayers. Each individual life was precious beyond measure.

* * *

After the memorial, we went to the cafeteria to register for classes. There were a lot of new students to replace the old ones—kids who came to Union to stay with friends or relatives following the deaths of their parents. Families everywhere were shapeshifting.

Almost none of the teachers had survived, probably because so many children who lost parents gravitated to the school seeking help, and the teachers banded together to try to do what they could. As a result, the entire teaching structure and curriculum had to be revamped.

Principal Sanchez introduced a new teacher, an oddly happy-looking man wearing a tweed sports jacket and matching golf cap. "This is Professor Greenberg, from CU in Boulder. He's agreed to come on board and will be teaching science and math."

The professor tipped his hat to the kids and said, "I promise to rock your world."

Oh, dear, I thought. *Our world's been rocked enough*.

Principal Sanchez then introduced Jesse's parents to the students. All of us who were from Union already knew the quirky couple, but the dubious joy of discovery awaited newcomers. "Mr. and Mrs. James have offered to help us out. Cosmic and Sunshine James will be teaching physical education. We've decided on yoga and tai chi this semester. Ah, our gymnasium was used as a morgue during the crisis and we've made the decision not to use it for the foreseeable future. It has been sealed." He paused and wiped the sweat from his face. "We'll be using a couple of vacant classrooms for the phys ed classes. All sports programs have been cancelled, but students are encouraged to use the tennis and basketball courts when weather allows. Oh, and Mr. and Mrs. James will also be working together to teach the arts."

Sunshine James, decked out in full tie-dyed hippie regalia, greeted everyone with, "And we promise to help you let the sunshine in again."

Carmela groaned. "Great, as long as we don't have to get naked and sing songs from *Hair*."

I smiled. Carmela had lived a sheltered "good Catholic girl" life until she saw the entire cast of the traveling Broadway show *Hair* strip down on stage. "All of them! Live on stage!" she had shouted at me via cell phone. "In the flesh! All that *flesh*!" After that, nothing much shocked her.

I leaned over to whisper in Jesse's ear. "I didn't know your parents were teachers."

He shook his head. "Well, they have questionable degrees obtained from the Berkeley School of Divine Hippie Arts and Sciences. Principal Sanchez has been forced to scrape the bottom of the barrel."

I doubted if there really was a Berkeley School of Divine Hippie Arts and Sciences, but you just never knew about such things. Jesse didn't have a lot of tolerance for his parents' lifestyle, which is why he rebelled by emulating an earlier generation of rebels.

"I'll be taking over Spanish, English, and Social Studies," Principal Sanchez said. "All grades will be combined. We'll do our best to teach given these limitations, and we trust you will all do your best to help us and each other. I'm afraid this is the new normal."

As the harsh realities crashed down, I fought the desire to simply walk away from my senior year and get on with my life. I had decided to become a professional photographer and could do it without the degree. However, part of me understood I needed the grounding and a semblance of normalcy that completing my education would provide—as odd as that final semester might turn out to be. Of course, nothing about my life would ever be normal again.

"Do you smell that?" I asked Carmela. My stomach clenched at a familiar, intoxicating smell.

She tipped her head back and sniffed the air. "Incense?" She leaned into Jesse and took a whiff. "Your parents been burning stuff again?"

He shrugged. "All the time."

I knew this smell, and it wasn't coming from Jesse. We stood in a long line, and people pressed into us from all sides. I stood on toes and strained to see over the heads of the crowd. My heart danced as I realized without any doubt what the smell was...who the smell was.

Then I felt him behind me. Like a needle irresistibly drawn to a magnet, I spun around and there he was. Dominic. My former bodyguard. My former guardian angel. One of two supernatural beings with whom I had fallen in love while on my quest to save the world. Here. Now.

He smiled, the sun broke through the clouds, and my heart took wings. I fell into his arms and inhaled his heavenly scent. Then our lips came together and I was lost.

"Hot damn," Carmela said.

A smattering of applause arose around us.

"Breathing is good, Glory," Jesse said. "Unless you plan to live fast and die young, that is."

I stopped kissing Dominic long enough to catch my breath, then dove in again. When I finally pulled away, my face was wet with tears of joy. "What are you doing here?"

"I'm enrolling for my senior year," he said.

I burst out laughing but stopped when I saw he was serious. Angels didn't enroll in high school. I shook my head. "Excuse me?"

He lowered his voice to a whisper. "A number of us are enrolling." His tone was cautious—careful. He glanced over my shoulder and deep into the crowd.

I followed his gaze. Standing alone was Micah. The crowd had edged away from him, as if it instinctively sensed his malevolence. Micah was a fallen angel who—only a couple months earlier—had tried to kill me. He grinned at me and winked.

My mouth went dry. "Why is your brother here?"

Dominic didn't reply. His eyes shifted to another spot in the room and I looked too. I gasped when I saw the dark-haired beauty with the ruby red lips. It was Nyx. The last time I had seen her, the demoness killed one of my friends. Now, however, she didn't magically manifest out of the mist. She wasn't wearing long flowing robes, but wore Levis and a tight sweater, *and she looked like she belonged.* Her hypnotic gaze and sultry smile reached across the room to capture me.

Every cell in my body heard the battle cry that my adrenaline announced. My fingers morphed into weapons, seized Dominic's arm, and swung him around to face me. "What are they doing here?"

Dominic unpeeled my fingers from their death grip and squeezed my hand. "Later."

This time Jesse said, "Hot damn." He gestured toward Nyx, cleared his throat, and added, "Tell me that's your sister."

"Not my sister," Dominic said.

Jesse ran his hand through his slicked back hair and affected a cocky expression. "No problem. I can handle this one on my own."

"*No.*" My voice was sharp.

Jesse looked at me with surprise. "Why not?"

"I know her. She's not a nice…girl."

A slow grin crossed Jesse's face. "All the better."

Panic caused my heart to gallop and I glanced at Dominic. He reached past me, extending his hand to Jesse. "I'm Dominic, a friend of Glory's."

When Jesse accepted Dominic's hand, a shift occurred that always happened when Dominic touched someone. The divine, peaceful nature of the angel's energy transmitted like a beam of light cutting through the darkness. The smirk instantly left Jesse's face and a softness I had never before seen replaced it.

"Jesse, Glory's best friend."

Dominic smiled. "Oh, you're the one she told me about who has so much class."

Jesse seemed confused, but pleased. "Yeah, I guess so."

Dominic dropped his hand and took Carmela's. Only he didn't shake hers, but kissed it.

Carmela rolled her eyes and giggled. "Wherever did you find this guy, Glory?"

"Nicky helped me find my mom when she was kidnapped."

Jesse and Carmela looked at me with curiosity. They had watched my mother's rescue from kidnappers as it unfolded live on CNN, but I hadn't yet filled them in on the details.

"I don't remember seeing you on the news report," Carmela said to Dominic.

"I was working behind the scenes."

"What are you doing here now?" Jesse asked.

"My family has relocated to Union."

I looked at him with surprise. How is it that a family of angels relocates anywhere? "Is Sasha here? I mean, um, in the flesh?" Sasha was my guardian angel.

He nodded.

"And Rebekah?"

He nodded.

Rebekah was the mothering angel whose family consisted of Dominic, Sasha, and Micah. When we had parted ways two months earlier, Dominic's assignment was to save Micah from Nyx's influence. Apparently, he had failed.

There was so much I wanted to ask Dominic, but we couldn't say much in front of everyone. "So, things haven't gone as you planned?"

Dominic's smile faded and his jaw tensed. "Things are worse than ever. The family troubles have become all out war."

"Family," Jesse said. "Can't live with 'em, can't shoot 'em. It's a mighty challenge."

Jesse had no idea how mighty a challenge this was.

Micah's spine-tingling cackle carried across the room and, despite Dominic's radiant proximity, chilled me to my core.

*   *   *

Dominic was even more attractive than I remembered. His dark eyes simmered, his dark hair shone, and he was beautiful. I had taken many photos of him, but they weren't a true reflection of his appearance. Certainly, it had something to do with the fact that he was an angel.

He stuck close to me throughout registration, signing

up for almost all of the same classes I did. Sasha joined us and signed up for the ones he didn't. It appeared they were determined to be my guardians throughout whatever was about to unfold. Sasha had always been my guardian angel, except for that critical week when the Caretakers of the World sent me on my mission to save humanity. Dominic stood in for Sasha during the crisis. Now the entire family of angels had taken physical form to deal with this new situation. But what was happening? Why had demons come to my town, my school, and back into my life?

When the student body completed their registration, claimed their books, greeted old friends, and introduced themselves to new ones, Principal Sanchez dismissed us for the day with the words, "Although we all now live with sadness, let us try not to live sadly. Tomorrow classes begin. Let it be a new beginning for all of us."

* * *

Jesse dropped Dominic and me off at the end of the long dirt road that led to my house so we could have some private time on the walk.

I took his hand and peace filled me. "What's happening?"

"An angelic war. Nyx, Micah, and the powers they represent weren't satisfied with the billion bodies their evil claimed. Now they want souls."

"Why here?"

"You and what you represent. Your courage saved the world. You're a very bright light. The brighter the light, the more it attracts the darkness."

Panic filled me. "I'll leave then. Let's go. Now."

"It's too late. The battlefield has been chosen. It's here. It's now. Before, the challenge for them was sheer numbers of victims. Now it's down to individuals. This town is their quarry. They're out to turn souls."

I thought about this pool of souls: my friends, their families, my mother. Me. The newcomers to town. All the survivors of the plague. And now evil had come to do something even worse than it had already accomplished?

He squeezed my hand. "How have you been?"

I shook my head at the disconnect. "You just told me Nyx is out to claim souls here. What does it matter how I've been?"

"One step at a time, Glory. I need to know how you've been."

I fought through the panic to find a reply. "Sasha hasn't kept you informed?"

"Sasha's required to keep your secrets."

I nodded. "That's good to know."

He waited.

"Oh, Nicky, I'm still trying to process a billion lives lost. I keep wondering if there was anything I could have done differently, or more quickly, to save more people. I miss my dad horribly—beyond words to describe. My mom, well, Mom's lost to me. She's disappeared into this pit of grief that is so huge...she's just gone. She blames herself for the plague." I thought back to the desperate race for the cure and those assigned to help me. Zane, one of my other guardians during the crisis—a vampire I had also developed romantic feelings for—crossed my mind, and my heart skipped a beat. "I miss Zane. What's become of him, do you know?"

Dominic looked at me and my heartbeat shifted into a different rhythm. The personal consequence of our mission was that I had fallen in love with two of my guardians: one forbidden, and the other, unwise. It had changed me in ways I had yet to fully process.

"Zane is on a quest to try to become human again."

I couldn't help but gasp. "Really? Is that possible?"

Dominic glanced at the sky. "I don't know if it's possible. However, Zane thinks it is, and he is most definitely on a quest."

I wanted to know details, but sensed Dominic would not provide them. Angels were frustratingly secretive. I hoped Zane would find his cure because he was tragically unhappy as a vampire. "Do vampires have guardian angels?"

Dominic shook his head.

Zane believed he lost his soul when he became a vampire, but I couldn't accept that. "So, God *has* forsaken him?"

Dominic gave me a look of surprise. "No, God doesn't forsake anyone. Ever."

I had more questions, but as we neared the farm my dog Hallelujah raced to greet us, her ears laid back, her speed faster than any Australian Shepherd should be able to achieve.

I laughed. "You are the love of Hallie's life. Brace yourself."

When Hallie was close enough, she took a running leap into Dominic's arms. He staggered from the canon ball blow of her forty-five pound body. She squealed, she squirmed, she licked, she howled with joy, she smiled the most beautiful smile I had ever seen cross her face.

Dominic grinned and struggled to hold onto the wiggling mass of lovesick canine. He gave her a gentle kiss and said, "I missed you too, sweetheart."

With that, she surrendered completely to him, went limp, and uttered a deep sigh. I swear I heard her start to purr. Hallie had accompanied me on my quest to save the world. On our journey, she had also fallen in love with Dominic.

As they snuggled, I pondered what it meant to be an angel, a living embodiment of God's love, and yet an individual with hopes, dreams, and personal relationships. I wondered what would happen to Dominic if he lost my soul to the dark side. Or Hallie's. I vowed to do whatever was in my power to prevent that from happening.

However, right now there was a moment of peace to be claimed, and I wanted it. Envying Hallie's obvious contentment, I slipped my arm around Dominic's waist, leaned into him and I, too, started to purr.

* * *

My family farm wasn't a working farm, but every year Dad and I had always planted a vegetable garden together, and there was a huge apple orchard. My dad was an artist and we converted the largest outbuilding into a studio for him. I hadn't gone into the studio since his death, however I did hang the black, paint-spattered sweatshirt he always wore on the front door—where it remained—in honor of his passing. As we passed the door, I faltered.

"Can you tell me where Dad is? How he is?" I asked.

Dominic lowered Hallie to the ground and slipped his arm around me. "Your father loves you. That's all you need to know. In the end, that's all that matters."

Tears spilled from my eyes and drenched my face.

"There was a time when you didn't think much of humans. Have you changed your mind?"

"Loving you helped me to understand why my Father loves all of you so much."

I wiped my face, twisted free of his arm, grabbed his hand, and led him toward the house. "Before we go in, I have to ask what the hell Mom's guardian angel has been up to? Why isn't Mom being helped?"

We stood at the open back door and looked at my mother, who sat at the kitchen table staring blankly into her coffee cup.

"Her guardian is standing behind her whispering words of hope," Dominic said. "We can only do so much."

I had never understood why the angels couldn't do more. It totally frustrated me.

Mom didn't notice us until we stepped inside and I spoke to her. "Hi," I said as brightly as I could manage. "How's your day been?"

She looked up and it seemed to take a moment before recognition crossed her face. "The same as always, I guess." Trembling fingers pushed greasy hair back from her face. I waited for her to ask how I was and greet our guest, but it was too much to hope for.

I directed Dominic to sit at the table and took a seat across from him. Grabbing a bright red apple from a bowl, I polished it on the leg of my jeans.

"Help yourself," I urged Dominic.

He grinned. "I stay away from apples. Eve, the whole Applegate thing."

I was grateful for the laugh. "Mom, this is Dominic. Do you remember meeting him in Georgia? He helped rescue you from the kidnappers."

Mom looked at him and blinked. "I'm sorry. Not really."

He extended his hand to her and she stared at it for a few minutes, seemingly uncertain what to do. So instead of shaking, he took her arm and gave it a gentle squeeze. The power of his touch brought life back into her face and she managed a small smile. "Oh yes. Glory calls you Nicky, right?"

He nodded. "Nice to see you again, Mrs. Templeton."

"Nicky and his family have moved to Union," I said.

"Really? Where are you staying?" she asked.

I looked at him, eager to know that myself.

"Well, ma'am, we haven't found a place yet. It's a small town and there aren't a lot of accommodations."

An idea came to me. "Um, Mom, do you think we could offer them Dad's studio? It has a bathroom and a kitchenette." It would benefit both of us to tear down the flag of mourning that shrouded the building and see life in there again.

An anguished sob escaped Mom, and she shook her head. "Oh, I don't know about that."

Dominic's hand brushed a stream of tears from her face and the warmth of his compassion dried it.

Mom's hand reached to clasp his. It seemed she instinctively knew his touch possessed healing power. "What about Mark's things?"

I didn't want Dad's things to disappear either—they were all we had left of him. I looked at Dominic.

"Do you have a storage shed or an attic?" he asked. "I would be happy to move them."

I thought about it. The attic wasn't used for much except Christmas decorations. It would be nice to have his private belongings in the house. There was unfinished art, his sketchbooks, journals, and pieces of his creative soul. I nodded and looked at Mom.

"She squeezed his hand. "How large is your family?"

"My mother and sister."

"That's a pretty small cabin for three people," she said.

"We would manage nicely."

How many angels could fit on the head of a pin? flashed through my mind.

"Well, I suppose it's the least I can do for you...rescuing me and all." The tone of her voice and heaviness of her sigh echoed her repeated declarations that she wished she had died and never been rescued.

Dominic was good at feeling people's emotions. "I'm glad I was able to help. Glory needs you."

Mom released his hand and slapped the table with sudden fury. "If it hadn't been for me, she would still have a father."

"If it weren't for you, Glory would be dead," Dominic reminded her.

It was true. The company my mother had worked for, Scorpio Pharmaceuticals, created the virus that started the pan-plague and only gave the vaccine she developed to a select group. Mom and her team discovered the conspiracy and developed a cure, but the company destroyed all but one vial of it. She had risked her life to steal that vial and give me the injection.

She looked at me, but it wasn't with love. When she looked at me these days, it was only with pain.

"I wish angels could whisper louder," I mumbled.

A harsh laugh erupted from her. It sounded almost maniacal. "Right. Angels. No angels, Glory. No God. Drive those foolish thoughts out of your head. Hasn't the pandemic taught you anything? There are evil people and bad luck. The only thing I believe in anymore is Hell...and this is it." She stood and stormed from the room.

My eyes flew to Dominic. He watched her leave, but he was looking at something invisible that seemed to trail about a foot behind her. "Whisper louder," he told Mom's guardian angel.

"I'll get the keys to the studio for you and show you the attic," I said.

He closed his eyes for a few moments, then looked at me. "All your father's belongings have been moved."

I glanced up at the ceiling. "That's sure a handy trick."

He shrugged. "There are some things even angels do well."

I knew there were many things angels could do well, but flushed and tried to change my train of thought. Taking a large bite of my apple, I thought about Eve and Applegate, then reminded myself that some of those things were still forbidden.

I stood, grabbed a key ring from the hook by the back door, and stepped out into the bright, fall sunshine. Hallelujah ran up to us with a Border Collie at her side.

"Milton?"

The dog looked frightened—frantic eyes darted and hackles stood at attention.

"What is it, boy?" I knelt down and urged him into my arms. "Milton lives next door at the Baxter farm," I told Dominic.

"Not anymore," a familiar, sultry voice said.

I glanced up and saw Nyx and Micah standing a few feet away. Terror filled me.

"The Baxters have gone," Micah said. "We've taken

over their property."

I struggled to find my voice. "Gone? Where to?"

Nyx shrugged. "I've always believed that humans go where they expect to go when they die."

Terror morphed into horror. "What did you do? The Baxters? The entire family? The kids? No!" Blind with rage, I launched myself toward them—desperate to beat someone to a pulp—but Dominic intercepted me.

Anguish crossed Dominic's face. "Don't do this, Micah. Please come back home and leave this evil behind. Father will forgive you."

Micah snorted. I noticed that the tattoos he wore on his face like war paint had changed over the past couple months. There was a more sinister quality to the designs—Nyx had seared him with her brand. I doubted he would ever repent the choices he had made. I knew how much it hurt Dominic, who still loved him dearly. I had developed an empathic connection with Dominic that was still strong, and I felt his anguish.

A red merle Australian Shepherd puppy stepped out from behind Nyx, baring needlelike teeth at Hallelujah and Milton. Her eerie growl sent shivers up my arms.

"I can send Milton to be with his people if you like or you can take the pathetic creature, but keep him away from our home or else Hex," Nyx's hand gestured to the pup, "will dispatch him with great delight."

There was a moment when all three dogs faced each other, obviously poised for canine chaos, but Dominic uttered a quiet command and Hallelujah and Milton backed down.

I couldn't speak.

"We'll take Milton," Dominic said.

Nyx smiled. "Well, we just wanted to come by and say

hello. We're looking forward to having a real neighborly relationship." She turned and slowly led her minions away, pausing only at one of the apple trees to grab a piece of fruit. As she bit into it, she turned back toward Dominic and winked. "Applegate. Good one, Nicky." Her laugh seemed to shake the world. "Who would have figured an angel with a sense of humor? With what's coming, you're going to need it."

CHAPTER TWO

KAIA

"I'm not giving you breakfast today," Kaia told Annie. "You're old enough now that you need to be hunting for your own food. I'll take you on a field trip and give you another lesson."

Annie's blue eyes reflected a mixture of disappointment and excitement. Kaia knew that Annie had grown accustomed to being spoiled, however she really did love to kill.

Despite the fact that Kaia was a vegetarian, she didn't begrudge Annie's blood-lust. It was natural for a mountain lion.

Annie's mother died a couple months earlier on the grounds of the Moonstone covenstead, and Kaia was raising the orphaned cub until she could fend for herself in the wild.

Kaia added more wood to her fireplace. She had lived alone since turning eighteen earlier that year and loved her cozy, rustic cottage. Even though it was only September, Crestone was at an elevation of 8,000 feet and the specter of winter hovered. The chilly air in the cottage surrendered to the fire, and Kaia breathed a sigh of contentment.

Carefully, Kaia swiveled the fireplace crane out so she

could remove the copper kettle and pour boiling water over the tea bag in her mug. She returned the kettle to the fire, lifted her mug, and inhaled the sweet smells of vanilla and maple. Settling onto a plush floor pillow next to Annie, she sipped her tea and nibbled from a bowl of trail mix. Ever since returning from her mission to protect Glory Templeton and save the world from the deadly pandemic-plague, Kaia had withdrawn from daily interaction with her coven. She now preferred to take her meals alone, work alone, and spend time alone. The horrific events had forever changed her.

"Over a billion people died," she told Annie.

Annie blinked, then flopped over onto her back to offer her belly for petting.

Kaia's fingers accepted the offering. "I'm not doing this for your pleasure," she said. "I'm doing it for mine." With wild animals, a human had to establish and maintain dominance.

After a few moments, Annie's passionate purr dispelled any illusion about who was pleasuring whom.

Kaia thought about sharing with Annie the other devastatingly haunting aspect of her mission—having briefly been possessed by a demon—but realized that might traumatize her. Annie's own mother had been possessed by a demon, an event that led to her grizzly death. Kaia hoped that Annie hadn't witnessed her mother's end, but the cub's memories were hard for her to read. Mountain lions viewed the universe in a decidedly unique manner that Kaia was still trying to decipher.

"Well, like me, you're going to grow up fast, my Little Orphan Annie."

Kaia sipped her tea and thought about her plans for the

day. Besides the hunting lesson, there was a scheduled meeting with the coven elders. She understood it had something to do with the coven's plans for generating income until the Renaissance fairs started up again. The coven members normally traveled the country from one Ren fair to the next selling their crafts and working as performers. Kaia used to work the fairs as a psychic, but didn't want to do that any longer. With all that had happened, she knew the desperation of people would be overwhelming. Her plan was to propose making herself useful as a pet psychic. She much preferred communicating with animals than humans, and people were willing to pay for that service. It was a trade she could develop from the covenstead, inviting clients to bring their pets to her or even just mail a photo. Time and space were irrelevant to a true psychic.

Along those lines, a local Catholic nun from the nearby Carmelite monastery had made an appointment with Kaia to inquire about her missing cat. She was due to arrive soon.

A mecca of spirituality, many people considered Crestone to be the Shambala of the Rockies. The mythical Shambala was the spiritual center of the world, and Crestone had a similar reputation. In the midst of a mountain range called *Sangre de Cristo*—Blood of Christ—Crestone had dozens of spiritual groups of many faiths, including Tibetan and Zen Buddhist, Hindu, Christian, Native American, and Pagan. In Crestone, there was no conflict between those of different faiths, so Kaia had not been surprised when Sister Colette contacted her.

The nun arrived at the appointed time, wearing a full-length black and white habit and a smile that was polite, but fearful. Kaia had seen that expression many times on people coming for psychic consultations. They wanted to know the truth, but really didn't want to face it.

Kaia ushered her inside the cottage, and directed her to the small, round bistro table that one of Moonstone's artisans had made for her. The top of the red oak table was inlaid with crystals and semi-precious stones. It served as a place to eat and a place to work, and fit perfectly in the small kitchen nook—a south-facing alcove surrounded on three sides by windows. Comforting sunlight streamed through the glass.

"I only know you through the notes we've exchanged," Sister Colette said with a slight French-Canadian accent. "I'm afraid I don't know how to pronounce your name."

"Ki-ya. It means, 'of the earth.'" Kaia sat down at the table across from her. "As a nun, I imagine you've taken the name of a saint?"

"Saint Colette helps sick children and women trying to conceive."

"I'm sure she's had her hands full with sick children of late, and I imagine many women who lost their children will want to conceive again."

Colette nodded. "I imagine."

"Would you like some tea?" Kaia asked.

"Thank you, no."

Kaia noticed a slight tremble in the nun's voice and tried to think of more to say to put her at ease before getting to the business at hand. "You're so young. Have you been a nun long?"

"I'm not so young, really. I've been a nun for fifteen years now." Her bright brown eyes swept Kaia's face. "You, on the other hand, are a mere babe. How long have you been a witch?"

Kaia smiled. "I was born a witch."

"Ah, I see. Well, not really, but I try." She looked down and laughed, then sighed.

From her bed by the fire, Annie uttered a squeak of sorts that Kaia knew was a demand for attention, and Colette noticed her for the first time. "Mountain lion cub?"

"She was orphaned. I'm raising her until she's ready to be set free."

"Her eyes are such a lovely pale blue."

"They'll change to a yellowish-brown by the time she's a year old."

Colette managed a sad smile. "My Topaz has yellow-brown eyes." She pulled a small photograph of a calico cat from her pocket and with seeming reluctance laid it on the table. "I fear I know, but I need to confirm. She disappeared a week ago."

"Topaz? When I was a child we had a cat with the same name." Kaia glanced at the photo and immediately saw what the woman needed to hear, but wasn't sure how best to say it. "Our Topaz wasn't nearly as beautiful as yours was."

Colette smiled. "I've had her since she was a tiny kitten."

Kaia centered herself and tuned more deeply into the spirit of the image. "She had a wonderful life and loved you very much."

A sharp intake of breath signaled Colette's understanding of Kaia's use of the past tense. After a few moments of shocked silence, she asked, "Did she suffer?"

"An owl took her. It was swift and merciful. Her last thoughts were of you."

Colette was unsuccessful at holding back her tears. Kaia had already placed a box of Kleenex on the table—the nun grasped a handful of tissues and buried her face for a time.

Kaia waited and surrounded the woman in a healing, golden light.

When she could speak, Colette said, "I'm taught that God knows each sparrow that falls. If that's true, why doesn't He catch them?"

"I've helped many animals cross over, and Spirit *is* there to catch them. They are often pulled from their bodies before death to minimize their suffering. They're comforted. It's the cycle of life, Colette. Animals don't murder, they kill to survive. It's the grand design."

"Oh God," Colette murmured.

"I'm sorry for your pain," Kaia said.

"She was like my child."

Kaia glanced at Annie. "With love, there's always loss. It's the price we pay for the gift of that love."

"I think of all that's happened in the last year, and I question my faith."

Kaia understood how fragile the world had become because of the great tragedy and feared the loss of even one of the light workers. Her mind scrambled to think of a way to save this one. "I don't know your religion very well, but didn't I read something in the Bible like 'the entire world travails in pain awaiting the manifestation of the sons of God?'"

Colette peeked out from behind the huge wad of Kleenex. "Yes, something to that effect."

"What do you do? I mean, what does a Carmelite nun *do* exactly?"

"Pray. Practice contemplation. We're committed to

being conduits, or channels, for God's love to pour into the world."

Kaia's mind probed hers. "Didn't I read about a scientific study which proved that the brains of Carmelite nuns in contemplation actually tuned into frequencies not accessed by ordinary brains."

Colette sat up straighter. "Actually, I was part of that study."

"So, you really do channel a higher frequency. You really are a conduit for spiritual energy to come into this world." She grasped Colette's hand. "Do you understand how important that is right now? Do you have any clue what's really going on in the battle between good and evil?" It was now Kaia who trembled. "Please don't lose your faith. We all need it now more than ever. 'The whole creation travails in pain awaiting the manifestation of the sons of God.' Manifest that. Take away the suffering. Your God needs you to do the work. Do you understand?"

Kaia had broken a sweat with her tirade and, for a moment, feared she had taken it too far. However, Colette's suddenly dry eyes were now regarding her with a fire in them that matched Kaia's own.

"Of course," Colette murmured. "Of course." She glanced down at the photograph of Topaz. "Will you tell my baby how much I loved her? How much I'll always love her?"

"She knows," Kaia said.

The two women stared at each other for a long time.

"What does a witch do, besides be psychic?" Colette asked.

"I've taken vows to fight the good fight against evil. Your vows are to God, mine are to Mother Earth."

Colette nodded. "Fascinating." She reached into her pocket, pulled out an envelope, and placed it in the middle of the table. "Your note said the fee for your services was a donation of whatever I felt was fair. I don't think this even comes close to what I owe you for what you've given me today."

"May the High Goddess protect and keep you," Kaia said in parting.

Colette smiled. "And may God bless and keep you, Kaia Moonstone."

* * *

The oversoul of the forest seemed to be paying attention to the hunting lesson Kaia was giving Annie. An air of expectancy surrounded them as she explained the rules to Annie, both verbally and psychically.

She crouched and looked into Annie's eyes. "All creatures have feelings just like yours. So, when you kill don't play with your prey or do anything to deliberately terrorize it." Kaia paused as she tried to convey her words as images the razor-sharp mountain lion mind could comprehend. "Kill fast and fair. Release the soul quickly with a strong bite at the base of the skull—break the neck. While you're young, you can kill rodents, birds, rabbits, squirrels, but I don't want you to kill any of your own relatives...especially cats. And when you grow up and move on to larger game like deer, I still want you to *never* kill any cats." Kaia was surprised at her own sentimentality—she was usually quite pragmatic about such things. However, she couldn't shake Colette's pain about Topaz. She wavered for just a minute, but then held fast to her resolve. "And never, ever, are you to kill humans. Do you understand?"

Annie blinked and Kaia felt the lion's impatience to get on with the hunt.

"Do you understand me, Annie?"

Annie understood but was trying to decide if she agreed.

Someone shouting Kaia's name broke the stalemate.

"Kaia! Kaia, where are you?"

"Damn." The coven knew she was having a training session. Who would be so inconsiderate as to intrude? "Over here!"

Annie started to wander off, but Kaia called her back. "Sorry, Annie. I know you're hungry and itching for a kill, but the game's probably been scared off now. We'll have to try again tomorrow."

Annie gave her a dirty look.

"Don't be so pitiful. I have some fresh venison at home."

Annie plopped down and rolled over to accept an apologetic belly rub. Despite her irritation, Kaia had to laugh at her very spoiled child. "I know you're letting me pet your belly because you trust me, but if you expose your belly after you've returned to the wild, you're dead meat. So, add that nugget of wisdom to what I'm teaching you."

Kaia was indulging Annie when a young girl crashed through the underbrush and entered the clearing. It was Rory, the twelve-year-old psychic from the Starlight coven in Georgia.

Kaia greeted her with, "What the hell?"

Rory rushed to Kaia, knelt, and gave her a clumsy embrace. "Omigods, I'm so glad to see you're still okay."

Kaia drew back and studied Rory's flushed face.

"Why wouldn't I be? What are you doing here? How did you get here? What's going on?"

Breathless, Rory readjusted her funky cool horn-rimmed glasses, pushed long tendrils of hair up into the casual bun she wore on top of her head, and then sat back on her heels. "I had a vision," she said in her soft, Southern drawl. "You're going to die." Rory had never been one to mince words. And her visions always came true.

Startled, Kaia had no idea how to respond.

"Since you live off the grid, I couldn't call or email, and every time I tried to connect with you psychically I got intercepted by this new obsession of yours." She poked Annie. "You really have merged with her. When I got a connection, instead of psychic static I got purring." She paused to give the mountain lion the evil eye. "So Evan drove me. We drove straight through from Atlanta."

Kaia's heart raced much more quickly at mention of Evan than news of her own predicted death. "Evan's here?"

Rory pursed her pretty lips. "I just said you're going to die and all you care about is if Evan's here? I swear, sweetie. And you refused to believe that I saw the two of you married someday? This just proves that I'm totally great at what I do. Only right now I wish I weren't."

When Rory had predicted a marriage between Kaia and Evan, the elders of both covens jumped on the idea with gusto and arranged the marriage—a medieval concept that Kaia adamantly rejected. It was a source of contention for all involved.

"Hah! If I die, that proves your marriage prediction wrong," Kaia said testily, and with a hint of smug satisfaction. "What do you think about that, little Miss

Totally Great at What She Does Psychic?"

Rory grabbed Kaia by her shoulders and shook her like a mad woman. "Get a grip. We're not talking about the dreaded arranged marriage here. Something's changed. You are going to die."

Kaia had heard her the first time, but was just trying to process the words. "How?"

"I think it has something to do with Glory."

"I haven't spoken to Glory since we left Savannah months ago."

A hush fell over the witches. A hush fell over the forest. Annie's tongue reached out and gave Kaia's hand an uncharacteristically affectionate lick.

Kaia had never felt her business with Glory was finished. "Can we prevent it?"

Rory shook her head. Her expression was miserable. "I don't think so. There's a quality about it that seems so fated."

"When?"

"I can't get a fix. There's something screwy about the timeline. It's all tangled. I've never encountered anything like it before."

Kaia took in a deep breath.

The forest exhaled.

And in that instant, Kaia knew with complete and utter certainty that she was going to die.

CHAPTER THREE

When I showed up for the first day of classes, the ivy hugging the school had already begun to die—I felt it knew that evil had invaded its home. I wondered how long it would take before the last leaf fell, and I took a photograph to record its slow decent into death.

Dominic watched me.

"Wouldn't you and Sasha being here offset the presence of Nyx and Micah?" I asked.

"The metaphysics of it is complicated," he said. "The influence of angels is on humans. We inspire higher and nobler states in humans. Demons can directly wreak havoc on anything in their environment, human or otherwise."

It was a bit too complex for me to process.

I glanced across the front yard of the school and noticed a new boy I hadn't seen before picking through a trash can. He pulled out a crumpled paper bag, peered inside, withdrew what appeared to be a half-eaten sandwich, and stuffed it in his mouth.

"Oh, how awful," I whispered, and despite the fact I should have respected the privacy of his humiliation, I grabbed my camera and shot pictures.

Dominic looked at the boy. "Post-apocalyptic survival techniques. This is a small town and pretty isolated. You should see what's going on in the cities." He shook his head. "No, actually you shouldn't see that at all."

I knew that life insurance companies had been unable to pay out claims and folded like houses of useless cards. I knew the unemployment rate was over fifty percent because businesses closed due to lack of live business owners. National food and supply distribution systems had broken down. The governments of the world were virtually useless in their ability to offer aid, their energy and resources more focused on quelling civil unrest.

Mom and I were relatively comfortable because the farm had been paid off years earlier, and Dad always made sure we had a well-stocked pantry and well-funded bank account. We stopped following the news because it was just too depressing, and I hadn't given much thought to the hunger or desperation that was the aftermath of the great tragedy.

I spied Principal Sanchez getting out of his car and rushed to intercept him. He looked at me with red, puffy eyes. He had lost his wife, parents, and infant son, and despite how hard he tried to be a good example to the students, his grief was poorly disguised.

"Good morning, Glory." His voice was weary. "What do you need?"

"Well, I wondered about the school lunch program. Will there be hot lunches, and have arrangements been made for kids who can't afford to pay?"

His chuckle was mirthless. "No and no. The kids are just going to have to fend for themselves."

I shoved my camera in his face and showed him the images I had just taken.

He sucked in air. "Oh dear."

"Look, my car is full of bushels of apples I was going to sell at the farmers market after school. How about if I put them in the cafeteria for kids who don't have anything to eat today?"

He regarded me with a surprised expression. "That's very kind of you."

I glanced at the river. "And how about if you start a class for fishing, and the fish that are caught be cooked up for the cafeteria? I mean, I know it's unorthodox and everything, but the river runs right by the school and is just loaded with all kinds of fish. And the school could start a cooking class to cover that one—you know, offer home econ credit. I'm sure Jesse's mom would love to take that over 'cause she fancies herself a gourmet cook." I was shooting from the hip here, but needed to try.

Principal Sanchez appeared thoughtful. "With all the local farmers, I'm sure we could put out a call for donations. The harvest is good this season. Maybe instead of sacrificing the first fruits to the Blood Mother River in the annual ritual, they could offer it to the schools."

"I know the home ec department has food dehydrators, and there's lots of freezer space in the kitchen," I said. "We could start putting away a store of food to carry us through winter."

"And when hunting season begins, I'm sure we could get some donations," Principal Sanchez said. "Hell, I bag an elk and a deer every year myself."

"We could make the food go further if we focus on making soup," I said. "Family legend holds that my great-grandma, who was an elementary school teacher during the Great Depression, made a pot of soup every day in class for her students. For many it was the only meal they had. I'm told she saved lives."

"Saving lives," Principal Sanchez said, a rare smile touching his lips. "Oh, yes, anything we can do to save lives." He broke all PC protocol and swept me up in an exuberant hug. "Thank you. What inspired ideas. I'll get right on organizing this, and I'll talk to Principal Murphy over at the elementary school about a joint effort. Maybe she can organize some field trips for her kids to go to the public areas round town and pick berries, grapes, wild asparagus, and such. I've noticed rhubarb growing like crazy over at Union Park. There are pear trees there too. Do you need help getting the apples inside?"

I laughed at his enthusiasm.

Dominic was behind me. "I'll take care of it."

Principal Sanchez's enthusiasm grew. "And my cousin has a pinto bean farm. He usually sells me a twenty-five pound bag of beans for ten bucks—" He juggled his armload of files and dug in his pocket, found his wallet, flipped it open, and examined his money. "Hey I've got forty bucks on hand and I know there are a couple of twenties on my dresser at home. That's two hundred pounds of beans we could stash in the cafeteria's pantry."

I found a twenty in my purse and handed it over.

Dominic slapped a thick wad of green bills into his hand as well.

Principal Sanchez examined the money with a look of wonder. "The children won't die," he whispered. "No more children will die." The man headed to his office with a bounce in his step I hadn't seen since before the pandemic.

I turned and looked at Dominic. "Thank you."

"For what?"

"Well, didn't you just tell me that angels inspired humans? Didn't you put those ideas in our heads?"

He smiled his radiant smile. "Sometimes noble ideas have nothing at all to do with angels."

As we headed inside, I noticed that the ivy seemed to

have perked up a bit and I felt a glimmer of understanding about the metaphysics of it all.

* * *

One of the largest classrooms had been cleared of all furniture and the floor covered with half-inch thick foam mats. This morning it was scheduled to be used for a girls' yoga class. Most of us dressed in sweat suits, but a few showed up in leotards, a couple in shorts, and several just wore jeans. We were a motley crew. The students were from all grade levels, including a few pre-school darlings who had come to school with sisters and—in the case of Belle Starr James—her mother, Sunshine. The daycare centers had closed due to the lack of anyone to run them, and so toddlers now attended school and/or work with relatives. Yet another aspect of the new normal.

Their parents had named Jesse and Belle Starr after outlaws of the Old West—no one knew why. (I thought it might have been as a form of rebellion against their own parents who were second-generation hippies. As I had once explained to Dominic, it was an ancient human tradition for children to rebel against parents.) Jesse had said that he was just grateful he and his little four-year-old sister hadn't been named Patchouli and Honeysuckle. (Although I, personally, thought Honeysuckle would have been a cute name for Belle Starr—she was just so blond and sweet. And if Jesse had been named Patchouli, I would have called him Patch. For inexplicable reasons my mind often pondered alternate realities.)

Sunshine James' own name worked well for her—she was usually annoyingly cheerful, and today was no exception. The CD she chose to play in the background was the meditative mantra OM, chanted on top of a pan-flute rendition of the Beatles' song, "Here Comes the Sun." It was all very yogaish.

"Today we will learn the Sun Salutation," Sunshine said. "It's comprised of a flowing series of twelve poses that will stretch your spine, move the prana, and balance those chakras. So, everyone stand up and follow my lead."

I chose a mat at the back of the room with Carmela on one side of me and Sasha on the other side. Sasha's human form was beautiful—I would have expected no less from an angel. Long black hair fell in curls around a perfectly sculptured face, and her silver eyes seemed outlined by faint eyeliner—although closer inspection revealed only thick eyelashes. And she smelled like jasmine. It wasn't perfume, but as with Dominic's scent of incense, seemed part of her aura—her essence. Carmela, on the other hand, had hardened her look over the summer—super short hair, skin-tight black clothing, and plum lipstick. She was still lovely, but harsh. I attributed the change to her grief.

"Stupid hippie dippy hokum," Carmela muttered, as she stood, and bent forward, and stretched out on the floor, and bent backwards, and did her clumsy, uncoordinated best to emulate the twelve "flowing" movements.

"Hippie dippy," Belle Starr echoed.

I hadn't noticed that the tiny girl had slipped in between Carmela and me.

"Hokum," Belle Starr said, and then dissolved into uncontrollable giggles.

"Hush," I whispered, looking around nervously for a

sign of Sunshine. For all her perkiness, Sunshine did have a nasty temper that I didn't want to experience today.

"Hippie dippy hokum," Belle Starr whispered, then reached out and grabbed me, knocking me off my feet.

I fell onto the mat and wrapped my arms around Belle Starr, burying my face in her soft belly to try to stifle my own giggles.

Belle Starr lifted my face so I could look at hers, then covered it with gentle kisses. Her sweet breath and tender ministrations warmed me in a way that no amount of sunshine could do. A thrill of gratitude struck me that this little bundle of precious love had not succumbed to the great tragedy.

"Thank you, God," I whispered.

"Thank you, God," Belle Starr echoed.

I hugged her fiercely. Then I glanced across the room and noticed that Nyx was watching us with a greedy expression.

* * *

Carmela and I took our time showering and getting ready for our next class. I had previously learned from Dominic that angels didn't need to bathe. In human form, they recreated their body every moment and so Sasha just sat with us in the locker room doing, I presume, her guardian angel thing. Unlike Dominic, she didn't talk much. I longed to get to know her better.

Carmela and I stood side-by-side at the wall mirror—she reapplied plum lipstick, while I touched up my lip gloss. As I always liked to say, I was a no muss, no fuss kind of gal. My hair was wash-and-wear, and I didn't use any makeup except a touch of clear gloss on my naturally rosy lips. I found it easy to be me.

"So, are you still a virgin, or did that hunky Nicky fellow finally wear down your resolve?" Carmela asked.

Carmela's blunt style never offended me. "Still a virgin," I said. "How about you?"

"Technically yes, but my love nest has been shared."

I blinked in confusion.

"I discovered I'm a lesbian. Always thought so, but was afraid to find out for sure. Then when it seemed like time was running out to discover much of anything, I dove in and, well, I'm in love."

My blinking increased rapidly as I assimilated. I felt like Seven of Nine from *Star Trek Voyager* processing a new world of information from my collective. "Who's the lucky girl?"

"TNT."

I gasped. "Tina Nancy Turner?" TNT was the head cheerleader and most desirable girl on campus. Hell, I would have gone for her if I were gay.

Carmela grinned and winked at me in the mirror.

"Congratulations," I said. "Great catch."

Carmela nodded.

"I haven't seen her around," I said. "Where is she?"

"They finally found the remains of her uncle. He lived alone in Denver and died in the plague as a John Doe so it took a while to identify him. The family's gone to bury him, but she should be back today."

"I'm sorry for her loss," I said, my words sounding hollow. Then I realized that in the chaos of my life, I had never offered Carmela proper condolences. "I'm so sorry for your loss too."

Out of the blue, a storm of hurricane proportions twisted Carmela's features, and an unexpected sob escaped its eye.

"My heart stopped. "What is it?"

She bit her fist, then slammed it into the mirror, moving as fast as a snake strike. I grabbed her wrist before she could do it again, and swung her around to face me. Her agony was so sudden and intense I was at a loss as to what to do, so I threw my arms around her and drew her close.

"Talk to me, Carmela," I whispered. "Whatever it is." I had never seen her like this. This was more than simple grief.

"The new priest said my family dying was God's punishment for me being gay."

I couldn't comprehend such a pronouncement by a man of God, and shock short-circuited my brain. The nice Catholic priest Father Michael—who helped me during the pandemic—had been reassigned to a different parish, but I knew nothing about the priest who replaced him. I shook my head in confusion. "What?"

"Father Hans said it was my fault because of my sin. He's forbidden me to even go to church now." A mighty sob escaped her. "Oh, Glory. Is it my fault my family died?"

"Of course not." My trembling of rage matched Carmela's trembling of guilt-laced grief, so I was grateful when Sasha stood and embraced us both.

"Your Father Hans is wrong," Sasha said.

Whether it was her angelic touch or the power of her authoritative words, I wasn't sure, but the storm dissipated in an instant. Carmela slumped into our arms and we led her to a nearby bench. Sasha sat next to her, tipped Carmela's head onto her shoulder, and said, "All God wants from any of us is love. To love Him, and to love each other. Never, ever would God punish anyone for loving."

Carmela used the back of her hand to wipe her tears. "Thank you. I pray you're right. I do miss my church though. So much. I need it now more than ever."

I looked at Sasha with pleading eyes. *Can't you do something? You've got connections at the top,* my mind implored.

Sasha answered me with a subtle shake of her head. There were just some things in which angels weren't permitted to interfere. Ironically, human religion was one of them.

* * *

Professor Greenberg was disconcertingly likable. He had an easy smile, a gentle manner, and oozed quirkiness. I also sensed there was more to him than the obvious, but it didn't raise my intuitive hackles so I chose not to worry about it. As I had repeatedly been reminded over the past few months, "There are more things in Heaven and Earth, Glory, than are dreamt of in your philosophy."

As soon as we all found seats in his science classroom, Jesse shouted out, "So, Professor, how does it feel to be slumming it at a lowly high school?"

He laughed and tipped his golf cap at Jesse. "Looking forward to teaching kids who don't believe they already know it all."

"Hah!" Jesse said. "You haven't met us yet. We're a bunch of arrogant little asses."

"Speak for yourself," Carmela said to Jesse, then winked.

"Arrogant little asses," a tiny voice next to me said.

I looked down to see Belle Starr. Oh dear, it appeared I was the one she was determined to shadow today. I lifted her up onto my lap. "Jesse, you might want to text your mom and let her know I've got your baby sister."

Jesse rolled his eyes, mumbled something about a little *pain* in the ass, and texted Sunshine.

Belle Starr snuggled into me, sighed, stuck her thumb firmly into her mouth, and promptly fell asleep. I was a bit on the lush side (or as my father always called it when I had whined about not being fashionably thin: voluptuous—chesty, hippy, and curvaceous) and I imagined I made a soft and comfortable place for a nap.

I looked up to see Professor Greenberg staring at me. "And you are?" he asked.

"At the moment, a bed. But you may call me Glory. Glory Templeton."

His easy smile vanished and he regarded me with a moment of intense assessment before he recovered his usual, casual demeanor.

He knows my secrets, I realized, unsure if that was a good or a bad thing.

Greenberg sat on the front edge of his desk. "I imagine that, after all we've been through, there might be some questions about the pandemic. Viruses? Vaccines?" He paused and looked at me. "Anything at all?"

"Is it really over?" The question came from the same boy whom I had earlier photographed raiding the trash for food. I had learned his name was Kenny. "I've heard pandemics happen in waves."

"That's usually true. Viruses mutate and subsequent waves can even be worse than the original. However, there were unique qualities to this one, which will prevent that from happening. It really is over and done with."

"Stupid, mean, cruel virus," Carmela murmured.

Greenberg grinned. "Don't anthropomorphize viruses. They just hate that."

The students' laughter lightened the mood.

"We'll be covering a variety of topics this semester, but I have planned my curriculum around quantum physics—always a controversial and fascinating subject."

Groans bounced off the walls.

Greenberg held up his hand to silence them. "Now, wait a minute before you tune me out. I assume that many of you enjoy being entertained by magic and fantasy? Well, I'm here to tell you that magic is real." He glanced at me with a disconcerting look that said, *You know it's real, don't you?* "And how does it happen? How do witches cast their spells and magicians manipulate reality? They do it by understanding quantum mechanics. They might not use the language, but they use the physics to slip behind the scenes of what manifests here to the place where it begins to form. From there they change and reshape this reality. This semester we will dive into the mystic waters of superstring theory and multiple universes, the famous double-slit experiment and what it proves about the effect of consciousness on reality, non-locality, interconnectedness, and why, ladies and gentlemen, anything is possible."

Murmurs of interest replaced groans, and an expression of satisfaction crossed the professor's face.

"We'll begin with an exploration of quantum entanglement, a theory which Einstein famously derided as '*spukhafte Fernwirkung*,' or 'spooky action at a distance.' He disliked the theory because it threatened his theory of relativity. But of course, everything in life is relative, including relativity." He chuckled. "In a nutshell, quantum entanglement theory proposes that two particles, once connected, sometimes will act together and become a system. They behave like one object, but remain two separate objects. This connection appears to work outside of the known laws of time or space. Indeed, it appears to transcend time and space."

The professor seemed to be addressing his words directly at me and I shifted uneasily under Belle Starr's weight. Who *was* this man?

"And what applications can this quantum entanglement be used for?" someone asked.

"Time travel, quantum teleportation, information exchanges through time," Greenberg said directly to me.

"That sounds like just so much science fiction nonsense," Jesse said.

"Quantum science is upsetting all known theories of time and space," Greenberg said. "It well could be that all things are happening right here, right now, at this moment and it's just our perception that interprets events in a linear fashion." He paused and caught my eye. "What do you think about that possibility, Hope?"

I froze. "What did you call me?" I managed to ask.

His eyes twinkled. "Oh, I'm sorry. I guess I called you Hope. It's Glory. Isn't it?"

* * *

"He called me Hope," I practically hissed at Dominic the minute I could get him alone in the hall after class. I grabbed Sasha's arm as she walked by. "He called me Hope," I repeated.

Dominic and Sasha shared meaningful glances. "Yes, he did," Sasha said.

"When Zane and I fell in love, I had memories of being his wife from the 19th century." I clenched Sasha's arm harder. "Her name was Hope."

Sasha nodded. "I know."

I looked from Sasha to Dominic and back again. "Are you going to explain?"

"No," they said in unison.

Sometimes I really hated angels.

Jesse came up to us. "You okay, babe? When you handed Belle over to me and ran out of there you looked like a ghost."

I managed a mirthless chuckle. "That's exactly what I felt like."

Carmela joined us. "What happened with you? You don't look so good."

"I don't want to talk about it," I said.

"Well, then let's go eat lunch," Carmela said. "I'm starving."

I hesitated. I wanted to go back into the classroom and confront the professor. What did he know? Was he with the scientists associated with Scorpio Pharmaceuticals, or maybe Nyx and her band of demons? Could he be with the mystical Caretakers of the planet or some group with which I was not yet familiar? Was he good or evil? Did he understand what neither Zane nor I could figure out—why we were both certain Hope and I had been the same person? I had to find out.

Dominic took my hand and my inner storm quieted. "Let's go have lunch," he said.

Although I resented his intrusion into my meltdown, suddenly all I wanted to do was have lunch with my friends. Together, we headed to the cafeteria.

Principal Sanchez had apparently made a store run.

Besides the apples, the serving counter contained jugs of milk, loaves of bread, peanut butter, and jelly. I had a feeling that the wad of cash Dominic gave him was substantial.

"From now on we will always have free food for those who need it," Principal Sanchez announced to the students after they filled the room. "Cosmic James will be teaching a fishing class, and the fish will be donated to the cafeteria. Sunshine James will be holding a cooking class to prepare the food. The classes will provide all who participate extra course credits."

Jesse grinned. "How cool is it that I get credits for fishing?"

"Very cool," Carmela said.

I noticed that after Kenny had filled his tray to overflowing he sat alone, carefully working his way through the unexpected bounty. I went over to introduce myself. "I'm Glory. We have several classes together."

He nodded. "Kenny."

"You're new in town?"

"I moved here from San Francisco after my parents died. I live with my grandparents, Takao and Mai Nakamura."

I knew the Nakamuras. The elderly couple lived in a small bungalow on the edge of town. It suddenly occurred to me that if Kenny didn't have food, it was logical to assume the Nakamuras didn't either. "How are your grandparents doing?"

His eyes avoided mine. "Well, you know that Social Security payments have stopped since the pandemic. My grandparents are too proud to ask for help. They're not doing well."

"I want you to take home some sandwiches and apples

for them—I'll square it with Principal Sanchez—and I'll make sure they get food delivered at home from now on."

His look of stunned gratitude almost made me cry. All he could do was nod.

"Why don't you join me and my friends over there?" I offered.

He glanced at my crew, but then shook his head. I could sense his shyness.

"Well, please feel free to join us anytime."

"Thank you," he whispered.

I returned to my friends. "I'm pretty sure his grandparents, the Nakamuras, are starving."

Jesse looked at me. "I'll make sure they get food." The James family owned a successful organic vegetable and dairy farm operation.

"He could use a friend and maybe an after-school job at the farm," I said. "And being a city boy, he could probably benefit from some special coaching on that fishing thing. Then he can fish for his family."

"I'll see to it," Jesse said.

"That's one of the many reasons I love you." I blew him a kiss.

Jesse caught it with his left hand and patted his heart.

Our love was something special and I valued it. I considered those I passionately loved: my mom, Jesse, Carmela, Hallie. My train of thought shifted from my dog to the Baxters' dog. "I can't get over the entire Baxter family dying."

Carmela nodded. "The great tragedy took so many wonderful people."

I shook my head. "The pandemic didn't take the Baxters. I just saw them last week. I only heard they were dead yesterday."

Carmela and Jesse looked at me as if I was crazy.

"Are you okay?" Jesse asked. "You couldn't have seen them. They died at the height of the pandemic."

"No, I'm telling you that I saw them last week. Little Joey and Cindy came over and picked apples." I had helped them pick the apples they couldn't reach so they could fill their basket.

Sasha laid her hand over mine and gave me a meaningful look. "Perhaps it was a dream. Grief can cause the most vivid dreams."

I felt betrayed but looked at her and sensed she wanted me to be quiet. Apparently, Nyx had thrown a blanket of illusion over the town, and what I knew to be true would make no difference.

TNT came up behind Carmela and greeted her with a lingering kiss on the back of the neck. All the humans at the table melted a bit at the sight. TNT was a gorgeous chocolate-skinned beauty who oozed raw sex appeal. She had charisma, and anyone with blood flowing through his or her veins responded to it.

Carmela lit up like a candle touched by flame, grasped TNT's hand, and pulled her down for a reunion of lips.

Jesse grinned. "Well, if one of us got to get her, I'm glad it was, well, one of us."

Carmela laughed her deep, throaty laugh. "Me too."

TNT smiled at Jesse and squeezed onto the bench between Carmela and me. Her arm grazed mine and electricity flowed. Her perfume was subtle, but it overrode the scents of angels. I decided the intensity was probably due to the thick pheromones that carried it. Her smile dazzled.

"What'd I miss?" she asked.

"New students, new teachers, new missions of mercy,"

Carmela reported.

TNT grabbed an apple and bit into it in such a seductive manner that I stole a glance at Dominic and asked, "Eve, temptation, Applegate?"

He cleared his throat. "You never know." His response floored me until he winked.

TNT laughed. "Eve was also an alluring African goddess. We're very hard to resist."

Carmela giggled. "Oh yeah."

"Tell me about the new students," TNT said.

Carmela pointed to Nyx, who sat a table across the room surrounded by a small crowd of students "She's the most interesting. I've heard she's from a Gypsy family. Supposedly, she's a medium and is passing messages between the worlds from those who died in the great tragedy."

I choked on my milk and threw my angels a look of panic. To prey on people's tragedies in order to amass followers and exert influence was unspeakable in its evil. Rage filled me as I tried to figure out what I could do to stop her.

TNT's eyes clouded a moment, then she said, "Well, we'll have to talk with her, won't we?"

"She's a fake," I said.

Carmela's eyebrows did a bit of a dance as she considered. "From what I've heard so far she has been spot on. I wouldn't be so quick to judge." Her voice fell to a mere whisper when she added, "I definitely want to hear what my family might have to say to me, you know, given Father Hans and his accusations."

TNT slipped a comforting arm around her.

Sasha said, "Your Father Hans is a fool."

Carmela stood and tugged on TNT. "Let's go find out."

Before I could protest again, they were gone.

"Wow. You really don't like that girl," Jesse said.

I shook my head. "You have no idea what a horrible...individual she is. Please stay away from her. You didn't lose anyone. There's no reason for you to get sucked into her wicked web."

"But she's such a babe, babe. How can I resist?"

"Try," I said.

"I love you lots, but you just don't understand about men and their glands. Maybe Nicky here will teach you." He gave Dominic a friendly nudge, and then stood to join Carmela and TNT.

"What are we going to do?" I asked the angels. A horrible sense of doom filled me to overflowing.

"Pray," they both said in unison.

CHAPTER FOUR

"I can't die now, my work's not done," Kaia said. "I've just begun to fight the good fight. I refuse to leave this world now. I've given my word to the Goddess to protect Her creation."

Kaia paced in frantic circles around her cottage. Rory and Evan sat at the bistro table, while Annie crouched beneath it. They all watched her, but none of them had said anything in a while.

Kaia gestured toward Annie. "What about her? I haven't finished teaching her how to hunt. And she can't be released into the wild until I teach her how to protect herself. No one around here can speak her language. She needs me. She loves me."

"I need you," Rory said. "No one but you speaks my language."

"I love you," Evan said.

Annie squeaked.

Kaia stopped ranting, looked at them, and sank onto the pillows in front of the fireplace. "I'm not afraid to die; it's just there's so much left to do."

"And so many of us who need you," Evan said.

Kaia looked at Evan. Despite every ounce of self-control she'd been able to muster, she had fallen in love with him somewhere along the way. When Rory first made her prediction about their marriage, Kaia was intrigued. She didn't rebel against the concept until the leaders of both covens inserted themselves into the situation and decided it would be a brilliant union that would bind two powerful covens and mingle the two family blood lines. They arranged the marriage before Kaia and Evan even met. After that, Kaia rejected the plan on principle. Nobody was going to arrange her life.

"Now I'm glad I didn't marry you, Evan. My death would hurt you worse."

He shook his head. "No, it'll hurt the same."

"You're the only one who has ever understood me," Rory said. Her mother had been killed when she was an infant, and she and Kaia had connected first psychically, then formed an intimacy that was like a psychic sisterhood. "Until you, I always felt so alone." Rory—who usually played the tough card—started to sob.

Frightened by the sound, Annie ran to Kaia and crawled into her lap. Kaia felt her fear and tried to soothe it, then reached out to Rory and urged her to come into her arms as well. She murmured soothing words to them both.

"What can we do?" Evan asked for the umpteenth time. He ran a hand through his stylish, short hair and then loosened his tie even further. It was obvious he had been at work—he was a reporter for CNN—when Rory had her vision of Kaia's death and demanded he drive her straight through from Atlanta.

"Tell me again what you saw," Kaia asked Rory.

Rory fumbled in her pocket for a tissue and blew her nose. "It was just a flash. I saw you and Glory together, and then I saw you dead on the ground. There was a lot of blood. I saw you leave your body. It was real. Final."

"So, you just need to avoid anything to do with Glory," Evan said. "You did the job the Caretakers asked you to do. You helped protect Glory until her blood could be used to manufacture the cure for the pan-plague. That's all they asked of you, and that's all you promised to do."

Kaia shook her head. "I made a promise to Glory to help find her sister. She said she would contact me when she was ready."

"But that's not a mission that has far-reaching consequences," Evan said, his tone pleading. "You don't have to keep your word."

Kaia's heart fell. Evan—for all his protestations of love—didn't know her at all. "My word is my oath. I will *never* break my word to anyone, whatever the personal risk."

"Tell Glory that if you help her, you'll die," Rory said. "She's a nice girl. She wouldn't risk your life."

"The Goddess gave me my gifts and I will use them to help others until the moment of my death, whenever that may be," Kaia said. "Besides, only the Gods know how far reaching the consequences of anything we do. Now, let's give it a rest, okay?"

There was a knock on the door and Kaia's Aunt Brennan stepped inside, her curious eyes sweeping the room. "I knew Kaia had unexpected company so we had our coven meeting without her, but now you all must join us for dinner. I'd feel a poor host if you didn't."

Brennan's imperious manner made her invitation impossible to refuse. As head of the family and the coven, she ruled more like a queen than a witch. "Is there something going on I should know about?"

"No," Kaia said. She wouldn't involve her aunt in this. Kaia's struggle for independence had been an ongoing battle ever since Brennan became her guardian.

"Very well," Brennan said. "Come then. Dinner is being served now."

Kaia instructed Annie to take a nap, closed up her cottage, and followed everyone outside. Evan grasped her hand and she tried to pull it away, but he wouldn't let go. Brennan was tall and regal and threw a mighty shadow over those who trailed behind her. Brennan and Kevin Moonstone had been twins, but besides their dark good looks, they were nothing alike. Kaia's father was warm and funny, loving and kind. Brennan's heart hid beneath many layers of ice—Kaia had never understood why.

A large, rustic lodge that served as a community dining and meeting hall stood in the middle of Moonstone Village. Inside, a giant fireplace blazed with fire, and the long tables overflowed with food. The covenstead was home to twenty-five people, and everyone appeared to be present. Noisy children running about the hall indicated that no one had yet begun eating the evening meal—they were awaiting the arrival of their leader.

Brennan invited Kaia and her guests to join the table of Elders, a round table located in the center of the room. Already seated at the table were Fiona, Mavie, Angus, and Owen—coven Elders in both rank and age. Kaia sat down between Evan and Rory, nodded a polite greeting to the Elders, and waited for Brennan to give the blessing.

Brennan stood by her seat, lifted the brass hand bell from the center of the table, and pierced the air with three sharp rings. Children scrambled for their seats and conversation halted. When the room settled, Brennan said, "Mother Goddess and Father God bless this food, this bounty of earth. We give thanks for the abundance You so selflessly share. May we use the nourishment to serve You and Your creation. So mote it be."

All in the room repeated, "So mote it be," and the meal began.

Because of her special bond with animals, Kaia was a vegetarian, but she was in the coven minority. Their own gardens provided abundant vegetables, the river surrendered trout, and their hunters provided wild game. As Kaia filled her plate with a brilliantly colored salad, she noticed that Evan passed on the grilled fish and chose to mimic Kaia's choice. He had once said to her that, for her, he could adopt a vegetarian lifestyle. He drizzled a dressing of olive oil, balsamic vinegar, and herbs on his own salad and then moved to do the same to Kaia's, but she snatched the cruet from his hands. "I can do it myself." She ignored his hurt expression and drenched her salad, then slammed the bottle on the table. *I'm perfectly capable of taking care of myself. I don't need anyone. I am strong and brave, and I can stand alone.* She mentally recited her lifelong mantra, forgetting for the moment that a mind reader sat beside her.

Rory grinned and said, "Sweetie, when will you figure out that you are all that, but can be—can have—more too?"

According to you it's a moot point now anyway, her mind told Rory's.

Rory's grin disappeared.

"I raised you with better manners than that," Brennan said.

"Yes, you did," Kaia said, but resisted the urge to apologize to Evan. She had been doing everything to discourage him for two years and didn't think now was exactly the right time to change her tactics.

"I was just trying to...sorry if I overstepped," Evan

said.

Everyone at the table ate in silence for a while.

Recently, Angus had begun plaiting his long gray hair and beard and he shook his head at every possible occasion to bring attention to it. He did so now with gusto. The glass beads woven into his braids tinkled.

Evan, who read people well as a good reporter should, said, "You're looking so much younger than the last time I saw you, Angus. Have a new woman in your life?"

Angus's smile revealed a bright new set of dentures. "Not dying in the pandemic gave me a fresh perspective on life. I figure I've got some unspent studliness. Looking for a hookup, if you know a lady who might enjoy fresh meat."

Brennan groaned. "*Please* Angus. I know we're a fertility religion and all, but try to behave."

Owen—who was equally ancient, but utterly hairless—chuckled suggestively. "I'm feeling my own juices rising lately too. Perhaps we could try that online dating thing I've heard so much about."

"A little hard to do without Internet," Kaia said.

Fiona and Mavie—twins who were even older than Angus and Owen—both chimed in. "Not anymore," they said in unison.

Kaia frowned in confusion.

Brennan set down her fork and lifted her goblet of wine. "We decided in our meeting today that since it is unlikely the Ren fairs will return any time soon, and because travel is dangerous with so much civil unrest, we're going to join the technological age. We'll get Internet up here, buy a computer, start a website, and sell our crafts and services online. It's the only way we're going to financially survive."

Kaia could feel the blood drain from her face. "But we made a pact when this covenstead was formed to live off the grid, to stay outside of time, to cling to the breast of the Mother. She'll provide for us."

Brennan took a sip of her wine and peered at Kaia over the rim of the goblet. "We voted on it. We have to be practical."

Kaia glanced at Evan and tried to ignore his smile. She had always told him she could never marry him because he was a city witch. Technology and everything related to modern civilization disgusted her.

"Think of it, Kaia," Mavie said. "We can advertise our jewelry, spell kits, Pagan arts and crafts all over the world."

"We've always known time and space to be an illusion," Fiona said. "The Internet has managed to prove that to the world. It's like another dimension where everyone is linked."

"Isn't it exciting?" Owen said, his smile practically reaching from ear to ear. His head looked like a cracked bowling ball.

"And there's online dating," Angus reminded everyone, emphasizing his glee with the tinkling of hair beads.

Kaia was heartbroken. Her dream life was coming to an end. Well, her life was coming to an end anyway, so what did it matter?

"Your psychic consultations can be arranged online now," Brennan told her. "We actually expect your services to be the most lucrative part of our new venture."

Dazed, Kaia stood. "Excuse me." She left the table and raced outside, trying to outdistance the profound sorrow that threatened to consume her. She stumbled to a bench next to the river and resisted the urge to bolt when Rory sat down next to her.

They sat together in silence for a long time.

Kaia stared at the rushing water and considered the obvious platitudes. *You can't stop the river. Go with the flow. The river of life has many unexpected twists and turns.*

"If you're going to live by the river, make friends with the crocodile," Rory said at last.

Kaia's laughter burst forth like a waterfall. "I love you, kid." She picked up a small stone and tossed it into the river. "My biggest regret in life is that I didn't slay Nyx. My biggest shame is that I couldn't stop Micah from possessing me."

Rory patted Kaia's knee. "Micah's possession happened when you were fighting to protect Glory, after you had been injured and almost killed in a car crash, and you had just nearly been broiled alive by witch hunters. Your psychic defenses were depleted. Don't beat yourself up over it. The important thing is that you overcame him in the end."

The sun disappeared behind the mountains and a frigid cloak wrapped itself around Kaia's heart. "It changed me."

Rory gave her a curious look.

Kaia shuddered. "I haven't talked to anyone about it, but a part of him remained with me. I...oh how do I describe what happened? He's a fallen angel, he's demonic, and I know his evil intimately. But I also—Goddess help me—have compassion for him. I experienced his memories and why he fell, and I have *compassion* for him."

Kaia felt Rory's flicker of alarm.

"Why did he fall?" Rory asked.

"As an angel his job was to help the souls of children who had starved to death cross over into the light. Thousands of children die every day due to starvation. And that was before the pan-plague. The suffering, the apathy of humanity about the suffering—it became too much for him to bear. He was created to love but grew to hate those who did nothing to help those children. I can understand that, Rory. I really can."

Kaia felt Rory's growing alarm.

"But sweetie," Rory said, "the fact remains that he chose to deal with his personal pain by turning to the darkness. Now he is one who creates suffering—who generates horror. You need to get a grip and some perspective, especially...." Her words died off and she uttered a miserable moan.

"Especially if I'm going to die soon," Kaia said.

Rory thrust out her chin. "I'm not with the camp who believes in praying for one's enemies. I say vanquish them so they can't hurt anyone else ever."

As full darkness finally embraced them, Kaia watched the dance of the river reflected by moonlight. She thought about merging with the river and wondered how best to deal with crocodiles.

CHAPTER FIVE

At the edge of the property line between my farm and the Baxters', I created a private memorial to the family Nyx so callously wiped out of existence. I put together a montage of photographs I had taken of them, laminated it, and nailed it to a tree. At the foot of the tree, I planted a small rose bush and pounded a handmade cross into the ground because I knew they were devout Christians. I said a prayer for them and cried a bucketful of tears. Their Border Collie, Milton, stayed by my side the entire time.

I sat on the ground trying to recall every single memory I had of the family. Jonas Baxter was a hard worker and always ready to offer us help. When Erica was kidnapped and my parents were still immobilized by shock, he jumped in to organize the search party and media interviews. He even started the reward fund using a huge chunk of his own life savings. His wife, Sally, took over my care until Mom and Dad were able to function again.

Joey wanted to grow up and be a farmer like his dad, and Cindy wanted to be famous. She was always after me to take pictures for her "portfolio." Truthfully, she was photogenic and might have forged a career in show business. Of course, in an instant, all the goodness, beauty, and promise of that family was obliterated. I hoped they hadn't suffered. A cry of anguish escaped me as I considered the possibility that they had.

Davina, a Caretaker of the planet, had once told me there was a grand plan to life. Was this tragedy part of that plan? The word "hokum" popped into my head and bitterness filled me. "Your grand plan is hokum, oh great Davina, Ms. Caretaker of the World!" I shouted to the universe.

Milton laid his ears flat against his head. Then I noticed his eyes widened to look at something behind me.

"It's not my grand plan. And, yes, sometimes things go tragically wrong."

I recognized the voice and sensed the shift in energy around me. I had only met Davina once, but memory of a Caretaker sticks with you. As disrespectful as I knew it was, I refused to turn and acknowledge her.

After a few moments, she sat down on the ground next to me. I glanced at her and saw she was as exotic as I remembered. With her long, wild hair, jeweled headband, flowing gown, and raw beauty, she was what I imagined Mother Earth would look like if She took a human form.

Zane had once used the term "awe-inspiring" to describe her.

"This world is the battleground between good and evil," she reminded me. "The grand plan holds that good should eventually triumph. Warriors such as you who are committed to the fight must make sure that happens."

I shook my head. "I couldn't do anything to save the Baxters. I didn't even know they were in danger until it was too late."

"However, you do know that there are now others in grave danger. Nyx and Micah are hunting souls, not just bodies. You must do what you can to stop it."

A fit of trembling seized me. "And just how do I do

that?"

"You're going to have to figure it out."

I waited.

Milton whined and crawled into my lap.

Davina said, "Their side has a grand plan too. This is just a small piece of theirs—almost inconsequential in comparison to what's coming."

"No soul is inconsequential."

"That's true, and that's the point of what's happening in Union right now. The pandemic was just the beginning of what they have planned. The world is teetering on the brink of the abyss. Terrible things are being planned."

I clutched Milton. "And what can I possibly do about that?"

"What's unfolding here has been designed to distract you from dealing with the larger issues. You don't yet understand how intimately involved you are in those larger plans. You're going to have to figure out a way to deal with all of it."

I stared at her in horror.

She met my stare with a look of compassion. "I told you when you agreed to fight the good fight that it wasn't going to be easy."

"You didn't tell me it would be impossible."

"Nothing is impossible, Glory."

I opened my mouth to reply, but she disappeared.

"What do you mean I'm intimately involved in evil's larger plans?" I shouted to the empty space where she had been.

Suddenly, Milton's tail started thumping against my leg at practically the speed of light. I noticed he was looking at the photos of his family. Hovering in the air in front of the montage was an image that appeared to be

Jonas Baxter. Jonas looked at me and said, "Remember what happened to Erica. That's when your involvement began."

Milton barked a happy yap and leapt from my lap toward his master's arms, but the image faded too soon. The dog yelped when he tumbled to the ground in a confused heap. Whining, he crawled on his belly back into my lap.

Milton whimpered, I wept, and we sat together for a long time. I don't know what he was thinking, but I was pondering the fact that if the fate of the world was resting even slightly on my shoulders, the future looked pretty damn bleak.

* * *

I hated that Nyx, Micah, and their wicked dog, Hex, were living within walking distance from my house. I could feel their evil and so, apparently, could most of the other living creatures in the area. Within days, they began showing up on our farm, and the guesthouse became Wild Animal Central.

Birds of every description appeared on the roof of the angels' new residence and built nests. Overnight, it became an avian condominium complex. A really loud avian condominium complex.

Hallie and I were standing in front of the angels' home looking up at the startling sight when Dominic opened the door. Hallie barked and bounded to him. He scooped her up into his arms and she surrendered to him with a sigh.

"I love you too, Miss Hallelujah." He looked at the roofline. "That's nothing. You need to see what's going on in here."

Curious, I stepped inside. The day bed in the corner captured my attention. On top of it were three distinct nests: a cat and her kittens held the place of honor on the pillow at the head of the bed. In the middle of the bed, a mouse nested with her litter of newborns. A squirrel and her babies had the foot of the bed. Poking their noses out from underneath the bed were a red fox and two of her cubs, and a family of skunks.

Milton stood nearby giving all the creatures his intense Border Collie stare, presumably to keep everyone in line. My gut told me it probably wasn't necessary.

I shook my head. "Seriously?" I looked around for a lion and a lamb.

Sasha, sitting on a stool at the kitchenette counter, giggled.

Dominic put Hallie on the floor and she studied the bed for a while, cocked her head from one side to the other, then sat down with a thud. She whined and looked at me with bright blue eyes.

"Since your bed is otherwise occupied, it's a good thing you guys don't have to sleep," I said. I knew from experience that angels had to recharge, but did so by phasing out of physical form for a time.

"We've let the animals with litters inside, but have had to turn out the others or we'd be too cramped," Dominic said. "We've rearranged the wood pile out back to give them shelter."

I had heard a coyote in the night who sounded close. I was curious about the farm's new residents.

"Isn't it a bit late in the season for some of these animals to be having babies?" I asked, my mind recalling litters I had stumbled onto in the past.

"Nature is confused right now," Dominic said. "When the supernatural and the natural worlds intersect as they've been doing in recent months, things change."

A brilliant light appeared around the edges of the closed bathroom door. Rebekah opened the door and stepped out into the main room. If one watched too closely and caught a glimpse of an angel shapeshifting between divine and human forms, the brilliant wattage of light could cause unconsciousness. I decided they must be using the privacy of the bathroom as a *Star Trek* type of transporter.

Although Rebekah didn't appear older than Dominic, Sasha, and Micah, she was their mothering angel and they were her family. I hadn't seen her since Atlanta, at the height of the pan-plague. Long brown hair flowed over fragile shoulders and her gown was white. Her aura of lilacs overrode all the other scents in the room.

She greeted me with a beatific smile. "Ah, the girl who prays for angels."

We had met when I was praying for Dominic and she expressed surprise that a human would pray for an angel's well-being. Now that I knew how far up the angelic hierarchy she was, I found myself intimidated by her presence. I fought the irrational urge to curtsy. "Thanks for helping us. I'm really scared about what the demons are planning."

"You do realize that angels can only inspire? We can't change what will be."

I was so tired of hearing that. "I came by because my mother wants to have your family over for dinner so she can meet all of you."

"That would be lovely," Rebekah said.

I couldn't take my eyes off of her youthful face and

wondered how we could pass her off as Dominic's and Sasha's mother.

She seemed to hear my thoughts. "Your mother will see me as an age appropriate to her expectations."

"Okay. Six o'clock tonight?"

Rebekah inclined her head in a gesture of assent.

Before I turned to leave, I blurted out. "My mom is in real bad shape. Can you all work your inspiration thing on her? Please?"

I expected a lecture about how Mom had her own guardian angel and they weren't permitted to cross lines, but Rebekah surprised me.

"We will all be at our inspirational best."

* * *

Okay, so it wasn't my mom who wanted the angels to come to dinner. I had devised the plan hoping that their influence would do something to pull her up out of the darkness.

Mom almost never left the couch. She sat on it by day and slept there at night, ate there when I brought her food, and I couldn't remember the last time she had bathed. Every day I turned on the TV for her, but she invariably shut it off, preferring to stare off into space. When she talked at all, it was to express guilt about her unwitting role in the pan-plague.

I sat down in the easy chair across from her and tried to ignore her zombie-like demeanor. "Mom, we're having company for dinner tonight."

Slowly, her eyes shifted from deep space to my face, but they appeared unseeing.

"I've invited Dominic and his family for dinner. Since

they're living in Dad's studio now, it seems like the polite thing to do."

Her head made a feeble attempt at a shake. "Oh no. No, no. Can't."

"I'll cook dinner. All you need to do is clean yourself up and be there. I'll draw a bath for you. It'll be good for us."

She groaned.

"Dominic saved your life. Having his family over for dinner is the right thing to do." I tried to inject some authority into my voice. "Dad would have insisted on it."

Her eyes focused. "Oh, your dad. How I miss him."

I swallowed, pushing a heavy knot of sorrow down my throat. "Me too, Mom. He would have wanted us to be hospitable. Please, let's do what he would have wanted?" I didn't even try to mask the unexpected whine in my voice.

She continued to stare at me and I could see her struggling with the concept.

"I'll cook," I repeated.

She frowned. "You don't cook."

"I found some of Dad's recipes."

She expelled a whoosh of air. "He was a good cook."

It was true. Dad had always been the househusband while Mom had been the career woman.

"I'll draw your bath now." I inserted as much bounce in my voice as I could and launched myself toward the bathroom. I didn't look back. I didn't want to give her another opportunity to argue.

Our house had a deep, old-fashioned claw-foot tub and I filled it with hot water, rose bath oil, and even threw in a few dried rose petals for good measure. I lit candles and tuned the radio to something soft. I grabbed a green chenille robe from her bedroom and hung it on the bathroom door, then returned to the living room. I led her by the hand to the bath and she didn't resist as I stripped her clothes and deposited her in the tub. I hated her docility—it wasn't the strong, amazing woman I had always known and respected.

"I'll leave you to soak." I handed her a bottle of shampoo. "Don't forget to wash your hair."

She murmured something I couldn't understand, and then I left her alone.

Mom had refused to see the family doctor for antidepressants, even though the medical community was practically force-feeding them to everyone who walked in their doors. I made her a fruit smoothie every morning and laced it with mood-elevating herbs from Jesse's mom, but it hadn't helped. I hoped a family of angels at the dinner table might snap her out of it.

Dad had inherited his mother's hand-written recipe book, and I stood at the kitchen counter flipping through it to find something that looked easy, could be made from ingredients I had, and might be a meal fit for angels. What did one feed angels, anyway?

A quick rap at the back door announced Jesse, who let himself in. He had Belle Starr in tow. "Hi, babe."

My heart warmed at the sight of him and the temperature grew when I saw Belle Starr's adorable smile. "Enjoying the afternoon off?" I asked.

There was a power outage at school and we had all been let go at lunchtime.

Jesse grabbed me in an enthusiastic hug, then Belle Starr stood on tip-toes to kiss me. I bent down and let her lips touch my face with their sweetness.

"Well, my folks put me to work in the dairy and then

assigned Belle to me for safekeeping," Jesse said. "I snuck out on the pretext of making deliveries." He thrust a package into my hands. "Here's a jug of buttermilk and some cheddar cheese. I can now honestly say I made deliveries."

I peeked into the bag at the unexpected bounty. "Yum. Actually, you just saved the day for me. I think I know what I can make for dinner now."

Jesse's laughter was hearty. "You're cooking?"

"For company no less. I'm having Nicky and his family over for dinner. I thought it might do Mom good to have some company."

He winked at me. "It'll do you good to have a boyfriend over too."

"Oh, Nicky's not my boyfriend."

"Could have fooled me and everyone else who watched you two kiss."

"Um, well, he's a real good kisser. I was just getting in some practice." It was lame and his expression told me we both knew it.

Hallie charged into the house to greet Belle Starr—the little girl was one of her favorite friends. They squealed at the sight of one another, gave each other a bunch of wet kisses, and wandered away to play.

I stuck the dairy products in the fridge, pulled out a pitcher of lemonade, grabbed a couple glasses, and Jesse and I sat down together at the table. As I filled the glasses, I noticed him watching me with a curious expression.

"Tell me what's really going on with you. What really happened when you disappeared? Why did you keep to yourself all summer? Talk to me, babe."

I had wanted to have this conversation with him for

months, but there was so much I still had to keep secret that I didn't know what to say. I met his eyes—the amazing windows to the special soul he was—and fought the urge to tell him everything. Instead, I chose my words carefully. "After Dad died and Mom was kidnapped I ended up connecting with a group of people who helped me find my mom. Nicky was part of that group. There was also another guy named Zane. I know it's crazy because we were only together for a little over a week, but I sort of fell for them both."

I expected Jesse to burst out laughing, or at least choke on his lemonade, but he did neither. "So, the first time you opened your heart two men snuck in?"

His response was one of the many reasons I loved Jesse so much. "Yes."

"Tell me about Zane."

"A young cowboy who lives with his family on a horse ranch in Texas." I left out the part about being a vampire.

Recognition dawned in Jesse's face. "Oh, the cowboy who made the citizen's arrest of your mom's kidnapper live on CNN?"

I nodded.

Jesse whistled. "Yeah, the girls went nuts over him. They wanted to know more, but he kept dodging the press."

"He's very private."

"A romantic triangle? Interesting that Dominic was the one who followed you home."

"When we were traveling to the east coast there was a car accident and I nearly died. Um, had one of those near-death experience things. When that happened, Nicky and I had a spiritual experience where we kind of merged. It was very intimate. Our hearts connected." I paused and took a big gulp of the lemonade. "On the other hand, from the moment I met Zane there was this intense electrical connection that blew me away. I'm crazy about them both, but in totally different ways. I couldn't make a choice." I groaned. "I'm *so* confused."

Jesse was quiet for such a long time that I grew nervous. He was never one to withhold his opinion or mince words. Finally, he said, "Well, I'd like to offer myself as a tiebreaker."

Startled, my eyes flew to his. In all the years we'd been best friends, he had never once even implied a romantic interest in me. That he would respond to the baring of my soul with a joke shocked me to my core. I could feel the heat in my face and hoped it showed. "That's not funny."

"I didn't intend it to be."

No, no, no. "Please don't," I whispered.

"Don't love you? I've always loved you. It was you who swore you'd never fall in love. I would rather have had your heart in friendship than your heart not at all."

"I never.... I didn't know."

"Now you do."

Belle Star and Hallie charged back into the kitchen. They were playing tug of war with one of my bras.

Grateful for the interruption, I stood to rescue it. "Were you two in my bedroom? You haven't played with my underwear in years, Hallie. Belle Starr you are a bad, bad influence on my dog."

Belle Starr erupted in delighted giggles.

Jesse stood. "Okay, Belle, time to go. We're headed over to visit Nyx and Micah. They're having a séance this afternoon. Sounds like a good time to me."

"No!" Belle Starr's shriek was completely out of character. "I don't wanna!"

Jesse blinked. "Why?"

"Please no." She trembled like a leaf in a hurricane.

Startled, I knelt and gathered her in my arms. Hallie licked her face.

"Do they scare you?" I asked.

"Scare me bad, bad," she whispered. "Stay here?"

My eyes flew to Jesse. "See? I told you they weren't good...people."

Jesse shrugged. "I just think the strange tattoos on Micah's face and his crazy cackle scare her."

"It's more than that. I know them."

His crooked grin seemed forced. "Ah, you're just worried that sexy Nyx will steal my heart away from you." He stood and quickly headed for the back door. "Keep Belle the rest of the day and I'll be back to fetch her later." His voice cracked when he said, "Catcha later, babe."

* * *

I resisted the urge to rant about Jesse's revelation because I knew Belle Starr would echo everything I said, so I kept my muddled thoughts to myself and put her to work helping me collect food for dinner. The garden that Dad and I had planted in the spring was ruined when I drove through it to escape Mom's kidnappers. However, some of the vegetables survived and others had returned. We dug up potatoes and onions, and harvested dill weed. Then we picked apples. After we hauled everything into the kitchen, I went to work.

Mom had managed to get herself dressed and was

back on the couch, so I turned the TV on and deposited Belle Starr in her lap. Startled, Mom tried to push her away, but Belle Starr's kisses melted her resistance. Hallie joined them, and the three merged into a contented pile.

I dug out the recipes for cheesy potato-dill soup, buttermilk biscuits, and apple cobbler, then did my best to follow the instructions. I brewed a big pitcher of iced tea, set the dining room table for six, and even found candles for the centerpiece. I changed from old blue jeans into relatively new ones and put on a clean tank top—which was as dressed up as I was known to get—and the angel family showed up right on time.

Apparently, angels read books on etiquette. They arrived with a bottle of wine and a bouquet of flowers, and all three of them were properly dressed for a dinner invitation. Dominic wore a sports jacket and slacks, Sasha was beautiful in a pale yellow dress, and Rebekah's white gown had morphed into a nice white pantsuit. With Mom, Belle Starr, and me in blue jeans, we appeared very much the peasants. At least the angels were too polite to mention it.

"This is a new tank top," I said in greeting, my fluster showing.

"It's lovely," Rebekah said.

Nervous, I looked around for the bra that Hallie and Belle Starr had been playing with, but thankfully it was nowhere in sight.

I put Hallie and Milton on the back porch with their dinner, then directed everyone else to their seats—and piled a couple thick phone books on Belle Starr's so she was above chin level. I put her on one side of me, Dominic on the other side, and placed my mother between Dominic and Rebekah. Sasha completed the circle.

I served wine to the adults and poured iced tea for everyone else. The soup was in a tureen, the biscuits in a basket, and the apple cobbler sat in its baking dish on a thick pile of potholders in the middle of the table. I lit the candles and placed the vase of new purple wildflowers in between them. Satisfied with my organizational brilliance, I was ready to say something to the effect of, "Ready, set, eat!" when Rebekah suggested saying grace.

I was at a loss, so gave Dominic a hopeful, somewhat panicked glance. He smiled that magical smile of his, took my hand, linked his other hand with my mother, I clasped Belle Starr's fingers, and the circle of hands continued around the table until we were all one.

He bowed his head. "Dear Father, we give thanks for the gift of food, the blessing of love, and the miracle of life. May we each live our lives in a manner that honors You. Amen."

Amens echoed—with Belle Starr the word echoed repeatedly—and I filled her plate before everyone else filled theirs so food might quiet her.

"Entertain often?" Dominic asked with a mischievous grin.

I knew he could feel my discomfort, but I restrained the urge to kick him for pointing it out. "You are the first dinner guests I've ever had and this is the first dinner I've ever made, so good luck everyone." I forced chipper into my voice.

"It smells good," Sasha said. "Thank you for all your effort."

"Well, Belle Starr helped me." I smiled at her. "Didn't you, honey?"

"How come she's so bright?" she asked, pointing her spoon at Sasha. Apparently, her innocent eyes saw the world more clearly than I expected.

Alarmed, I looked at Mom, but she was so engrossed in buttering her biscuit that she didn't appear to have heard.

I leaned down and whispered, "It's a secret we'll talk about later, okay?"

"Is it a secret why bright mommy is younger than her kids?"

"Yes," I practically hissed. "Now hush."

"Okay, I'll hush," Belle Starr whispered and made a big production of zipping her lips and throwing away the key.

It occurred to me that those were the first truly articulate sentences I had heard Belle Starr speak since the great tragedy. She had reacted to the horror with a kind of posttraumatic stress disorder that affected her speech patterns. I wondered if the positive change was due to being in the presence of angels.

After my mother buttered her biscuit and ladled soup into her bowl, she stared at it for a time as if trying to figure out what to do next. "Did your dad help you cook this, Glory? I think he learned to make this soup from his mother."

Fear cut through my stomach. Just how far had Mom's mental illness progressed? "I used Grandma's recipe."

Mom tasted it cautiously. "It's good."

I breathed a sigh of relief. "Thank you."

Mom looked at Rebekah. "It's nice to finally meet you."

"I travel a lot," Rebekah said. "I'm glad to know my children are safe here with you."

Mom's eyes swept those who sat around the table. "The little one isn't yours, is she?"

"Belle Starr is Jesse's sister," I gently reminded her.

"Oh yes, Jesse. Nice boy." She looked at Dominic and Sasha, then her attention returned to Rebekah. "So, tell me about your children."

"I have three actually. Sasha is a perfect angel, and has a beautiful singing voice. Dominic loves movies and I think is handsome enough to be an actor. However, he has other career plans. His most recent choice has stunned the family, but we'll adjust. My other son, Micah, is a troubled boy and I'm working hard to bring him around."

"And their father, what kind of work does he do?" Mom asked.

"He's an artist. Creates beautiful things—breathes life into them. He travels extensively as well."

"What's his medium?"

"Mixed."

"Would I know his work?" Mom asked.

"Oh yes," Rebekah said.

I tried to think of something to say before Mom could ask his name, but Belle Starr beat me to it.

"Micah is a bad, bad boy."

Rebekah's crestfallen expression mirrored what I knew she felt about her son. I stuffed a biscuit in Belle Starr's mouth before she could echo herself.

"So, Kate, tell me about your daughter," Rebekah said.

Mom perked up. "Oh America—we call her Erica—is a delight. Such a beautiful girl. Just like a little princess. Incredibly intelligent, too. We had her IQ tested, and she's going to grow up to change the world." A dreamy expression crossed her face. "Mark and I are so proud of her."

I dropped my spoon and cheesy potato-dill soup splashed everywhere. A silent pall fell over the table. Well, except for Belle Starr.

"America's a silly name for a princess," she said. "Does she live in a tower?"

"Yeah, hidden away in the crown of the Statue of Liberty," Jesse said softly. I hadn't seen him come in. He walked over to me, leaned down, and kissed the tears off my cheeks. "And what about your other daughter, Mrs. Templeton?"

Mom blinked in confusion. "Oh, right. That would be Glory. She wants to be a photographer. Never understood that." She grinned at Rebekah and threw her a conspiratorial wink. "Those troubled children of ours. What are we to do with them? Sometimes you've got to wonder if they're worth all the trouble."

I felt as if I was going to throw up. I reached for Mom's untouched wine glass and downed it. Hell, I'd show her what a troubled child could really be.

She's sick, I heard Sasha say in my mind. *Don't take it personally.*

Jesse lifted Belle Starr off her phone books, knocked them off the chair, sat down, and settled her into his lap. Then he reached over and took my hand.

"Since everyone else is being too polite—or cowardly—to point out the facts, Mrs. Templeton, Glory is sitting right here and Erica has been missing for eleven years," Jesse said. "Your husband is dead. He died in the pandemic. The company you worked for withheld the vaccine that would have saved lives. You blame yourself, but it's not your fault. As a matter of fact, if it wasn't for your discovery of the conspiracy a whole lot more people would have died." He paused to take a breath, but quickly pushed on. "You've got to get a grip and snap out of this. It's ridiculous everyone's been coddling you."

I gasped and tried to pull my hand from his, but he wouldn't let go. Mom's eyes widened and her face bloomed red. I noticed the angels regarding Jesse with a look of admiration. Then Belle Starr asked, "So does the princess live in a tower or not?"

"I don't know where Erica is living, or if she's alive at all," Jesse said. "But there's a Gypsy medium next door who could tell us. She's totally amazing."

I panicked. "No."

Jesse squeezed my hand so hard it hurt. "If it'll help your mom move on, it doesn't matter if you like the girl or not." He captured my mother's wild eyes and held them still with the force of his indomitable will. "Her name is Nyx, you can walk to her house—it's the old Baxter farm. Go ask her about Erica, and start treating Glory better. I'm sick and tired of seeing her hurt." With that, he let my hand go, tucked Belle Starr up under his arm, and walked out of the house.

"Oh I'm so sorry, Glory," Mom whispered. "I don't know what's come over me lately."

I wanted to tell her it was okay, but it didn't feel okay.

"I'm going next door right now and talk to this Nyx person." Mom turned to our guests. "Please excuse me." Before I could stop her, my mother rushed away.

"That certainly went well," I said with as much sarcasm as I could muster. "What happened to inspiring and uplifting her? And between the three of you and her supposedly hovering-but-invisible guardian angel, why the hell couldn't you keep her out of the clutches of a demoness?"

Dominic started to respond, but I knew what he was going to say and I was tired of hearing how they couldn't interfere. "Get out. All of you. Just. Get. Out."

Slowly, one by one, they stood and walked away.

I sat there for so long the candles burned down and their flames flickered away to smoke, filling the air with the smell of bitterness. Then I walked upstairs to my room, removed a file from its hiding place behind my bed's headboard, and spilled its contents onto my bedspread.

I dug through the photographs, addresses, and phone numbers I had collected during that incredible week spent working to save the world from the great tragedy.

I picked up the business card of a feisty helicopter pilot named Cookie who had nicknamed me Sweet-cheeks and called Zane a Stud-muffin. She told me if I ever needed a helicopter to get me out of a jam, to call her. Her number was burned into my memory—not that I figured I'd ever need a helicopter again.

I studied the photos of those I had met that week. Despite the horror—or maybe because of it—I had tried to capture a piece of soul from most everyone I encountered. I had beautiful images of Dominic and Sasha, but never had the opportunity to photograph Rebekah. I wondered, with the ability she apparently possessed to change her appearance, how the unbiased eye of the camera would see her. I would have to find out.

And there was Micah. Desperately loved by his family, he had fallen and no one had been able to stop him. Until encountering these supernatural beings, I didn't realize that angels had free will. Dominic told me that all created things had free will. He also informed me that all created things were imperfect. I studied Micah's face and the crazy tattoos he wore like war paint. I noticed how he had stained his lips a permanent bloodlike red. I thought about the similarities between a human child rebelling against his or her parents and a divine one going rogue. I wondered if there was hope for Micah. Dominic clung to that hope. However, I felt that once he had teamed up with Nyx he truly was lost forever.

Then there were the photos of the vampires.

Gorgeous Zane without his shirt on, revealing a perfect physique carved from flesh that had spent well over a century working on ranches as a cowboy. Hunting down wild animals with nothing but his bare hands as weapons also carved that muscle—Zane was a vampire who only drank animal blood and felt obliged to earn his meals the hard way.

Zane's sister, Trinity, was incredibly photogenic. Her inner beauty actually eclipsed her physical beauty, which was quite a feat. On the other hand, the image of Trinity's pretty sister-in-law, Leah, revealed the utter bitterness that consumed her soul. She appeared ugly in her photo. My camera really did have a way of capturing that which lurked beneath the flesh.

Then there were the Goth Girls, an all-girl gang of vampires who had been friends with Zane since the 1800's. Photos of the sexy band of women—a rainbow of races—revealed the power that self-confidence bestowed. They astounded me then, and their photos astounded me now.

The witches were fascinating. Little twelve-year-old psychic Rory with her horned-rim glasses, pouty lips, casual pile of hair, and cocky energy glowed so intensely in her photograph that it threatened to spontaneously combust. What I remembered most about her was the day she told me in her soft Southern drawl, "Let me make this *condescendingly* clear; I'm totally great at what I do so just let me do it, okay?" Her sass was charming.

Then there were the images of Kaia and Evan. Tiny Kaia, a spitfire with cascades of wild red hair, bright green eyes, a nose piercing, and hippie clothes. Evan, a sophisticated young man who looked as if he stepped right out of *GQ Magazine*. On one level, they were like night and day: country witch meets city witch. However, when their eyes looked at each other love oozed from the pictures, dripped to the floor, and flooded to cover the world. Their love was epic. The only one who didn't realize it was Kaia. My dad had been known for quoting poets. "Take away love and our earth is a tomb," was Dad's Robert Browning mantra. When I looked at Kaia, I thought of that mantra. I hoped it wouldn't be Kaia's epitaph because, tragically and inexplicably, she seemed determined to deny herself love.

I turned the photo of Kaia over and found her mailing address, a post office box in the town of Crestone. That was what I had been looking for. I was finally ready to accept her offer of help. I had to find my sister before I lost my mother too.

CHAPTER SIX

Kaia spent two days trying to send Evan and Rory home, but they refused to leave. "Well, if you're going to stick around, could you at least find something to wear besides a suit?" she asked Evan. "It's a bit overdone for the wilderness." She winced at her own rudeness.

"I'll take a trip to the store in town," Evan said. "While I'm there, I'll see if there are any errands the coven needs handled."

"Aunt Brennan will probably want you to stop by the post office and check the mail." Kaia made a face. "I guess all that will become obsolete when we get the Internet." She said *Internet* like it was a dirty word.

"Maybe I can help get that organized while I'm here. I do know a bit about modern technology."

"Where does CNN think you are?" Kaia asked him.

"I'm on personal leave due to a family crisis."

"I'm not your family," Kaia said.

"From the minute we met, you've been my family. Long before that, I imagine."

"Your connection goes back lifetimes," Rory offered, less than helpfully.

Kaia grunted.

Rory sat cross-legged on the floor by Kaia's fireplace brushing Annie. "You'd better teach me everything I need to know to help Annie after you die. I'm not especially psychic with animals, but my gifts help some."

"You have to get home," Kaia said. "You can't take her back to Atlanta."

Rory shook her head. "I know my daddy will let me stick around here until I've fulfilled this duty. I'm home-schooled anyway and am sure I can learn a lot here. I promise you I'll make sure she's okay."

"Will you two stop talking as if Kaia's death is already a done deal?" Evan was not handling this at all well and Kaia really did want him to leave. His presence made things so much harder.

Brennan let herself into the cottage after a sharp knock on the door. She looked around and gestured toward the two sleeping bags on the floor. "We do have better guest accommodations, if you two plan on staying a while."

"They won't," Kaia said at the exact moment Evan said, "We will."

Rory said, "The sleeping bags are fine. It's cozy here. We're good."

Brennan waved a US Post Office Express Mail envelope in the air. "Gabrielle went into town this morning for groceries and picked up mail. This is for you, Kaia. It appears to be from Glory Templeton."

So there it was. Kaia, Evan, and Rory all stared at it waving at them and no one stepped forward to claim it. Eventually, Kaia said, "Thank you, Aunt Brennan. Please set it on the table."

Brennan's eyebrows merged in consternation, but she didn't ask questions. Before walking back out the door she turned and said, "I'm here if you need help with whatever this is." She gave Kaia an especially poignant look. "I promised your mother I would always care for you as my own if she was unable to. I would move Heaven and Earth for you, Kaia dear."

After she closed the door behind her, Kaia shook her head. "What the hell was that? Where did all that *niceness* suddenly come from?"

"Omigods," Rory whispered. "I saw something when she was talking. Something I don't think I was meant to see."

It was hard to keep secrets among witches, but strong shields sometimes allowed it—shields like a wall of ice around one's heart.

"What did you see?" Kaia asked, not certain she wanted to know Brennan's secrets.

Rory adjusted her glasses and grew pensive. "She was in love with your mother. It was a big love."

Not much knocked Kaia off her feet, but that revelation did. She scrambled to the nearest chair before her knees gave way entirely. "Did they have a relationship?"

Rory's eyes clouded for a moment and she nodded. "But your mother loved your father more and chose him. Your aunt never recovered."

Kaia's mind raced. It would explain why Aunt Brennan never married. "She's been so cold to me all these years. Why?"

"Sweetie, it was because of what just happened. She let her guard down for a moment and her secrets spilled. If she let them down with you, given your psychic gifts, you would have always known. From what I saw, she promised your parents to keep their secrets. Out of respect."

Evan cleared his throat. "I've said it before, but it bears repeating. You can't choose whom to love. It's wild, and magical, and beyond our rational control."

"If that's true and she understands that, then why does

she persist on pushing the two of us together?" Kaia asked him.

"Because she knows you love me, even if you won't admit it."

Kaia moaned, then glanced at Glory's letter. What would love matter to her now? She tried to stand up, but still couldn't find her strength. "Would you read it to me, Evan?"

Evan approached the envelope as if it contained a bomb. Gingerly he ripped it open, reached inside, and pulled out two items. He looked at the photograph and handed it to Kaia, then he read the letter aloud.

"'Dear Kaia, I hope you have recovered from the difficult events surrounding the great tragedy and are doing well. You once said you would help me find my sister, America, and I need to ask for that help now. Nyx and Micah have shown up in Union and are seducing everyone with their evil. My mother is the latest to come under their spell. I feel if we can finally resolve the mystery of what happened to Erica, it would free Mom from them. I am enclosing the only image I have of my sister. As my parents never took photographs of us when we were young, all I have is a photo I took of my dad painting a portrait of Erica from memory. I am also enclosing a necklace that belonged to her. She was wearing it the day she was kidnapped, but it fell off her in the struggle. Please let me know what we must do next. Sent with love, Glory.'"

From the bottom of the envelope, Evan withdrew a gold star on a broken chain. He put the envelope down, then placed the necklace to his forehead and closed his eyes. Evan's magical gift was psychometry—the ability to see images imprinted on objects by people's magnetic fields.

While Evan read the necklace, Kaia studied the photograph. She tried to ignore the expression of anguish on Mark Templeton's face as he painted his daughter. It was obvious that it was their father whom Glory was trying to capture in the photograph, but the image of Erica was telling—it told Kaia that the soul of that girl was still alive, although contrary to all reason it felt as if she was buried underground. Without saying a word, Kaia passed the photo to Rory, who looked at it and gasped.

"I saw her," Rory said. "I saw her in the vision I had of you when you died."

Kaia cocked her head. "You said you only saw me and Glory."

"I saw this girl's—well, now this woman's—reflection in your sunglasses. The birthmark on her cheek is exactly the same."

Evan lowered the necklace. "The girl who owned this necklace knew the men who kidnapped her. I feel recognition. She knew them from her mother's workplace."

Kaia thought about that. "My understanding is that Glory's mother worked for Scorpio Pharmaceuticals since before her daughters were born."

Evan took a seat at the table across from Kaia. "About a month ago I talked to Glory by phone, as a follow up to my story about the pan-plague. In that conversation, she mentioned that someone tried to kidnap her right before the pandemic started. One of the Caretakers later told her that the reason she was targeted for kidnapping was the same as her sister."

"What reason was that?" Kaia asked.

"The Caretaker didn't elaborate."

"Damn Caretakers anyway," Rory mumbled. "You'd think they'd be more helpful to those of us who agree to work for them."

Kaia looked at Rory with surprise. "They've asked you to be a light warrior? At your age?"

Rory appeared both offended and proud. "I was told I was special."

Kaia laughed. "And that you are, my dear."

"I've always had the feeling that Scorpio was just one branch of a massive organization created with world domination as its goal," Evan said.

Kaia managed a humorless laugh. "Nyx and Micah. A mother's soul in danger. A huge organized conspiracy designed to do Gods know what. I can't very well *not* help now. It's much more complex than just finding a missing person." She looked at Evan with a defiant expression, daring him to argue the point.

To his credit, he didn't. Instead, he said, "Marry me first. A handfasting will bind us into the next life. We'll be more likely to find each other again."

Kaia shook her head. "I can't afford to love you right now. My parents' love doomed them because they were distracted by each other. I need my focus."

"But we love each other."

Kaia's eyes filled with tears and her voice fell to a whisper. "You have my heart and I want it back. Oh please Evan, give it back to me."

"No."

There was a long silence. After a while, Rory said, "I'd like to read you something Glory sent to me this summer." She scooted across the floor to her backpack, dug in one of the zippered pockets, and withdrew an envelope. "She wrote a letter thanking me for my help, and she ended with something that was so moving I want to share it with y'all." She slipped the letter from its envelope and read it to them, her voice soft and tone deliberate. "'There is nothing that transforms a person more than love. Not discovering that the world is a mysterious place populated with witches, angels, and vampires. Not almost dying from disease. Not being the only known cure for that disease. Not watching family or friends die. Nothing transforms a person more than love because love is the light that pierces the darkness of the world. It is what makes the profane holy. It is the highest magic there is.'" She looked at Kaia. "Stop being a fool. You love Evan and you know it. You've turned out just like your aunt. Your heart is like one of those marble statues at Savannah's Bonaventure Cemetery where we buried Vanni—beautiful, cold, and shrouded by mist. Don't die before you're dead."

The universe stood still. Even Annie's roar of a purr paused in the presence of the shock that permeated that timeless moment. No one breathed. Kaia couldn't think, and from that place of clarity the most unexpected words emerged. "Evan, you need to formally ask Aunt Brennan for my hand. Then we need to put together a handfasting in record time. I've got work to do."

* * *

Kaia, Evan, and Rory made an unannounced appearance at Brennan's cottage. Unlike Kaia's Spartan decor, Brennan's home was lush: velvet-covered furniture, Tiffany oil lamps, marble fireplace, mantel, and hearth. Kaia always felt that Brennan had been royalty in a past life, and her innate regality certainly seemed to be a carryover.

The plush sofa swallowed the visitors while Brennan perched expectantly on her matching red throne.

"I'm here to ask permission to marry Kaia," Evan said.

Kaia noticed the self-satisfied expression that crossed her aunt's features. She could feel the little girl in Brennan jumping up and down shouting, *I win! I win!*

"Of course, Evan," Brennan said, her smooth voice masking her inner excitement. "We all knew it was only a matter of time. Between our coven and Starlight we will throw you the most glorious handfasting ever in the land."

Yes, definitely former royalty, Kaia thought. "It has to be now and it has to be fast," she said.

Brennan sat straighter, her eyebrows stood at attention, and her entire demeanor grew as imperious as Kaia had ever witnessed. "I think not."

Rory shook her head. "Now and fast. Kaia's going to die and they want to marry first. No time for a lot of explanation. Just do this for them. Okay?"

"Die?" Brennan whispered.

"Yes, she's going to be killed," Rory said. "Soon. Let them do what they want to do while there's time."

Brennan stood to her full six feet, threw back her shoulders, and said, "We will not let her die. We have an entire coven—two covens—and strong magic. We will stop whatever it is—"

Rory stood to her full four-and-a-half feet, carefully adjusted her glasses, and said, "Ain't gonna happen, sweetie. Let's give them what they want while there's still time."

Brennan's intense gaze met Rory's and her expression

morphed from defiant, to disbelieving, to accepting, to grief-stricken. Slowly, she sank back into her chair. "It will be done tonight. Leave now so I can get it arranged."

"Thank you," Kaia said.

"Thank you," Evan echoed.

"Be brave," Rory told Brennan. "They need your strength."

Kaia hung back. "I'd like to talk to my aunt alone."

Rory and Evan left.

Kaia stood respectfully in front of Brennan and struggled with a tsunami of emotions. "I know about you and my mother now—Rory saw. I'm glad Mother was so loved. There should be no shame attached to that and no secrets anymore to hold. Now that you have nothing left to hide, could you possibly allow your heart to open and love me too? I would love to be loved by you before I die."

Brennan's faced paled and she uttered a tiny gasp. "I have always loved you."

"I never knew that," Kaia said.

Brennan moaned. "I'm so sorry for the pain I've caused you. I'm truly ashamed." She stood to embrace her.

Kaia stood on tiptoes so they could kiss. "With the time that's left, let's allow ourselves to love. Okay? In the end, it's all that matters."

* * *

The huge, roaring bonfire built in the middle of the encampment softened the evening chill. Adding light to the night, a ring of flaming torches defined the magic circle. Brennan shared the reason for the suddenness of the marriage only with the Elders because she wanted joy to be the energy that blessed the union, and for that kindness, Kaia was grateful.

Rory helped Kaia get ready for the wedding. Kaia still had the gown her mother wore for her own handfasting, and it fit Kaia perfectly. As both mother and daughter had a petite pixie-like beauty, the flowing dress with its whimsical style worked. Made of chiffon and cobweb lace, the skirt and sleeves were scalloped and wild. Cut on the bias, it gathered at the hip and was secured with a silver dragon clasp. Spectacularly, it was the exact shade of green as Kaia's eyes. A gorgeous crown of wildflowers topped her full, curly hair, and Brennan presented her with a green emerald nose ring for the occasion.

Although the men of the coven offered Evan all manner of Renaissance-style clothing—which is what they always wore—he insisted on wearing his suit. He was a city witch to the core. Angus presented him a boutonniere that matched Kaia's crown.

Rory stood with Kaia, Angus stood with Evan, and Annie was ring bearer. They attached the silver dragon rings—hastily designed by the coven's silversmith—to Annie's collar, and Rory kept her on a leash to prevent wandering.

A handfasting was one of the most ancient forms of a wedding ceremony. It was the root of the phrase "tying the knot." Witches had kept alive the tradition into modern times.

Coveners threw handfuls of scented herbs, pine needles, and cedar boughs in the bonfire, and the aroma filled the night with a fragrant cloud. Brennan blessed the circle, invoked the Gods, and created the sacred space between the worlds. Kaia and Evan held hands and Brennan tied their wrists together—his left to her right—with a red cord that represented blood, life, and passion.

Then Brennan spoke the Moonstone Coven's traditional handfasting vows. "Above you are the stars and below is the earth. Like the stars, your love must be constant. Like the earth, your love must be firm. Be close, but don't lose yourself in the other. Be steadfast in your love because storms will come, but they will go quickly. Be free in giving of affection and warmth, and make love often and with great passion." Brennan's voice broke and tears streamed down her face. "Have no fear of what lies ahead, for the Goddess and the God are with you. With the binding of wrists, the exchange of rings, and a kiss, your family and the High Gods witness your union and declare you united in a sacred bond that binds you in this life and into the next. Blessed be these two very special souls."

Rory and Angus handed the rings to Kaia and Evan. As the bride and groom placed the rings on each other's fingers, Kaia experienced the intense presence of her parents and their special bond of love. She felt her mother's and Brennan's timeless love also reach out to bless them.

Before they kissed, Evan said, "I claim you as my one, true soul mate. A bond never to be broken, it will remain forever."

Kaia said, "All my forevers are in the magic of your lips right now."

The extreme passion of their kiss brought the crowd to silence.

Kaia and Evan shared the goblet of sacred wine, and when they drained the last drop they raised their bound wrists to the crowd in a triumphant gesture. The coveners responded by shouting, "So mote it be!"

Children threw flower petals, musicians played, singers sang, and the couple jumped over the broom, which represented the threshold from their old life apart to their new life together. For that moment in time, Kaia was happier than she had ever been.

* * *

Despite all the fanciful tales of witches dancing naked by the light of the moon, and even though witches are a naturally passionate lot without Puritanical notions about sex, Kaia had never before been naked in the presence of a man. She was shocked to discover a vein of shyness in her that she didn't know how to pierce.

When they were finally alone in her cottage, Evan easily stripped his clothes and lay down to wait for her.

Kaia stood next to the bed uncertainly. Candlelight illumined the room, and she found herself breathless at the sight of his incredible beauty. "Your dragon is so sexy," she whispered.

He grinned. "Which one?"

She giggled and was dismayed to find herself blushing. "Your tattoo." A magnificent and colorful dragon covered his chest and arms. "And, well, the other one is pretty special too," she managed to mumble.

His grin vanished. "Oh, you're new at this, aren't you?"

Her blush deepened and she averted her eyes. "I'm sorry."

Evan jumped to his feet and enfolded her in a gentle embrace. "Sorry? Oh, I'm the one who should be sorry for being so insensitive." He kissed her neck. "Amazing how little we really know about each other."

"We have a lifetime to learn," she said, fully aware of the irony but needing to affirm that—however brief it would be—it *was* their lifetime together.

"A moment can be an eternity."

"It'll have to be."

Kaia, who had always been strong, independent, and never needed anyone, surrendered for the first time in her life. With a sigh, she relinquished her need for control and allowed Evan to teach her the mysteries of love. He undressed her, lifted her into bed, and covered her body with kisses. Time lost all meaning as the thrill of touch and the merging of hearts held sway. When their bodies united, Kaia closed her eyes and floated in a sea of pleasure where—contrary to their handfasting vows—stars exploded and the earth shook.

CHAPTER SEVEN

Professor Greenberg seemed to have a different golf cap for every day of the week. Today's was tie-dyed. I decided that it must be because he was from Boulder, which had always overflowed with hippies, yuppies, and New Agers. And Boulder's spillover was pooling here in Union.

I smiled at him when I walked in the classroom door, then made my way to the back of the room to grab a seat with my friends. Jesse was already there with Belle Starr on his lap, and I noticed he had saved a seat for me next to him. Dominic and Sasha were in chairs on the other side of mine.

Belle Starr was whining and trying to squirm out of Jesse's arms. When I sat down, she instantly lunged for me.

"Fine," Jesse mumbled. "Go to Glory. See if I care. I don't like you much lately either." It was unusual for Jesse to be peevish.

"Brother-sister tiff?" I asked while Belle Starr tried to settle into my arms. She was leaning as far away from Jesse as possible, and it was threatening to tip me over.

Dominic reached out for her. "Here, I'll take her."

Eagerly, Belle Starr scrambled from my lap to Dominic's. She greeted him with face kisses and then settled down.

"What are you, some kind of pervert?" Jesse asked

Dominic. "You like little girls, Nicky-boy?"

I gasped. "How dare you. Belle Starr is just being Belle Starr."

Jesse stood to claim his sister. "Yeah, well as her brother it's my job to protect her from pervs."

Belle Starr screamed as Jesse approached and struck at him with tiny fists. Sasha quickly swept the little girl off Dominic's lap and onto her own.

"Is there a problem back there?" Professor Greenberg asked.

"No," Sasha said. "Everything is just fine."

"Let her stay with Sasha," I told Jesse. "And apologize to Nicky."

Jesse sniggered. "Can't tell me what to do, babe. I'm not your boyfriend. Yet."

"Yeah, well the way you're behaving you'll never be," I said.

Jesse looked at me with a cool, unreadable expression. "You never know about the future, do you?"

Thankfully, Jesse sat back down and left Belle Starr in Sasha's arms. The little girl glared at Jesse, thrust her thumb in her mouth, twisted around so her back faced us, and promptly fell asleep.

I wondered what the hell was happening. Belle Starr had always adored Jesse, and Jesse was always such a gentleman to everyone. Was it Nyx's influence? He'd spent a lot of time with her lately.

I opened my notebook and sneaked another quick peek at the letter I'd received from Kaia. *I believe America is still alive and am searching. Rory and Evan are helping. Will let you know when I have something.* She signed it, *Mrs. Kaia Moonstone-Killian.* My heart leapt at all the messages the brief letter contained. I had always believed

Erica was still alive. And I always knew Kaia loved Evan and was thrilled that she finally figured it out too. I glanced at Jesse and said a silent prayer they would find my sister before Nyx had an opportunity to influence our mother as much as she was apparently influencing my best friend. The angels had talked me out of trying to kill Nyx, but I wasn't convinced. Why couldn't a human slay a demon? It made no sense to me at all.

Professor Greenberg slapped his hands to bring the class to attention, then sat on the front edge of his desk. "Time, consciousness, reality. What are they really?"

"Totally messed up," someone said.

The professor grinned. "In a manner of speaking, yes. There seems no rhyme or reason to the universe or our experience of it."

Jesse leaned into me. "Sorry."

"Apologize to Nicky, not me," I whispered.

Jesse straightened up and grunted.

"I'm sure most of you are familiar with the famous quantum mechanics double-slit experiment," Professor Greenberg said. "It proved that the mere act of observation can change the outcome of an event. Observing matter makes it behave differently. The power of consciousness can change what something is. Think about that. Consciousness can change reality."

He stood and walked to the chalkboard where he wrote: SPACETIME AND CONSCIOUSNESS. "String theory postulates that physical spacetime is made up of multiple dimensions—at least ten and probably more. Then there is phenomenal spacetime, which is the reality we are commonly aware of. The renowned scientist Sir Arthur Eddington said, 'Events do not happen: they are just there, and we come across them as the observer on his voyage of exploration.' Consciousness observes them." He sat back down on the edge of his desk. "Everyone please close your eyes."

I closed my eyes.

"Take a moment and simply be. Don't think, don't feel...just be."

I did as he asked.

"That awareness is your consciousness, pure and simple. It's not your body, it's not your emotions, and it's not even your thoughts."

He gave us a few moments to "just be" before giving us permission to open our eyes.

"A new theory of consciousness suggests that it exists outside us in one of these other dimensions postulated in string theory. It wraps itself around our phenomenal universe, and the point where it and our phenomenal universe converge is the *now* that we experience as this moment in our individual life. If you examine your experience of consciousness, you'll realize that you always exist *right now*. However, the you that is experiencing this *now* is really in a parallel universe that is converging with this one, and you, my dear students, are really spacetime travelers on a voyage of exploration."

There was a long silence while the students tried to absorb his words. I looked around and saw confusion and skepticism, but I understood what he had said with utmost clarity. I raised my hand. "Didn't you begin this lecture by saying that consciousness has been proven to change reality?" I asked.

He tipped his hat to me. "Yes I did. Gives one *hope*, doesn't it?"

This time I didn't come unglued when he pointedly

used the *hope* word.

"So, theoretically, timespace could be changed?" I asked.

"Who could possibly do that?" a skeptical voice asked.

"Someone with an extraordinarily powerful consciousness," the professor said and winked at me.

*   *   *

"He winked at you," Jesse said as we walked to our next class. "What's going on between you two? Perv Nicky here, a chick-magnet cowboy who is God knows where, and magnificent me don't provide you with enough romantic choices?"

His uncharacteristic peevishness was really getting on my nerves. "One thing I learned a few months ago was that jealousy makes a guy really unattractive," I said, trying to avoid Dominic's eyes. For an angel, he had been a dreadful green-eyed monster. And Zane was even worse. What was it with men, anyway? "If you care about our friendship at all, Jesse, just lighten up."

Belle Starr, holding hands with Sasha and trotting alongside her, asked, "Magnificent who?"

Jesse glared at her. "Me."

Belle Starr thought that was uproariously funny, and after a wild bout of laughter, stuck her tongue out at Jesse.

I struggled mightily to keep a straight face as I led the way to art class.

Cosmic and Sunshine James were in charge of Union High's new art program. They had decided that instead of the town's annual offering of the first fruits of the harvest to the Blood Mother River on the fall equinox, there was going to be an art and music festival.

"Creativity is what Mother Earth is all about," Sunshine said, enthusiasm gushing from every pore. "As we previously discussed, instead of sacrificing first fruits to Her, we will offer up the fruits of our spirit." She stood at the front of the classroom with her husband while he wrote UNION HIGH'S FALL EQUINOX FESTIVAL on the chalkboard.

"I hope you've already begun your projects because time is running out," Cosmic said. "We've received permission to set up the art exhibition on one end of the Blood Mother Walkway Bridge while our music students perform on the other end. There will also be booths along the greenway for students and teachers to use for their own projects. The newspaper will promote the event, and we should have a great turnout. The deadline is just around the corner, so let's see what you've done so far."

I was surprised by how many students had their projects either completed or nearly completed. There was a flurry of activity while everyone unloaded backpacks or boxes and displayed their artistic creations on their desks.

For my project, I had framed large photographs I took of the three men in my life. The first was of Dominic holding Hallie, both of them looking into each other's eyes with utter love. The second one was Jesse holding Belle Starr; he was smiling his crooked smile at her, and she was bursting with giggles. Then there was a black and white photo I had taken of Zane. However, with his image I had done some clever magic and superimposed a photograph I had taken of a tintype image of his wife, Hope, who had died in 1882. I had caught Zane in a moment where the agony of his soul reflected in his face, and Hope's tintype displayed her utterly joyful nature. The pairing of the two images was haunting.

"Your cowboy?" The harsh voice behind me was Jesse's.

"Yes."

"Who's the woman?"

I hesitated. "A relative from the 1800s."

"He's not wearing a shirt," Jesse said.

Now I was becoming peevish. "Yeah, he's got great pecs, don't you think?"

"Bitch." He stormed off before I could respond. I felt like he had slapped me.

Okay, so I had been insensitive, but he was turning into someone I no longer knew.

Belle Starr emerged from her hiding place behind me and struggled to climb up onto my chair. She seemed quite intent on her mission, so I steadied her as she reached out and touched the photograph of Jesse. Specifically, she very carefully touched each of his eyes. "They're different now."

"What's different, honey? Jesse's eyes?"

Solemnly, she nodded. "I miss them. They loved me." She touched each of his eyes again, then climbed into my arms. I embraced her tightly and closed my own eyes as I tried to recall Jesse's new ones. Belle Starr was right. Panic washed through me like an out-of-control oil slick destroying all life in its path, which was exactly the effect Nyx was having on all life in her toxic path.

I struggled to calm my nerves, lifted Belle Starr to my hip, she wrapped her arms around me, and we walked around the room looking at other displays.

Kenny Nakamura was cradling a large, stuffed rainbow trout. An empty soup pot sat on his desk.

I approached him. "Kenny?"

He held the fish up to me, his smile full of pride. "I caught this and Grandfather suggested we make a trophy out of it. I'm trying to think of a way to display it with the empty soup pot to demonstrate the contrast of hunger and abundance."

Cosmic overheard and inserted himself into our conversation. "That's a very cool concept. Let's brainstorm it."

I smiled at Kenny and moved on.

Sasha had made a dream catcher. "I brushed Hallelujah and spun her hair for it," she said.

I looked closer and could see the delicate fibers were indeed comprised of copper, silver, white, and black hair. Woven into the web were tiny pinecones, acorns, dried flowers, and small colorful stones.

"It's gorgeous," I said.

Belle Starr reached out and touched it almost reverently. Then she pointed to a framed charcoal drawing on Dominic's desk. "It's Glory!"

The portrait of me was excellent.

"Wow," I said.

Dominic shrugged. "I used some of your father's art supplies."

I shook my head in amazement. "I didn't know you were an artist."

He laughed. "I didn't either."

"You're an angel of many surprises," I whispered.

"Angel?" Belle Starr asked.

"Whoops," I said.

Belle Starr gave Dominic a pensive look. Then she studied Sasha for a few moments and pointed at her. "She's an angel."

"Whoops," I repeated, and quickly walked away from them before Belle Starr could say anything else.

Carmela and TNT had set up their projects side-by-side.

"I used clay from the Blood Mother River to make a goddess," TNT said to me. The small red statue of a naked woman was a true piece of fertility art. Her breasts were lush, her hips wide, and her belly pregnant.

"Amazing," I said.

"Pretty goddess," Belle Starr whispered. "Pretty, pretty," she echoed.

Carmela had made a carving from a blackened, burned hunk of wood. "It's the angel of death."

I had noticed Carmela's depression worsening every day. My efforts to snap her out of it had been in vain.

From her perch on my hip, Belle Starr reached out and gently touched each of Carmela's eyes, who closed them but didn't even seem to have the energy to flinch. "Death angel," Belle Starr said. "Death, death."

Carmela's eyes did look lifeless. As had been the case with Jesse, I hadn't noticed the change before. How could two people have changed so profoundly in such a short period of time?

TNT gestured for me to follow her, and we left Carmela sitting at the desk, staring listlessly at her carving.

"That Gypsy girl is evil," TNT whispered the moment we were out of Carmela's earshot.

I nodded. "I know. No one will listen to me."

"My baby doll is taking drugs now. Nyx told her it was some sort of ancient Romany cure for depression, but I think it's opium and other stuff too. Carmela gets a buzz, sees visions, has dreams, then comes down hard."

TNT blinked away tears. "It's a vicious cycle and I'm losing her, Glory."

"Well, that would explain why things seem to be moving so fast." I looked up into TNT's questioning eyes. "Nyx's bad influence is overtaking people at record speed."

"Subtle isn't in that woman's vocabulary," TNT said. "What can we do? Should I let the cops know?"

The Baxters flickered across my mind and I knew that if TNT did anything like that she would be wiped out of existence as quickly as they had. "Don't do that. Please trust me. I know Nyx and Micah from before they moved here. I understand things you don't. Please just let me handle it with my own connections, okay?"

TNT looked doubtful. "I'm losing her."

"Keep loving her and let me take care of the rest, okay?"

"Oh, I can keep loving her good."

"Love good," Belle Starr echoed, then reached out to TNT and comforted her with kisses.

I marveled at the angel I held in my arms. There were angels, and then there were angels.

TNT returned to Carmela's side and I moved on, trying to avoid Nyx's group. However, Jesse came up behind me, grasped my arm, and pulled me toward their side of the room.

"You've got to see our art," he said.

The first thing that I noticed was a colorful oil painting that oozed horror. The Blood Mother River was personified as a hideous woman who exuded fury and hatred. Standing in raging waters, mutilated corpses of humans and animals swirled around her, and she regarded the carnage with an expression of pure evil. I gasped and tried to turn Belle Starr's face away from the sight, but what she then saw made her scream. I swung around and followed her gaze. Sitting on the desk in front of Nyx was a bird's nest filled with dead baby birds. They looked as if they were newly hatched.

"If the Blood Mother River doesn't get her sacrifice of the first fruits, she's going to be really pissed off and a lot of Mother Earth's babies are going to die," Nyx said.

Mr. and Mrs. James raced across the room and Sunshine snatched Belle Starr from my arms, but the little girl continued to scream.

"What kind of art is this?" Cosmic asked, waving spastically toward the dead birds.

"Art that imitates life," Nyx said. "The river expects a sacrifice and not the wimpy art festival you have planned."

"Get that out of my classroom right now," Sunshine said. Belle Starr's screams had shifted to shuddering sobs.

Cosmic pointed to Micah's pen and ink drawing—a skeletal image of a dead child. "And what the hell is that?"

"Every three seconds a child dies," Micah said quietly. "There'll be even more death without the sacrifice of first fruits."

Belle Starr's sobs turned to moans.

Cosmic shook his head and gave Jesse a look of utter confusion. "Mother Earth is divine, not vengeful. Mother Earth does not demand sacrifices, but only to be honored and respected. We've taught you better than this." His arm swept the spectacle of Jesse's gory painting, the dead birds, and the tragic drawing. "Get it all out of my classroom now. And you and I, young man, will be having a serious discussion later."

Jesse, Nyx, and Micah took their projects and left the room. Jesse smirked when he walked past me.

"Do you think it's true?" Carmela asked TNT. "If we don't offer the Blood Mother the first fruits, will there be more death?"

TNT grasped Carmela's hand and kissed it. "Of course not. Silly superstition."

The students exploded in a spirited debate about the entire affair and I walked back to my desk. That's when I saw that someone had vandalized my three photographs. The pictures, removed from their frames, were covered in obscenities.

In my heart, I knew that Jesse had done it.

CHAPTER EIGHT

Rory saw the albino bear. Kaia didn't.

Evan saw the albino bear. Kaia didn't.

A flustered Annie told Kaia she saw a big white bear in Kaia's cottage.

Even Brennan saw it.

"How come I didn't see it?" Kaia asked. Was marriage diminishing her powers? It had been her biggest fear and now—

"What's the significance of the bear?" Rory asked.

Rory, Evan, Brennan, and Kaia sat around a table in the central lodge. They shared a pot of tea and a platter of warm raisin and walnut cookies.

"It came to me once before, during my parents' execution." Kaia shivered at the coincidence. "I always believed it was the familiar—the totem—of a friend of my parents from Arizona."

"White Bear?" Brennan asked.

Kaia nodded.

Brennan grew pensive. "White Bear is a powerful medicine man. He was your father's best friend." She chuckled. "And, like Kevin, a true rebel. He owns a store in Sedona—I order from him occasionally."

"I feel you need to go see him," Rory said. "I'll stay here with Annie. You can use me to keep in touch with the coven. Now that I'll be the one with Annie, I expect not to hear purring when my mind tries to connect with yours."

"If White Bear is calling you, I would definitely listen," Brennan said.

"I'll drive," Evan said.

Kaia nodded. She felt that the events leading to her final days were beginning to unfold.

* * *

As they drove to Sedona, Kaia had a lot of time to think about the past, the present, and her future. For someone on the threshold of death, she was surprised to realize that she had never felt so alive.

A flash of lighting did not come from the sky, but from the energy of the earth rising to meet it. The earth Herself was given life by the connection. In the same fashion, passion had recharged Kaia and balanced her energy field. The transformation was exhilarating. It was no wonder that desire was life's sweetest mystery.

Kaia remembered something Dominic had once said. *Yearning preceded creation, caused creation, and sustains it. It's what holds the atoms together.*

She had worried that marrying Evan would weaken her resolve to face what was coming, but it only made her stronger. Kaia now knew that she could face anything the Goddess asked of her.

* * *

White Bear's shop, WHITE BEAR, had a flashing neon sign on the building that was a white bear. Another sign said it was "Sedona's Native American Medicine Bag." Also announced were, "Tours to local power vortexes!"

Kaia and Evan got out of his BMW and approached the

small store. The window advertised a product called *Vortex in a Can*. It said the contents had been "humanely gathered during the full lunar eclipse by nonsmoking vegetarians."

"Seriously?" Kaia said.

Evan laughed. "Sedona is known as a touristy place for New Agers, but this does make me wonder about White Bear. I mean, why would someone with real power be so commercial?"

Kaia struggled to catch the hope that threatened to slip away. Had this trip been a foolish waste of precious time?

Evan opened the door and the scent of sage and the sound of Native American flute music greeted them. The newlyweds held hands and stepped inside.

Kaia immediately noticed the Native American blankets, full-feather headdresses, peace pipes, garish art, and touristy items like Sedona tee shirts and mugs with sayings like, *Sedona: where old age meets New Age* and *Sedona: Vortex Power Rocks!* However, tucked away in corners were crystals, herbs, handmade jewelry, and authentic medicine power items.

Evan leaned over and whispered, "I'm sensing there's more here than meets the third eye."

Kaia chuckled. "I sure hope so."

A big, burly man around fifty years old sat behind the counter. His long, dark, gray-streaked hair was in a ponytail, and he wore jeans with a light cotton shirt. When he looked up at them and saw Kaia, a brilliant smile crossed his face. "Why Kaia Moonstone, fancy meeting you here."

She recognized him from when she was a very little girl—before the family moved to Colorado. She smiled. "I got the impression you wanted me to come."

He stood, stepped out from behind the counter, and embraced her in what crossed her mind as a classic bear hug. "It's been a long time." He extended his beefy hand to Evan. "You must be the new husband. A mountain lion cub told me there was an interloper sleeping in Kaia's bed. The cub is not happy to share, by the way."

Evan shook his hand and introduced himself. "Evan Killian. Yes, I noticed Annie was a bit grumpy with me."

"She did enjoy being part of the handfasting ritual, though," White Bear said. "So there's that, at least."

Okay, Kaia thought. *Despite the appearance of things, he really is a man of power*. She found herself breathing a bit easier.

White Bear held onto Evan's hand longer than was necessary and regarded him with assessing eyes. "You chose well, Kaia." He released Evan and looked at her. "But I would expect no less from the daughter of Kevin and Deirdre."

Emotions burst through the dam of Kaia's reserve and she clutched at him. This time, their embrace involved both their hearts. Filled with sudden memories of her parents and a childhood that predated Crestone, she felt as if she had come home.

He patted her back gently and murmured soothing words in a language Kaia didn't understand. "You're tired and hungry after your long trip," he said at last. "Let me lock up the store. I've got dinner ready for you."

* * *

White Bear lived above his store in a simple apartment that simmered with magical energy. It was in stark contrast to the commercial atmosphere below.

He gestured for them to sit at his small kitchen table and removed warm pans from the oven. He served them barbeque beans and cornbread filled with cheese, corn kernels, and jalapeno peppers. He set out glasses of ice water, grabbed a cup of coffee for himself, then sat down across from them.

His chin jutted toward the water glasses. "It's special water from a deep well in the center of Sedona's most powerful magical vortex. It was collected by naked vestal virgins at midnight on Midsummer's Eve."

Kaia blinked.

Evan regarded his glass with interest. "Naked virgins, huh?"

"Seriously?" Kaia asked.

White Bear erupted in a giant belly laugh. "Hell, no. You were so worried about *Vortex in a Can*, thought I'd yank your chain."

Well, Kaia quickly decided as she dug into her food, *I guess I can't hide anything from him.* "Why do you do it? You know, be so commercial?"

He shrugged. "Sedona, like where you live in Crestone, is one of the most powerful places on the planet. It was sacred to Native people long before Europeans arrived. Word's gotten out. I figure if I play it up silly enough, maybe some won't take it so seriously and go away." His hand slapped the table. "The spirit of this land does not want to be a tourist attraction. We're getting over forty thousand visitors a year now. I do what I can to help."

Kaia could understand his logic. She would be horrified if forty thousand tourists descended on Crestone.

"What about your vortex tours?" Evan asked.

"I steer them away from the truly powerful ones. If they really knew what's here...well, they would be so affected that word would get out and things would become worse."

"Aunt Brennan did say you were a rebel," Kaia said.

He smiled. "Oh your dad and I were total hell-raisers. And don't let that crafty woman fool you—Brennan was too. They defied their family to leave the city and start the Crestone covenstead. Their parents were successful doctors in Phoenix, and despite their magical heritage—or perhaps because of it—worked hard to blend in and not bring attention to themselves. The whole witch commune concept caused their parents to disown them."

Kaia was startled. She remembered her grandparents and wondered why they had never visited, but Brennan always evaded her questions. "What about my mother's parents? I never knew them at all."

A shadow crossed White Bear's face and shields came up. He didn't respond and she couldn't read him, so decided to drop the subject.

"Thank you for being there with me when my parents were killed," she said at last.

"I've been looking out for you your whole life. I took a sacred oath at your birth that I always would. Do you remember me helping you in the car accident last summer?"

Kaia thought back to when Micah had flipped the Explorer she was riding in with Glory, Dominic, Zane, and Hallelujah. At the time, she didn't recall White Bear's presence, but now she remembered him manifesting and wrapping big, white furry arms around her. "Oh. You held me the entire time."

"If I hadn't, your head would have split like a ripe

melon."

Gratitude filled her. "Thank you."

He shrugged. "I'm your guardian."

"Why did you appear to everyone else but me the other night?"

His eyes twinkled. "I did try but you were exuding a bridal glow of joy that was spinning and flashing out in all directions like a supernova gone wild. I figured the others would convey my message."

Kaia was afraid to ask. "Why did you call me here?"

He hesitated for a moment. "I saw your death not too far from here and not too far in the future. I took a sacred oath to take care of you."

Someone who was not a witch might have asked, *Then why did you bring me to the place of my certain death?* But Kaia asked, "So you called me here to help me meet my fate?"

Evan set down his bread and pushed himself away from the table, his meal only half-eaten.

Kaia touched his arm. "Eat. You must stay strong."

White Bear watched their exchange with obvious compassion. "This news doesn't appear surprising to you. Tell me what you know."

Kaia took a sip of water and collected her thoughts. There was so much to tell him. "During the pandemic, I was called upon by the Caretakers to assist a girl named Glory Templeton, whose blood contained elements needed to stop the plague. I—"

White Bear held up a hand to silence her, then pointed at Evan. "I knew you looked familiar. You were the reporter who broke the news on CNN about the vaccine having been found."

Evan nodded.

"You never said anything about this girl."

"Glory didn't want to be labeled a savior. She just wanted it to all be over and get on with her life."

White Bear's eyes narrowed. "In your report you said that a pharmaceutical company had found the vaccine early in the great tragedy, but kept it from the public for unknown reasons. That kidnapped scientist you helped rescue was the one who had discovered the conspiracy."

Evan nodded. "That was Glory's mother. She injected the last vial of the cure into Glory to save her life, and it made her a living vial of that cure. Ah, I mean vaccine."

White Bear grew pensive. "No, you said cure. Twice."

Uh, oh, Kaia thought. Powerful people had ordered Evan to reveal only a fraction of the truth about the panplague in his reporting of the events. He had successfully kept many secrets, but White Bear was good at disarming shields.

"Well, let me just throw some things out here," White Bear said. "Now, it makes sense to me why the supposed vaccine was curing people who already had the virus. The doctors explained it away as an unexpected fluke. Since there was a *cure* for the virus, then I would guess the virus itself was manmade because there ain't no cure for true influenza virus. And since the real vaccine and cure were both initially withheld from the general public, I would guess that this conspiracy was related to a planned program of world depopulation."

"What would make you come to such a conclusion?" Evan asked in his most neutral, reporter's voice.

"Because there's a powerful group comprised of the world's wealthiest people, members of secret organizations, and some crazy mad scientists, who have an agenda to do just that. I call them the shadow government."

Kaia was astounded. He was absolutely correct. That's what they had discovered while helping Glory. She and Evan shared nervous glances.

"You seem so certain of your hypothesis," Evan said.

White Bear shrugged. "There are many dark spirits who work in the shadows with these groups. They've formed an unholy alliance. I speak to spirits and they tell me things."

Kaia psychically assessed the situation and said to Evan, "There are no secrets to be kept here. Go ahead and tell him what we know."

Evan nodded. "According to the group of scientists who are working to depopulate the planet, they claim a noble motive. They say there are too many people for the planet to support. The group claims that they are sacrificing some so others may live. But their goal is to eventually kill billions—at least five billion more than they've already managed to eradicate—one way or another."

"They're also working to destroy religion," White Bear said. "Their plans for that are in motion."

"How do you know?" Evan asked.

"The spirits tell me much. Once humanity has surrendered its spiritual faith, dark spirits will have a field day. It's all in the damn plan."

The three of them sat in silence for a long time, lost in their own thoughts. Then White Bear said to Kaia, "You were going to tell me what you know about your death."

Kaia nodded. "I promised Glory that I would help her find her sister who was kidnapped eleven years ago. Erica would be eighteen years old now, and I feel she's still alive. Rory, the psychic from Evan's coven, saw me die in the process of helping Glory." Kaia dug around in her purse and withdrew the photograph Glory had sent. "Erica's very distinctive looking—she's got that beauty mark on her cheek. Rory saw a reflection of her in the sunglasses I was wearing. Erica and Glory were looking down at me."

"What else did this Rory see?" White Bear asked.

"A barren landscape. Red earth. Nothing else."

"What did you see?" Evan asked White Bear.

"Two girls staring down at Kaia's body. One—tall, thin, beautiful—had that mark on her cheek. The other was real pretty, a big girl—buxom, hippy."

"That would be Glory." Kaia chuckled. "She's very proud of her curves."

"I'll remember that." White Bear tried for a smile, but settled for a sigh. "I know the place. It's an access point to a secret underground facility. The earth tells me they perform scientific experiments there that disrupt time and space. It's a natural vortex, a powerful planetary spot where time and space are naturally distorted. Scientists discovered its power and are utilizing it."

"So, Erica might have been kidnapped to be part of that experiment?" Kaia asked.

White Bear shrugged. "For over forty years every newborn's DNA is sampled before they're released from the hospital. There's a DNA database that is monumental in scope. They're looking for markers—markers that will either create a super race or at least be in harmony with the plans they have for the planet. Add to that, something like two thousand children are kidnapped every day and most will never be heard from again. Yeah, there's something big going on."

Shocked, Kaia looked at Evan, who said, "It's true—

the DNA database thing. And I've never personally believed that all those kidnapped children are related to pedophiles. No, it's something much more organized."

Kaia processed everything that she had just learned. It appeared as if she would be able to help Glory find Erica, and then be killed so she wouldn't reveal secrets. "Someone tried to kidnap Glory last winter. Davina, one of the Caretakers, later told Glory that the kidnappers wanted her for the exact same reason they had taken Erica."

White Bear's eyes narrowed. "Some special DNA going on in that family?"

Kaia shrugged.

"With as many years as Erica has been with them, is it possible she's on their side now?" Evan asked White Bear.

"Could be. I'll take you to the spot tomorrow as if we're on a tourist vortex tour. You won't see them, but they'll see you, so we need to have you in disguise— there are more surveillance devices out there than on the roof of the CIA building. Then, later, Kaia must return alone with Glory."

"Do we tell Glory what we know?" Kaia asked.

White Bear nodded. "She should be prepared. Is she a smart girl?"

"Scary smart," Evan said. "Gutsy. Clever."

"Good. She'll need to be. We're delivering her into their hands and no one will be there to help her."

"Davina asked Glory to be a warrior of light," Kaia said. "This isn't just about a missing sister but about good versus evil on a huge scale."

Evan moaned. "Isn't there anything we can do to prevent Kaia's death?"

"I'll stay up tonight and talk to the spirits," White Bear said. "But my heart says no."

* * *

There was a tiny balcony off the guest bedroom. Kaia and Evan curled up together on a chaise lounge and watched the brilliantly clear sky.

Kaia cleared her throat. "There are some things I want to say tonight that you're not going to want to hear—"

"Please don't—"

"But I've got to say them and if you respect me and our religion, you'll listen." She groped in the dark to clasp his hand. "You will love another woman and make sweet love to her, plant your seed in her, create life with her, and even marry her if it will bring her joy, because love changes the world from black and white to color and there's another woman out there who deserves that gift from you. You are in service to the Goddess, and the Goddess lives in all women. Find another one to serve and worship. The Goddess in me is commanding you to fulfill this divine decree. It is my dying wish."

Kaia felt his resistance, his anger, and his ultimate surrender. She had played the Goddess card, and the command of the Goddess was supreme in their religion. Embedded in the genes of men from time immemorial was the act of sacrificing their essence in the creation and service of life. Thousands of years of genetic memory fought its way to the surface of this 21st century male, and he replied with reverent obedience in the words common to their ancient faith.

"As you wish, my Lady."

*   *   *

Sedona really was magical. The land was serene, and it filled Kaia with overwhelming peace. If she had to die, she was glad it would be here. It felt like sacred space—she could almost hear the whispered voice of Mother Earth Herself chanting creation into being, moment by moment.

On their drive to Sedona the day before, Kaia and Evan had passed through a lush forest of pine trees, descended into a sixteen-mile winding gorge with spectacular streams, waterfalls, and verdant greenery wedged between sheer rock walls, and then spilled out onto the high desert of Sedona. Stunning red buttes and towering monoliths hovered over the town like mystical sentinels guarding holy ground. Yesterday Kaia hadn't paid too much attention to her surroundings. Now that she knew this was where she would surrender her body, everything held enormous fascination for her.

After breakfast, White Bear provided them tacky touristy tee shirts, oversized sunglasses, and big hats in order to hide their identities, loaded them into the vortex tourmobile, and headed out into the bright day.

"Every time I got up in the night I saw you in the backyard tending your fire pit," Kaia said to White Bear.

"I was talking to the spirits."

"Anything new to report?" Kaia asked. She couldn't disguise the hopefulness in her voice.

"They revealed many things to me. But, no, you are still destined to die as we thought."

Kaia took a deep breath. Air had never smelled so sweet.

"If we tell Glory that Kaia's going to die, she might

call the whole thing off," Evan said.

"That's true," White Bear said. "Kaia shouldn't tell her."

Evan didn't even try to hide his disappointment.

"However, I want Kaia to tell her to pay attention to everything that happens. Make Glory wear a watch and tell her to take note of exactly when things happen. If she asks questions, just tell her to shut up and do it." He dug in his shirt pocket, pulled out a folded slip of paper, and pressed it into Kaia's hand. "These are the geographical coordinates for the entrance to underground base I call The Time Vortex. Tell Glory to memorize them."

"Why?" Kaia asked, hoping he wouldn't tell her to just shut up and do it.

"Remember that she's going to have to figure out a way to escape."

Kaia thought about it. "Can't you rescue her?"

"You have no idea what's going on there."

Kaia took that to be a definite no.

"Tell us," Evan said.

"Are you asking as a husband or a reporter?"

"Both."

White Bear sat in silence for a long time before changing the subject. "There are a few popular vortexes in Sedona. We're going to tour a couple and then drive out to the one that matters."

"If we're being watched—" Kaia began.

"I go there all the time," White Bear said. "Sometimes I take people; sometimes I don't...depends on the people. The hidden cameras and mics are used to me. I must make them nervous, which is why we might be under surveillance. However, no men in black have visited me in the middle of the night, so they probably think I'm a harmless fringe nutcase." He grinned. "Every once in a while I go out there in full feather headdress regalia, drink water out of a vodka bottle, and dance my ass off."

Kaia laughed. "I'd like to see that."

White Bear shook his head. "I dance like a drunken monkey. It ain't pretty."

The first stop on the vortex tour was the Airport Vortex, located off Airport Road. They parked and hiked into the sacred site.

Sparse sage green groundcover adorned the red earth. There were two hills that Kaia, Evan, and White Bear walked between, then they followed a path that didn't appear heavily trodden. Suddenly, a change in atmospheric pressure hit them.

"Whoa," Evan said. "Feel that?"

Kaia could almost see the funnel-shaped energy field emerging from the ground. She knelt down to examine a juniper tree that had grown in a spiral design. Even its branches twisted in a slow helical spiral growth pattern. "Fascinating."

"The spiral dance," Evan said. In their religion, the spiral design was sacred, representing connection to the divine.

"Rebirth, evolution, always circling in on itself, always reaching higher," Kaia murmured. She glanced down at the Celtic dragon tattoo on her wrist and it brought her a measure of comfort. Of course she knew that death was just a transition, and there would be growth and rebirth involved. She tried to focus on that, instead of what she was leaving behind.

"The energy here is strong in courage," White Bear said. "Soak it up. Both of you." He walked away and allowed the young couple time to absorb the gift the

Mother offered.

When they returned to the SUV and settled in, Evan said, "Okay, how about if I ask as a husband and not a reporter?" He obviously was not going to let White Bear ignore his questions.

"We're going to Cathedral Rock Vortex next," White Bear said. "Compassion is the gift of that vortex."

"Off the record?" Evan said. "Please?"

Kaia reached out, took his hand, and was surprised to feel it trembling.

White Bear opened a cooler on the floor and tossed them each a bottle of water, then started up the engine. "There will come a time when you will use the information as a reporter. It isn't now. What's happening now pales in comparison to what they're planning down the road. That's when you'll be a reporter."

"Okay," Evan said.

White Bear twisted open his own bottle of water and chugged, then stuck it in the holder in his console. "I call the special place I'm taking you to, The Time Vortex. The energy there warps time and space. It's not a wimpy vortex that emerges in relatively small areas like the others, it's a monster that spans a great deal of the Four Corners area—where Arizona, Colorado, Utah, and New Mexico meet. Native peoples have known about it for...well, forever. Races of people have emerged from it and disappeared into it."

"The Anasazi?" Kaia asked.

White Bear nodded. "And others. Some races in this region have disappeared entirely and others, like the Hopi, claim to have emerged from it. About three thousand feet down from the surface you have an aquifer that is a veritable great lake of fresh water. The entire underground region around here is full of enormous sandstone caverns, underground rivers, tubes from extinct volcanoes. Large self-sustaining communities are believed to be there. Our people have seen construction equipment go down but never come up—there are a number of entrances throughout the Four Corners. It's believed ancient peoples existed there and modern people have rediscovered the hidden world. But what makes it special besides the geological assets, is the vortex. Time and space are fluid here. What may have begun as a massive underground survival bunker built by the shadow government for catastrophic situations has become much more. And the spirits tell me it's all tied into the plans to depopulate the planet and take control of the survivors."

"So, possibly a new race of people being engineered by selective breeding, a self-sustaining bunker of ginormous proportions, unlimited financial resources, the best scientific minds, and the means to control time?" Evan said.

"Wow," Kaia whispered.

The enormity of the situation brought the conversation to a halt, as each withdrew into thought. They remained silent until they were at the Cathedral Rock Vortex.

"The gift of this vortex is compassion," White Bear reminded them.

The beauty of Cathedral Rock was breathtaking, but they did not need to scale the towering red rocks to experience the vortex. They followed the creek to an area where it was closest to the rock formation and surrendered to its warm, nurturing energy. The enchanting beauty of the massive red rocks rising majestically against the backdrop of the royal blue sky and then reflected in the perfect mirror of the water was the Earth Goddess at Her most alluring. The arms of compassion She wrapped around Kaia melted away any quiet whispers of lingering resistance the young witch had about laying down her life for the sake of others. She was at peace.

* * *

"We'll be there soon," White Bear said. "Evan, since you're a public figure and could easily be identified with all that Homeland Security facial recognition technology stuff, you should just stay in the car. Pretend you're asleep. Kaia can pitch a fit about being tired too, and we can get out of here quickly. When Kaia eventually shows up with Glory, they're going to seize the opportunity to snatch her since their last attempt failed."

"Why can't I bring Glory?" Evan asked. "Why does Kaia have to do it? I'd gladly die in her place."

White Bear gave him a look of admiration but shook his head. "I asked the spirits if I could ferry Glory out here myself, but it's gotta be Kaia for some reason."

"Why can't we just program the GPS to bring Glory here?" Evan asked. "Then no one has to die."

"If no one dies how will Glory know that what's happening here is evil?" Kaia asked.

Evan shrugged. "We'll tell her."

"No, it's not the same thing," Kaia said. "Besides, I have plans when I die."

Both Evan and White Bear turned to look at her.

"I'm not going into the light. I plan to stay behind to vanquish Nyx. It was a vow I made as a child and the only thing I've not accomplished that I must. Now, because of me, Nyx is stealing the souls of Glory's loved ones. If I had already vanquished her.... No, I've got to stop her."

Evan groaned.

"That wouldn't be wise," White Bear said. "It's one thing taking on a demon when embodied. Out of body, you're so much more vulnerable." He whistled. "Man, that wouldn't be wise at all."

"I'll vanquish Nyx," Evan said. "I'll assume the vow you took."

"The vow is mine. Besides, you're not a demon hunter. It takes special talents."

"You stand to lose your soul if you fail," Evan said.

"It's my risk to take."

Evan pulled Kaia into his arms and wept.

* * *

The Time Vortex was a rocky, barren area of land north of Sedona, up along the Mogollon Rim. Large rock formations and brown scrub dotted the red landscape. There was nothing civilized in sight.

"Is this what you brought us all this way for?" Kaia shouted at White Bear. "This isn't what I'd call magical—not like the other places you took us."

"It's a great power spot," White Bear said. "Can't you feel it?"

Kaia stamped her foot. "All I feel is the need to pee and then go to sleep." She flailed her arms toward the SUV. "Look. He's already crashed. We're exhausted. Just take us back."

"Do you want to pee first?" White Bear asked patiently.

"Not out here. My butt's likely to get stung by a

scorpion or something. Just take us home, okay?"

White Bear opened the car door for her. After she got in and he closed it, he said, "Ungrateful little brat." He spread his arms wide, looked at the sky, and shouted, "Oh Great Spirit, why does no one ever believe me?"

* * *

In parting, White Bear embraced Kaia in a lingering bear hug. "I am proud of your spirit. Your great courage brings honor to your ancestors." He shook Evan's hand and said, "Be strong."

CHAPTER NINE

Sasha loved ice cream. I decided it was a good thing that when the angel family had been sent on this mission their Father had provided them with an apparent unlimited amount of money—because a huge chunk of it seemed to be paying for every flavor of ice cream available in Union. With the James Family Organic Dairy Farm churning out a multitude of flavors, and problems with the truck lines that normally transported it, there was a lot of ice cream stranded in Union. This seemed to make Sasha a very happy angel.

"Dad and I used to sit at this picnic table eating ice cream on hot Saturday mornings like today," I said. The shade from the cottonwood tree draped us in a cool cloak. "Dad used to recite poetry in between mouthfuls of his favorite flavor, pistachio. He'd pick out chunks of nut and set them on the table to tempt brave squirrels." I blinked back tears at the memory. I missed him more each day.

Sasha looked at me. "Your father still recites poetry." Her tone was kind.

I struggled for my voice. "Some of it was a bit, um, colorful."

Sasha nodded. "Yep. It still is."

I managed a laugh. I thought about what Dad took with him and what he left behind. "I was surprised that Nicky bought Dad's truck." The Chevy Silverado had been out by the road with a big FOR SALE sign for months until Dominic decided to buy it. "Your Father must be loaded."

Sasha giggled and scraped the bottom of her bowl. "You could say that."

"I appreciate the rent money too. Mom seems in no hurry to find a new job, and I heard her on the phone with Nyx last night. She's actually giving Nyx money for mediumship services." My fist slammed onto the picnic table. "Why can't I stop Nyx? Tell me again why I'm not allowed to vanquish her, turn her over to the cops, burn her alive, drive a stake through her heart, or something equally satisfying? I'm a warrior of the light and not allowed to fight for crissakes. It's making me crazy, Sasha."

Sasha licked her spoon. "There are special magical skills needed to destroy a demon, and you don't possess them. You'd just get yourself killed, which would be really counterproductive at this stage of the game."

"But my mom, my friends. How can I protect them?" I was trembling with a mixture of fear and rage.

"You're very much in the same position we angels are. You can only encourage others to make the right choices. They have free will."

"Tell me again what angels are permitted to do?"

"Encourage, support, love our charges. In certain circumstances, we can intervene and save their lives, but we can't do a thing about their souls. And neither can you." Sasha's spoon poked toward my bowl of melting chocolate chip ice cream. "You going to finish that?"

I pushed my bowl across the table to her.

"Jesse may be running with the wrong crowd, but his family dairy sure does wonders with the nectar their cows provide," Sasha said.

I smiled. "True that." I glanced at Dominic, who was lying on his side in a hammock that stretched across the studio's front porch. His eyes were closed, and the orange-striped barn cat whose litter now lived on the bed inside the studio alongside the mice and squirrels was curled up in the curve of his belly. "Where are the kittens?"

Sasha dove into my bowl of ice cream. "Milton is guarding them, while Hallelujah is guarding us." Her spoon flickered in the sunlight as it poked in the general direction of Hallie, who sat a few yards away near the property line. She was trying to stare down the little red demon puppy from Hell. Hex lay at the edge of her property line staring back through slit amber eyes.

I groaned. "That's not going to end well, is it?"

"Hallelujah is conflicted. Hex is such a cute little puppy, and Hallelujah's latent maternal instincts are wrestling with the desire to nurture her while at the same time wanting to tear her to pieces."

Noticing my attention, the adorable-looking little Hex bared a mouthful of needlelike teeth and hissed like a nasty old Tomcat.

Despite the afternoon sun, gooseflesh swept across my body.

"Keep up the good work, Hallie," I said.

Hallelujah grunted.

I studied Sasha, who seemed to be around my age. "When you were created as an angel were you a baby or have you always been like you are now?"

"Like I am now. I'll always look the same when in human form. It has to do with morphogenic fields and the image God had in mind when I was formed."

"So, when I'm an old lady will I still have a teenage guardian angel, or will I be assigned someone new who's age-appropriate?"

Sasha smiled. "I have no idea. I'm not very experienced at all this yet."

I thought about it. "Nicky told me that he only ever guarded one other human—before he took me over from you for that little while during the great tragedy." I faltered, unsure whether it had been a mistake to bring it up. Things didn't end up well with the boy he had guarded. "Since you and Nicky were created at the same time, was I your first charge?"

A flash of pure panic crossed Sasha's face and she dropped her spoon. "Um. Well, yes and no." Her sigh was loud. "And, well, yes." Her hand accidentally knocked the ceramic bowl onto the ground where it cracked in half. "And no."

Her eyes refused to meet mine.

I wanted to ask questions but was too confused by her reaction to formulate anything specific. When I opened my mouth hoping something articulate would come out, Dominic rolled over onto his back and started to snore. The fat little orange cat yowled in protest and moved to the crook of his arm.

Sasha looked at Dominic and her expression of panic increased. She jumped to her feet. "Um, I'll go get more ice cream now." Her voice quavered as she bent down to pick up the broken bowl. "You want some?"

I grasped her wrist and forced her back into her seat. "What just happened there? Is Nicky actually snoring?"

"I...I think he's got some sinus issues—"

"Which have to do with *snoring*." As my grip tightened on her arm, its luminosity increased and I could feel her intent to dematerialize. "Oh no. You're not going anywhere, Sasha. Tell me."

Her eyes met mine with as miserable an expression as I had ever seen on an angel—and I had seen some miserable angels in my day.

"Angels don't sleep," I whispered.

She nodded.

My mind raced down the logical road and ended up crossing the finish line in two seconds flat. "He's not an angel anymore?"

Sasha groaned. "I never told you that."

I released her wrist and fought to catch my breath—it was trying to escape having to ask the questions. "When? How? Why?"

Sasha lowered her eyes and examined the two halves of one previous whole that her hands held. "You should ask him."

"I'm asking you. You're my guardian angel. Your purpose is to protect me. I'm feeling in some desperate need of protection right now." It was true. My heartbeat was struggling to find a less ominous rhythm.

Sasha set aside the bowl and looked at me with an expression of pure compassion. "He asked to be released from his birthright so he might have a chance to win your heart. He loves you, and he didn't want to put either of you in a position of violating the rules that forbid romantic love between a human and angel."

"But...but—"

She took my hands in hers. "He realizes you haven't made a choice yet between him and Zane. He's not trying to force your heart. He just wanted to be honorable."

"But...but—"

"What if you don't choose Dominic? He knows that's

a possibility. It's a risk he's willing to take."

"But he can become an angel again if that happens, right?"

Sasha shook her head.

I snatched my hands from hers and ran them through my hair. "Is God mad at him? Is he damned?"

"God is not mad and, no, Dominic isn't damned. If you reject him, he'll live his life out as a human being."

I looked at Dominic. The mother mouse scampered up to join the mother cat and the two of them curled up together in his arm. "But the peaceful effect he has on everyone. His magical smell. He still has all those things."

"Human or angel, he's a spiritual being. Very evolved. Saints of many religions have the same effect on people and animals. Many have been said to smell of roses or sandalwood. Their auras vibrate to a high frequency."

That flustered me even more, and I groaned. "I can't be in love with a saint. That seems even stranger than romancing an angel."

"Love is love. Don't let your head cripple your heart."

"Is God mad at me for tempting Nicky away from his calling?" It was a weird question for me. I wasn't even sure I believed in God. Confusion clouded my senses as I found myself in the midst of a swirling, dark hurricane. I struggled to find its eye.

"When Dominic was assigned to be your guardian during the pandemic he hated humanity. Your goodness opened his heart to your species. Your love awakened his. We're all grateful for the influence you had on him."

I slammed my fist on the table again and winced—it was becoming sore from all my abuse. "How come I—who had never been in love with anyone before in my life—fell in love with two guys in one short week?"

"With Dominic it was because when you died and he helped you return, you formed an empathic connection that was born outside of time and space. With Zane it was because of, um, well, that special connection you have with Hope." Sasha's expression grew miserable again.

"I want to understand the Hope thing. Please explain it to me." I was desperate for answers.

She shook her head.

"How am I supposed to make a choice between them when I don't understand why I feel like I do?"

"Please trust me when I tell you that you will find your answers. In time." She giggled.

"It's not funny."

The smile instantly left her lips. "No. No, it's not funny at all. I'm sorry. I...I'm pretty overwhelmed myself."

I thought of the more experienced angel in the family. "I had better talk to Rebekah about Nicky, shouldn't I?"

"She's inside, if you'd like to see her."

Unsteadily, I got to my feet. Quietly, I tiptoed up the porch steps, past Dominic, and slipped inside the studio. Rebekah sat cross-legged on the bed, petting all the baby creatures. There seemed so many more than the last time I had visited.

Rebekah tickled the belly of a tiny skunk who lay on its back with all four perfect feet in the air. I could have sworn it was smiling.

Without looking at me, Rebekah said, "Love is the energy upon which this entire creation is based. Love is what matters most. God celebrates love, however it manifests."

"What if I hurt Nicky?"

"That's the risk faced by anyone who chooses love."

I stood there awkwardly, wanting more from her. Finally, she said, "Give him a chance to truly win your heart. If it doesn't happen, be honest. Be kind. Be the honorable human being I know you to be."

* * *

I decided to join Hallie in her staredown with the demon puppy from Hell. It gave me something to do at least, so I wouldn't have to think about my own personal *Book of Revelations*.

I reached out and ran my fingers through Hallie's long black, white, copper, and silver hair. "Do you still miss Dad?" She had been his dog before the pan-plague stole him from us.

The expression in her sky blue eyes as they flickered in my direction, told me she did.

"You've taken such good care of us since he left. He'd be so proud."

She leaned over and kissed my face.

I glanced at Hex. "I bet you don't even know what love is. Could that be why you're so evil?"

"She's evil because she's mine." Nyx's smug voice emerged from the shadows a moment before she stepped into the light.

I slipped a protective arm around Hallie. "Why pit the dogs against each other? What's the point?"

Nyx sat on the ground next to Hex. "It's fun. I told you that I'm after souls. All the pretty souls. Human, angelic, canine...they'll all be mine before this is over."

"You'll never take Hallie or Milton. Our love will keep them safe."

"Is your love keeping your mother safe?"

My stomach did a somersault. "I'm working on that."

Nyx laughed. "Really? I always heard you were such a heroic little creature. Not really seeing it."

I would much rather have punched her than the picnic table, but Sasha warned me not to. I wasn't very good at following rules and my internal battle raged on, so I channeled my rage into sarcasm. "Have you contacted my sister's soul in the afterlife yet and passed on messages from her to Mom?"

Nyx tossed her head. "Oh, yes. Erica has been most helpful. Of course, everything has a price and your mother is more than happy to pay it. For every message I manage to squeeze out of Erica, we're squeezing an awful lot of money out of dear Katie. Pretty soon there will be no boundary between your property and mine because it'll all be mine."

"I won't let that happen," Dominic said from behind me.

Nyx looked up at him. "Oh, do angels have golden wings now? Gold is worth quite a lot these days. Or are you just independently wealthy?"

"Yes," Dominic said.

Nyx's eyebrows lifted in surprise and she waited for him to elaborate, but he didn't.

Jesse stepped out from behind a tree near Nyx. "Angels? What are you talking about?"

Nyx rolled her eyes. "Whoops. Let the cat out of that bag, didn't I?"

I realized I could now tell Jesse the truth and felt a surge of hope that maybe it would bring him back to me. "Nyx is a demoness," I said. "Micah is a fallen angel. You're in way over your head, Jesse. Are these creatures who you really want as friends?"

Jesse paled and closed his eyes. I could practically see his brain processing all the facts. After a few minutes, his color returned, he opened his eyes, and smiled. "Hot damn. Well now I'm a rebel with a cause, and a mighty exciting one at that." He winked at me. "Bad boys are way more fun than angels, Glory. The fire is much hotter."

My heart broke for Jesse. I stood, took Dominic's hand, and called Hallie. "Let's go home. There's love there." We turned and walked toward the house.

I squeezed Dominic's hand. "I know about you," I whispered.

"I know you do," he said.

We were still empathically connected. I supposed we always would be.

* * *

Dominic asked me out on a date. In my entire life, I had never before been out on a real date.

"The theater department at the university in Boulder is putting on a play," Dominic said. "Apparently they were already in rehearsals before the pandemic closed the schools, so the survivors got the production ready in record time."

"What is it?" I asked.

"*Godspell.*"

I choked on my iced tea—we were sitting at my kitchen table. "Seriously?"

He grinned. "Nah. Actually, it's *Jesus Christ Superstar.*"

"Really?"

His grin widened, lighting up his gorgeous face.

"Okay, well it's really *Romeo and Juliet*."

I thought about it. "Do you know the story of *Romeo and Juliet*?" His first charge as a guardian angel was a teenage boy who loved movies, and that was how Dominic developed a passion for them. I couldn't imagine the boy ever watched *Romeo and Juliet*.

"I know it's Shakespeare. I've never seen Shakespeare."

"Okay." I wondered if I should warn him about the ending.

He sensed my hesitation. "Is it something you would enjoy? With things so slow to return to normal since the meltdown, it's our only choice. Well, there is one movie playing at a theatre in Boulder, but it's one of the *Twilight* movies and I just didn't think that would help my case to win over your heart."

I burst out laughing. "No, the glories of vampire love would probably be counterproductive to the whole taking me out on a date thing. Shakespeare's good. Every former angel should experience Shakespeare once in his or her life."

"Professor Greenberg told me that a popular pizza parlor has reopened on Boulder's Pearl Street Mall. I remember from Atlanta that you like pizza."

His earnestness touched me. "Been doing research on taking women on dates?"

His smile turned shy and he nodded.

Oh, boy, he was serious. If his family's appearance when they came for dinner was any indication, I figured I had better find something besides old jeans and a tank top to wear. "Well, give me some time to primp and, ah, stuff. Like girls, you know, do." I panicked as I wondered what the hell girls did do in these circumstances.

"Okay, so I'll pick you up at one. It'll be about a forty minute drive into Boulder. We can have lunch and the play starts at three. Because of the new curfew laws, they're just doing a matinee." As he left me alone I was struck by the look of hopeful eagerness plastered all over his face. I tried not to think about what might happen if I did end up breaking his heart.

*   *   *

I had no idea how to dress for the occasion. I went to my bedroom and rummaged through my closet but found nothing promising. Maybe Carmela would have some ideas. I dug out my cell phone from the back pocket of my jeans and dialed.

TNT answered.

"Hey there!" I said. "Carmela around?"

"Glory?" TNT's voice sounded muffled.

"Yep. I'm getting ready for my first date. How's that for an exciting turn of events?"

"Better late than never," TNT said. Her tone was kind, but her voice, strange.

"Everything okay? Where's Carmela?"

"Hold on." I could hear footsteps and doors opening and closing. Then TNT came back on the line. "She's passed out, Glory. I just came over to see her and she's out cold."

I was confused. "Booze?"

"Drugs. She's been spending time at Nyx's. A lot of time. I don't know what to do."

I thought about it. "Maybe we should talk to her dad. Maybe he would forbid her to hang out with Nyx."

TNT groaned. "I've thought of that, but Carmela would hate me. We've been invited to some kind of barbeque over there later today. I think I'll confront Nyx directly. Maybe threaten her with Carmela's dad."

My stomach turned over. "Oh, I don't know if threatening Nyx would be a good idea. She's dangerous. Please trust me on that—I know things about her." For the umpteenth time I thought about telling Carmela and TNT what Nyx really was, but besides it sounding like crazy talk, it could get them in more trouble. No telling what Nyx would do to random people who found out what she really was. I considered what might have happened today when Jesse found out. If he had walked away from her, would Nyx have killed him? My mind continuously went back to the fate of the Baxters.

I heard Carmela call TNT's name and TNT respond. There was a flurry of activity, muffled voices, and Carmela came on the line, her voice hoarse and her words tangled.

"Was up?"

I tried to sound cheerful. "I've got a date with Nicky and was calling to get some ideas for what to wear." I managed a laugh. "You're my cool friend. Figured you'd know."

"Where ya goin'?"

"Lunch and a play in Boulder."

There was a long silence and I wondered if she had passed out again. "Um. Don't you got a red dress? I remember, ah, yeah a red dress."

My mind tried to place the dress in question. "Well, last Halloween I dressed up like Little Red Riding Hood. Short dress. Hooded cape. You want me to wear *that*?"

Carmela yawned. "Just dress. The white blazer you

wore with your jeans when you came to church with me that time." Her voice faded for a few moments. "Um, and I think your mom has some very cool white sandal heels. You wear same size, right?"

"I thought about it. That would be perfect. "Thanks, Carmela."

"No prob."

"Hey, Carmela, you don't sound too good. Are you okay?"

"Just tired. Gotta go." The line went dead.

"Oh, Carmela," I whispered. Then I said a silent prayer to the God I wasn't sure existed to please save my friend's pretty...no, her *beautiful* soul.

I located the Halloween costume tucked away at the back of my closet and was pleasantly surprised to find the dress still fit. It was simple but clung nicely to my curves. The white blazer was linen and looked perfect with the dress. Its large pockets would be useful so I wouldn't need to carry a purse, since I didn't have a white one anyway. I could slip my camera in one of them, too—this was a date I wanted to capture for posterity. I found Mom's white heels in the hall coat closet. I fluffed up my hair, put on an extra layer of lip gloss, and examined myself in the mirrored shower door. I looked pretty damn good.

Buoyed by excitement, I went to find Mom and tell her my news. I found her lying on her bed, her face soggy with tears, a pile of used Kleenex next to her. Carefully, I sat on the edge and took her hand. "Are you okay?"

The look she gave me was withering. "Do I look okay?" She snatched her hand from mine.

"Do you want to talk?"

"Erica is dead. She died a torturous, gruesome death."

An anguished moan shook the room. "It was worse than I had feared."

"Did Nyx tell you this?"

Mom nodded and blew her nose, filling another tissue to add to the pile. "It's hard on her to tell me—it means she has to tune into the hell that Erica endured—but I'm getting it out of her a little at a time."

And paying her for the performance. "I know you believe in psychics because of the lab experiments you ran, but I have a friend who's also a psychic and she says that Erica is still alive."

Mom's bloodshot eyes looked at me. "That girl I met in Georgia?"

I nodded. "Kaia. The one who helped us find you. She's a *real* psychic. I have doubts about Nyx's abilities."

Mom cocked her head. "Why?"

"I met Nyx in Georgia when you were still held captive. She has a bad reputation."

"But she's told me things about Erica that no one could have known. Private conversations. Silly secrets we kept from your dad." She shook her head. "Nyx is real." Mom moaned again. "Oh, God, all the horrible things those men did to your sister." Huge, shuddering sobs shook the bed and I reached out to try to embrace her, but she pushed me away. "Leave me alone. Just go away and leave me alone."

I couldn't understand her anger at me until she added, "You could have done more. You could have screamed. You always were jealous of Erica. Shame on you. You should be so ashamed."

Appalled, I stood and backed out of the room. What had Nyx been telling her? Even when and if Kaia found

Erica, could this evil be undone? The shocking realization dawned that I likely had lost my mother just as effectively as I had lost my father. Trembling, I raced up the narrow stairs to the attic where Dad's things were stored. I recently discovered it to be a place of comfort where I felt close to his spirit. I often came up here to sit and talk to him.

I grabbed the black paint-splattered sweatshirt that he always wore when he worked and buried my face in it. I could still smell his cologne and inhaled the woodsy scent until it filled my lungs and overflowed into my soul. I imagined his presence. I remembered his laugh. I felt embraced by his love.

"I have my first date today, Dad," I whispered. "You'd like Nicky. He's a good...man. Just like you."

I heard something behind me and jumped, but it was only Hallie. Relieved, I sat down on a low stool. Hallie sat down a few feet away and stared at me with those all-too-human eyes of hers. Then, after a time, she stood and walked over to a small table on which a crate filled with Dad's sketchpads balanced. Before I could stop her, she reached up and used her front paws to knock over the crate. Sketchpads flew.

"Hallie! What did you do?" I leapt to my feet and scrambled to pick up the mess. I was dismayed to see that some of the pages in the books had bent when they fell. "Hallie, why would you do such a thing? This is all we have left of Dad. I can't imagine why—" I gasped when I noticed one of the open pages, and my mind twisted in disbelief. Slowly, carefully, I lifted the pad and moved to the bright sunlight streaming through a nearby window.

It was a colorful sketch of me in a red dress, white blazer, and white high-heeled sandals. Tucked behind my right ear was a luscious white rose. A trickle of blood streamed down my right cheek. The title of the work was FIRST DATE. It was written above Dad's signature, which was dated last Christmas and followed by a string of X's and O's in the unique design he always used when he signed cards or letters to me. *How could this be?* I stared at Hallie, who stared right back at me. "How could this be?" I asked her.

If she had answers to give, I could not hear them.

"Thank you for showing it to me," I said to her.

"I love you, too," I told my dad.

* * *

Dominic arrived precisely at one o'clock with a potted plant of white roses. He handed them to me and said, "I didn't want to murder them. I hope you don't mind they're not a bouquet cut for a vase."

Their smell was sweet. "They're lovely. Thank you." I set them on the kitchen table. "I'll plant them in the garden by the front door."

He reached into his pocket and withdrew one lone rose. "I accidentally broke it off. It would look beautiful in your hair."

He waited expectantly and so I nodded. Gently, as he slipped it behind my right ear, one of the thorns stabbed me and I flinched.

His expression turned grim. "I'm so sorry. And you're bleeding too."

My hand flew to my cheek where I could feel the trickle of blood. *How did Dad know?*

Dominic reached out to do something, then stopped. "I can't heal you. I'll go get Sasha." His air of dire urgency amused me, and I reached out to grab his arm before he could rush off.

"It's fine. More than fine, really." I grabbed a tissue from my pocket and dabbed it dry.

"What can I do?" It was obvious he wasn't used to being helpless in these most common of human situations.

"Just kiss it and make it better."

Confusion crossed his face. "How will that make it better?"

"It's something people do to soothe the wounds of their loved ones."

Relief smoothed away his anxiety; he leaned over and kissed the scratch. When he did, I inhaled his magnificent scent. Mingled with that of the rose, it created the most exquisite smell and I realized that as long as I was with him I would never need to wear perfume—it would be a pale imitation that would only mask the real deal.

"All better," I said.

His eyebrows furrowed. "Really?"

I laughed. "Really." I gave him the once over. He was wearing spiffy slacks, a shirt with a few buttons strategically undone, and a light sports jacket. "You look good."

He smiled his megawatt smile. "You do too. I've never seen you in a dress before. It does your legs justice."

Fluttery heat rose from my stomach to my face and I blushed, remembering the time—when both dressed in only short hotel bath robes—we had first seen each other's bare legs. That was also the occasion of our first kiss.

He noticed my flush and concern washed over his face

again. His hand flew to my forehead. "You sure you're okay?"

Life with a former angel was going to involve some major adjustment for both of us. I tugged his hand away from my face and squeezed it. "Let's go have a date."

"It's my first one ever," he admitted, as if I didn't already know.

"So far, so good," I told him with a strong emphasis on sincerity.

Hallie and Milton followed us out to the truck.

"You can't come," I told Hallie.

"You can't come," Dominic told Milton.

Their despair was evident. I laughed, which offended Hallie and she trotted off in a snit. Milton just cocked his head and his eyes said, "Please?"

"Stay here and protect everyone," Dominic told him. "I'm counting on you."

Dogs loved having a job to do, and Border Collies loved it most of all. He ran off toward the studio.

"You might lick Hallie's ear to comfort her," I shouted after him, then noticed Dominic's confused expression. "Girls like that," I said, feeling mischievous.

"I'm learning something new every day," he said, opening the door for me.

As I stepped up into the cab, his lips brushed my ear and a chill swept through me that felt good. Better than chocolate chip ice cream on a hot day.

Union was on the high plains east of the mountains. From its vantage point, the Rocky Mountain range was postcard picture perfect. As we drew nearer to the foothills where Boulder was nestled, the mountains towered and threw wild shadows. The landscape rolled, raw and powerful. I loved Boulder, and it was always a treat to visit. I knew we had crossed the city line when a slick red Porsche flew by us sporting a bumper sticker that read, MY KARMA JUST RAN OVER YOUR DOGMA. Boulder was a yuppie New Agey kind of place. In the heart of downtown, in the historic district, was an open-air four block pedestrian mall called the Pearl Street Mall. The magnificent Flatirons—a soaring rock formation that provided a dramatic backdrop to the city—loomed over the mall, which was paved with red bricks, beautifully landscaped with colorful flower beds, and lined with restaurants, bookstores, art galleries, coffee shops, and bars. However, what I had always loved most about the place were the street performers. They ran the gamut from classically trained violinists to mimes and lone guitarists playing for cash thrown into open guitar cases. I wondered how the great tragedy might have affected things and was pleased to discover that, except for many of the shops and restaurants yet to reopen, not much at all had changed since my last visit a year earlier.

Dominic and I sat together at one of the outdoor cafes and ate my favorite pizza in the entire universe: a fire-roasted white pie with artichoke hearts, sun-dried tomatoes, fresh basil leaves, black olives, and ricotta cheese. I was in heaven and made a lot of unladylike noises.

At one point, Dominic asked, "Does that mean you're enjoying it?"

All I could do was moan and nod.

A nearby trio of Irish musicians who played fiddle, flute, and hand drum serenaded us. Passersby stopped to jig, clap, and toss coins into the little gold-painted cauldron that sat on the ground in front of them.

I ate half the pizza before I could gather my wits enough to actually converse with Dominic. I cleared my throat, rearranged my legs beneath the table (how did women manage to sit ladylike wearing short dresses anyway?), took a sip of my iced tea, and said, "So?"

"It's very good pizza," he said.

I eyed the last piece with undisguised lust and managed an, "Uh-huh."

Dominic grinned and flagged down the waitress. "We'll take another one of these to go, please."

She giggled, leered at him for the umpteenth time since our arrival, and said, "No problem, hunky...I mean, honey."

I burst out laughing. Despite my single-minded, obsessive pizza-eating orgy, I noticed that many of the women—and some of the men—had been giving him the eye.

He gave me a look of confusion. "Was it something I said?"

"No, just something you are."

"I don't understand."

I dug my camera out of my pocket and took a photo of him. "You look like a movie star. Your smile is like the sun. You simmer with sexiness." A startling thought crossed my mind, and I tried to keep it there, but it insisted on being heard. "Nicky, you think you want me, but I'm the only girl you've ever been close to. Before making any decisions about what you want to do with your humanity, you might want to date other women. Explore this island in space and time that you're now shipwrecked on."

He looked wounded. "Are you, in a tactful way, trying to tell me that there's no hope for us?"

"Nope, tact isn't one of my strong suits. I honestly care about you and just want you to be as happy as you can be. You deserve that."

His eyes captured mine. "I know who I want. You're the one who has to make a choice."

I thought of Zane and wondered if I would ever see him again—there might be no choice to make. And what about Hope? "Since you're not an angel anymore can you reveal the secrets you've kept from me? I mean, can you finally explain the mystery of Hope?"

"I'm still bound to holding secrets."

"When exactly did you stop being an angel?"

"It's been a gradual shift over the past couple weeks. As of today, it's complete."

"And irreversible."

"My choice."

His expression was so unabashedly eager that I had to look away. *Oh God, what if I end up hurting him?* I glanced at the Irish trio. Their music was rousing and fun. I noticed a woman, perhaps in her early sixties, who had joined the gathering crowd and danced an Irish jig. Although her dress may have once been nice, she was dirty and probably homeless, like so many who frequented the mall. A half-empty pint of gin in her hand told me she was a drunk. She laughed with delight at the music, managing to find joy despite her apparent challenges. I aimed my camera and took pictures. There were so many interesting characters in this world.

Dominic took notice of her too. "'All the world's a stage, and all the men and women merely players: they have their exits and their entrances; and one man in his time plays many parts.'"

I shook my head. "There you go quoting Shakespeare

again—you do it often. Yet you told me you've never seen his plays."

"My family spent a lot of time playing games like trying to figure out which famous human quotes were from Shakespeare or the Bible."

"Get out. My dad and I used to do that too." I thought about it. "But wouldn't an angel know exactly what quotes were from the Bible?"

He shrugged. "It's just one of many holy books."

"But, um, isn't it *the* holy book—I mean for angels?"

He gave me a curious look. "God doesn't have a religion. Religions are how men understand God. God doesn't need any organized philosophy to understand man."

"But aren't there right religions and wrong religions?"

"All God cares about is that we love Him, each other, and His creation."

"Hmm." It seemed so simple. Maybe there really was a God after all. It was the complexity and hypocrisy of religion that had led me to doubt. "Do you have a guardian angel now?"

"Rebekah."

That made sense. I thought about all the money he suddenly seemed to have. "It was nice that you were given seed money to start your new life with."

He smiled. "I'm very blessed."

"What do you plan to do, you know, for a career?" I thought of the likely choices for a former angel who loved movies and could do a perfect imitation of Sean Connery as James Bond: doctor, social worker, preacher, actor.

"I want to be a farmer."

"Really?"

"To make things grow from the earth. Oh, yes, I *really* want to do that." His face glowed.

My mind engaged in a brief flight of fancy and I imagined myself as a farmer's wife. "You know that I want to be a photojournalist?"

"That would be a great job for you. You'd be happy."

Hmm. Well, if I somehow ended up with Zane, I'd be a ranch hand's wife. At least with Dominic I'd have a home of my own. Hmm.

I glanced at the homeless lady dancing her joyful heart out a few feet from us. Her bright eyes were watching us. "Nice that you two sweethearts still have each other," she said. "My Cecil—may he rest in peace—and I did the Irish jig at our wedding. And we taught our daughters—may they rest in peace—to jig from the time they could walk. Now, of course, there's no one left for me to jig with." She kicked up her heels and smiled through a sudden onset of tears.

Dominic stood and walked over to her. Wordlessly, he removed the gin bottle from her hands and slipped it into a big pocket in her dress, then he took her into his arms and, together, they performed a flawless Irish jig. The couple shuffled, twirled, pivoted, and their feet perfectly pounded the bricks to the music's rhythm. She laughed and hooted. He smiled and maintained piercing eye contact with her. Me? I shot photos like crazy.

When the song ended, she grabbed him in a tight hug and seemed disinclined to let go. "Thank you."

"Thank you," he said. "It was delightful." He took her hand and tugged her in my direction. "I'm Dominic and this is Glory. We're sorry you weren't able to join us for dinner, but why don't you take this and share it with these musicians here. You all look like you could use some food."

I watched as the woman accepted the box containing my beloved white pizza pie—she seemed completely overwhelmed. She nodded to me, then to Dominic. "My name's Mary. Mary O'Donnell. Thank you for your kindness." She reached in her pocket and pulled out the pint of gin. "This is all I have to offer in return."

Graciously, Dominic accepted it.

Mary's smile widened. "God bless you, young man."

"May God bless you too." As he leaned forward to kiss her cheek I saw him stick a big wad of money into her pocket, then he tossed a few dollars into the musicians' pot of gold.

Mary apparently felt Dominic's hand slip into her pocket and she examined the gift he had left. "Oh," was all she could manage to say.

"Your life is not over, Mrs. Mary O'Donnell. Your Cecil and your girls wouldn't want it to be."

Dominic left money on the table for the waitress, took my hand, and we headed off in the direction of the campus. As I looked back over my shoulder, Mary had settled down on the ground with the musicians and they were diving into the pizza.

"We can stop back by on our way home and get you another," Dominic said.

Deeply moved, it was hard to get the words past the lump in my throat. "No need. It's just an excuse to get you to bring me back here sometime."

His eyes flashed. "Oh, no excuses necessary. Just say the word. I am the proverbial putty in your hand." He slipped his arm around me, drew me close and we walked in comfortable silence down Broadway and toward the campus.

* * *

Usually, the Shakespearean plays at the university were summer events held outside. However, demand for tickets had been extraordinary—people were hungry for entertainment—and so the play was moved indoors to the large Macky Auditorium. While Dominic and I waited at the back of the line to pick up our tickets, a young woman approached us. She was dirty and reeked of liquor.

"Will you help me?" she whispered. "I really need a drink."

Dominic's compassionate eyes met her frantic ones. "Why?"

"My heart hurts so bad I just gotta have a drink. Please help me. I'll do *anything*...if you know what I mean." She took a step closer to us and I fought the gag reflex as her sour odor wrapped around me like a hideous blanket. "I. Will. Do. Anything."

"Do you have family?" Dominic asked.

She shook her head and managed to spit out the word, "Pandemic."

Dominic took Mary's bottle of gin from his pocket and put it in her hands. "I'll give this to you on one condition."

"I'll do anything," she whispered, clutching it to her chest.

"Walk on over to the Pearl Street Mall. There's a pizza parlor there. Sitting in front of it are some Irish musicians and a woman named Mary. Mary lost her entire family in the great tragedy as well. She needs someone to love her. Just someone to love her. Can you find it in your heart to do that?"

The young woman's eyes blinked fast, like the beating of a bird's wings in a mighty storm. "Who would need me? I'm nothing."

Dominic reached out and drew her to him in a gentle hug. She resisted for a moment, and then surrendered with an air of desperation that was tragic.

"I would love to love someone again," she said. "It's not the *not* being loved that hurts so bad; it's having no one at all to love."

"She needs you, Sweet Angel Pie. Go to her."

She pulled back from him with a startled expression. "My daddy used to call me that. How did you know?"

Dominic cocked his head. "I have no clue." He shrugged. "None whatsoever."

The woman's face paled beneath multi-layers of grime. She opened the bottle of gin and took a deep swallow from it. Then she examined the bottle with a curious expression, closed it up tight, looked at Dominic, and returned it to his hands. "I'll go find Mary and see what I can do to help her."

"Her name is Mrs. Mary O'Donnell," I said.

"Mrs. Mary O'Donnell," she repeated. "Yes. Okay." Sweet Angel Pie scuttled off in the direction of the mall, glancing back over her shoulder at us twice before she was out of sight.

"How *did* you know that?" I asked.

"Glory, sometimes miracles just do happen, whether one is an angel or not."

Before we entered the auditorium, Dominic tossed the bottle of gin into a trash bin. Its job was done.

* * *

I wished that the play had been a rousing musical number to lift the huge crowd out of the sadness that permeated the planet, but I understood this was the play the drama department had been ready to premiere when the pan-plague hit. They had lost much of the cast, but it was the strength of those involved in theater from time immemorial that the show always went on. To the immense credit of all involved, it did.

Executed with passion and consummate skill, the acting was brilliant, and the costumes and scenery, glorious. The ending was, as always, tragic. However, given the tragedy everyone in that theater had endured in recent months, reaction to it was magnified. After the final words, a hush fell over the audience that felt timeless. The actors, moved by the same spirit that embraced everyone, remained as statues. Finally, like a tsunami of enormous proportions—like one erupting from a silent earthquake in the deepest part of the ocean—applause began slowly, then grew and roared and reached its peak as a standing ovation that rose to crash down on the stage with such force that I witnessed some of the actors actually stagger. When the wild waters finally receded, everyone in the theatre collapsed into their chairs and gave vent to tears that went far beyond hearts moved by the death of two teenage lovers. Over a billion deaths were mourned in a group purging that was more unselfconscious than I ever thought possible.

Dominic sobbed in my arms and I rocked him as I would a baby.

Love, loss, the whole gamut of human experience telescoped in over two thousand hearts in that auditorium. I finally understood that what Dominic had said was true—the only religion that mattered was love.

CHAPTER TEN

"No, you can't go with me, Nicky. I need you here to take care of Mom and the dogs. Besides, Kaia said for me to come alone." Kaia had texted Glory via Evan's cell phone and told her to head for the covenstead in Crestone as soon as possible.

"I'll be with Glory," Sasha said. "I'll stay embodied until we near Crestone. But I'll stay with her, um, through it all." Sasha's voice held an ominous sound when she spoke those last three words, a point that didn't escape me. Was something bad going to happen? No use asking. They never told me anything useful.

I sat on the edge of my bed and reread Kaia's message. MEET ME AT MOONSTONE ASAP. COME ALONE. LEAVE CAMERA. WEAR WATCH.

The instructions were odd.

One thing I did want to take along was a wedding gift I had made for Kaia and Evan. A few months earlier, when we were on the roof of Evan's Atlanta penthouse, I had shot a photo of Kaia looking at Evan with tremendous love and longing. One of those intimate moments in life rarely caught on film, I framed the image for them.

Hallie saw me packing and gave me an expectant look. "You can't come," I told her.

She did something I had never seen her do before—she turned her back to me and sat down with a decisive thud.

I looked at Dominic and Sasha. "Would you leave us alone for a while?"

They walked out of the room and shut the door.

I knelt on the floor and rubbed Hallie's ears the way she liked. She was Dad's dog and I had done my best to forge a close relationship with her, but she hadn't received a lot of attention in the midst of all that happened. She seemed to have the uncanny ability to understand everything said to her, so I poured out my heart. "I love you more than I can express. After Dad died you saved my life, not only literally, but emotionally too. I want us to have what you and Dad shared. I know it'll never be the same for you—I don't even come close to being as good a human as Dad was—but I promise you I'll try to do better."

She leaned into me.

"I need you to help me hold our home together. Mom's in a real bad place and she's slipping away fast. Dominic left his family for us—we need to give him a new one. And poor Milton has lost everyone and everything he's ever loved. Then there are all those animals who came here for safety. There's so much work to do, and I *really* need your help."

She uttered a guttural sound and pressed into me harder.

"You'll be with Nicky. You love him. I thought you loved him more than me."

She looked at me with a startled expression and cocked her head. Hmm. Maybe I was wrong about that one.

"I promise that when things settle down, you and I will go visit Dad's grave again. Just us." I slipped my arms around her and sang a refrain from the song that Dad had named us after. "*Let us live to make all free. Glory, glory, hallelujah.*"

* * *

"So what did your mother say when you told her you were leaving?" Sasha asked me. We were alone in my Honda, on the way to Crestone, which was about a four-and-a-half hour drive southwest of Union.

"Not much. Didn't ask where I was going, why I was leaving, or how long I'd be gone." Her lack of concern really hurt. "Her only comment was that she hoped I didn't miss the Blood Mother River Festival." I blinked back tears.

Sasha reached out and touched my arm. "Please don't take it personally. She's under a wicked influence right now."

I knew that. It still hurt.

"So..." Sasha paused. "So, I've been dying to ask if you're in love with Dominic?"

My stomach got all warm and fuzzy. My heart tap-danced at the thought of him. I could feel my face flush. Desire swept through me like wildfire. I had always felt love for him, but the desire was new. "Yes, I think I am."

Sasha squealed. "Glory's in love with Dominic," she sang in a silly, singsong voice.

I had to laugh. She was so sweet and innocent. A newly created angel. So young.

"Have you ever known an angel to leave the angelhood, or whatever it's called, to be with a human?" I asked.

"There are legends, but I've never known anyone who

actually did it before. Of course, I'm very young."

Yep. "What's it like being an angel?"

"Like living with one foot in the most magnificent love and light, and one foot in the shadows. It's hard to keep my balance sometimes. Everything gets all crookedlike." She looked at me. "I can't imagine why they assigned me to you. I mean you're so hugely important in the grand scheme of things." She clasped her hand over her mouth and her silver eyes widened in horror. "Oh, I wasn't supposed to say that."

"Do you know what's going to happen?"

"I know some of it because some of it has already happened." She groaned—she had done it again.

"You'd make a really lousy spy. The enemy wouldn't have to torture you to reveal secrets. You'd just blurt it out given enough time."

"That's what Dominic always tells me. Except he does it in his Sean Connery as James Bond voice."

We both erupted in welcome laughter.

I thought of Kaia. "Do witches have guardian angels?"

"They have guardians of a different sort, more in line with their beliefs."

I thought of Zane. "And vampires?"

Sasha's sigh blew through the car like a cold wind. "Oh, poor vampires. See the thing with vampirism is that it's a blood-borne virus. Vampires are born human and transformed by the virus."

Zane himself had told me that. He said that some scientists he knew had suggested the viral theory.

Sasha said, "One of the side effects is that a barrier goes up between the soul and spirit, and connection with God is lost. Their challenge is to somehow overcome the blood lust that consumes them through sheer blind faith."

She made a whimpering sound. "It's so hard to explain. God is still there for vampires, but until they push through the darkness by the power of faith, the grace of God can't save them. It's all between them and God with no intermediaries at all. Those who do overcome are, in my opinion, the strongest of all souls."

I thought of Zane, his sister, her husband, and the Goth Girls. All of them had managed to find a way to live with their vampirism without succumbing to the dark side.

Sasha read my mind. "Amazing, aren't they? That they can do that? Such noble spirits they have. So amazing."

I thought of the evil vampires I had met.

"And they're the ones I pray for the hardest," Sasha said, once again reading my thoughts.

I glanced at her. As always, her sheer physical beauty impressed me. Dominic and Rebekah were equally beautiful. Even Micah would have been if he hadn't marred it with the war paint tattoos—which I felt was a deliberate action to disguise the glory of his birthright.

"Do angels ever fall in love with each other?" I asked.

"Angels are love. We don't fall in love with each other."

I tried to understand, but failed. "Why do you think you were assigned to me?"

"Well, angels are individuals with souls that need to grow and learn too. I think that when Dominic was assigned to you, it was to find something loveable in the human race because he was so bitter after what happened to his first charge."

I knew that the teenage boy who was Dominic's first assignment had fallen into the darkness, murdered others, and ultimately committed suicide. Dominic blamed the violence that society seemed to celebrate.

"Your willingness to sacrifice your life for the rest of the human race changed that," Sasha said. "Dominic grew—changed. So, I suppose Rebekah thinks that there is something I can learn from being your guardian."

"And what could you possibly learn from me?" I asked.

She lit up like an angel Christmas tree topper. "Oh, Glory, as humans go, you're my hero. You have no idea what you are. I do."

"But I'm only seventeen and, until this year, nothing much extraordinary has ever happened to me."

"Well, seventeen years in this life and twenty-four in the other—" She rammed her hand over her mouth and turned crimson. After a few minutes of uncomfortable silence she asked, "Do you think we could stop somewhere for ice cream?"

* * *

There was something wrong at Moonstone. I felt it the instant I saw Kaia and Evan. The newlywed joy that should have been pouring out of them was so muted it was barely noticeable. On top of that, Rory wouldn't meet my eyes. Most unusual of all, was the fact that Brennan was being nice to Kaia. Very wrong indeed.

I took a seat at the central round table in the big lodge and gratefully accepted lunch. Kaia, Evan, Rory, and Brennan sat with me, watching me eat my bowl of tomato-basil soup and a small loaf of freshly baked whole grain bread.

"I think I know where your sister is," Kaia said at last.

"There's a secret, underground community of scientists living in Arizona. We believe your sister is there."

I chewed and waited for them to reveal more.

Evan cleared his throat. "Last summer when we discovered the plan to depopulate the planet by the shadow groups—well, it turns out that Scorpio was a very tiny tip of a gigantic iceberg. We believe your sister was kidnapped by the central group and is ensconced with them, possibly working on a project that's related to time travel."

I chewed and eventually remembered to swallow.

"Besides me, another psychic saw her," Rory said. "White Bear, a Native American who is Kaia's magical guardian."

"White Bear took us to the spot," Kaia said. "Above ground, of course. It's heavily monitored, and we believe that if I take you there they'll see you and invite you in. However, the visions have shown you going in alone which means that, in essence, I'll be delivering you into the hands of the people who likely tried to kidnap you earlier this year."

"Once you're inside their space, we can't help get you out again," Evan said. "You'll be on your own."

I took a long sip of spiced sun tea and tried to absorb everything they had said. "I won't be alone," I said at last. "I'll be with my sister."

They all looked at each other with wary expressions.

Rory, who was the spunkiest twelve-year-old I ever met, said, "Your sister may be one of the bad guys."

I choked on my tea. "She may be the enemy now too?"

All four of them nodded.

The lunch didn't want to stay down. I stood and raced

outside in case it came back up. I paced back and forth for a long time until I reached the only decision there was to make. When I returned to the lodge, all four of my hosts were still sitting together in a cloud of miserable silence. I wondered what more they knew that they weren't telling me.

I said, "If I don't make it out, I need your word that you'll do what you can to help my mom. It's not just a matter of her losing another daughter, it's that Nyx has her soul tethered like a puppet on a string."

Kaia nodded. "I'm totally committed to vanquishing Nyx." Her expression changed to reveal a fierceness I had never witnessed in her before. "And I want you to remember that *whatever happens*, nothing will change my vow. I can vanquish her from any level of existence."

I cocked my head as I considered the implication of her words. "Are you telling me that you might die?"

"We could both die," Kaia said. "I'm just telling you my intentions, whatever may happen."

"If you believe you might die on this mission, I think I should go alone," I said.

"Ain't gonna happen," Kaia said. "We're in this together."

"After you and Kaia leave for Arizona, Rory and I are heading for Union," Evan said. "We're going to see what we can do to help from that end."

"Thank you. We need all the help we can get there. Go to my house and check in with the angels. They're staying in my father's old studio out back." I realized I had better update them on the news. "Oh, and there's something you should know. Dominic isn't an angel any longer. He sort of resigned."

That news conjured the first smile Kaia had given me.

"Because he loves you?"

I nodded, feeling a mixture of pride and guilt.

Evan put his arm around Kaia's shoulders and drew her close, which reminded me of the wedding gift I had for them. I reached into my roomy handbag and handed them the framed photograph. "Congratulations on your marriage."

Kaia took it from me and ripped away the gift-wrap. They both stared at it for a long time before Evan ran from the room.

"Thank you," Kaia managed to say.

I looked from one face to another and felt I knew what they didn't want to tell me. "Kaia, I don't think—"

She raised her hand to stop me. "I'm taking you. What will be, will be. That's life."

* * *

On the drive to Arizona, I memorized all the information Kaia provided. I didn't ask why, I just did what she told me to do. She coached me—I repeated the geographical coordinates so many times they would be stuck in my brain forever. I tracked the time. I listened to every word Kaia said as she explained what White Bear had revealed to her. And every time I tried to bring up what I feared was about to happen, Kaia cussed at me quite colorfully until I shut up.

In turn, I told her everything that had happened in Union since the demons arrived.

"I find it unusual that Nyx is so fixated on stealing a handful of souls when there's such a big world to conquer," Kaia said.

"It seems personal," I said, my fingers tightening on

the steering wheel. "It's like she's out to get me. Why would I matter to her so much?"

"I've always felt that you've got a special destiny, but I haven't been able to see it," Kaia said. "Didn't the Caretaker Davina say to you that someday your name would be legend?"

I nodded and my face grew hot with embarrassment.

"The shadows don't like the light. They can't stand it. It's a threat. They want to dim your brilliance."

"But I'm so ordinary," I said.

"No one ever knows their destiny. There are higher powers that decide that. Our free will just allows us to work with or against it, day-to-day, in each choice we're called upon to make."

I thought about the choices Kaia and I were making now. "I love you, Kaia."

"I love you too, Glory."

* * *

I followed the preprogrammed GPS to the exact coordinates that led to what Kaia called The Time Vortex. A rocky, barren piece of land in the middle of nowhere, it was unimpressive.

"I'll leave the keys in the ignition," I said. "So you can, you know, get home."

"Thank you," she said.

We sat in the car for a while, silent except for the rapid breathing of our shared fear. Then our eyes met and we spontaneously embraced, hugging hard.

I thought of something Sasha had said to me when we drove to Crestone. "Light will always dispel the darkness. Always."

"Let's do it," Kaia said.

We stepped out of the car and stood together under the blazing sun, silently waiting.

From the time we pulled up to the site until an enormous boulder slowly slid to one side revealing a hole in the earth, fourteen minutes and thirty seconds had passed. I knew this because Kaia had told me to time it. From the hole, three people emerged—two men dressed in nondescript dark jumpsuits and a tall, beautiful young woman whom I instantly recognized as my sister.

Although only a year older than me, she seemed far more mature and sophisticated. An efficient bun held her long brown hair, her makeup was light but striking, and her pantsuit, practical. However, the thing that jumped out at me in the first seconds of seeing her was that although her smile was bright, it was cold like ice.

"Glory," she said. "Fancy meeting you here."

At the sound of her voice—still familiar even after eleven years of change—a cascade of emotions welled up in me: relief, disbelief, and yes, love. Behind my sunglasses, I blinked back tears. "Erica," was all I could say.

Erica glanced at Kaia with a look of distaste. "And one of the supernaturals in your life. They have made it so hard for us to get close to you, which makes it quite a relief you sought us out."

"Mom needs to know you're alive," I said.

"Ah, Mother. She did manage to complicate our plans with the pandemic." Her voice did nothing to disguise her irritation.

So, Erica had sided with the enemy. My mind struggled to accept this, but failed. Perhaps the brainwashing would vanish with a visit home, a mother's passionate embrace, and a good home-cooked meal. Of course it would...wouldn't it? Evil was evil and good was good and people basically were born a certain way and—

In a move as fast as lightning, Erica pulled a silver pistol from her pocket, and without saying a word, shot Kaia in the chest. "The supernaturals have really been getting in the way of things," she muttered as Kaia slumped to the ground.

The gunshot echoed, and my scream split the world in two. I had never been so shocked and horrified by anything in my life. I fell to my knees and crawled to Kaia's side. I ripped off her sunglasses, and when her eyes looked at me, I saw that there was still life.

Desperation filled me as I tried to put pressure on her wound. "It's okay, Kaia. Hang on. Light always dispels the darkness. We'll win. Don't go. We've got work to do. Brides don't die. Evan needs you. Annie needs you. I need you. *Please don't leave.*" My inane rambling continued until the light in her eyes faded and I knew the darkness had won.

I shrieked and pulled her up into my arms, then howled, sobbed, and shrieked some more. I had thought perhaps one or both of us might die, but I imagined it the result of some sort of heroic battle—certainly not such a cold, meaningless death.

"Oh, chill out," Erica said, stepping away from us. "You're being utterly ridiculous."

"*Ridiculous?*" I jumped to my feet and charged her, fists flying wildly, hatred propelling them forward with intent to pummel that smug look right off her face.

One of the two men yanked me back before I could attack her.

A long time ago when considering the situation

between Dominic and his brother Micah, I had assured myself that I would always love Erica, even if she chose to ally herself with evil. I was wrong.

Erica's chin jutted toward Kaia's lifeless form. "Get rid of it. The car too. Bring Glory down the rabbit hole."

One man pushed me forward while the other went to carry out the rest of her orders. I followed Erica down a spiral staircase to a steel door which opened to an elevator that took us deep into the secret world I learned was called Wonderland.

* * *

Wonderland was a sprawling underground city the likes of which I could never have imagined. We rode a high-speed rail train past rivers, parks, power and sanitation plants, apartment complexes, restaurants, and I even noticed a small television studio. There was no sky, but a radiant light did mimic sunlight, and since vegetation grew, I presumed it was a full-spectrum type of technology. The city appeared populated by people of all races and ages—most dressed in diverse colors of jumpsuits. Everyone seemed to ignore my presence, even though my unconventional clothes were drenched in blood. My tears now spent, I just felt numb.

We went to a laboratory in a science and technology center that was at the far outskirts of the city. My guard deposited me at a conference table in the middle of the room, and Erica took a seat across from me. I noticed that her eyes still had flecks of gold that flashed like fireflies when she was upset. They were flashing like crazy.

"Are you upset about something?" I asked.

"No, should I be?"

Well, you just murdered someone. Your long-lost sister has discovered you and your secrets. Maybe you aren't the ice queen you appear to be. "The virus you people created killed Dad," I said.

She shrugged. "That was designed by a different branch of this project than I'm involved in."

"Is that all you can say?"

"He wasn't special. You and I, we got our good genes—the ones that make us useful to the future—from Mother."

I was appalled. "But he loved you so much."

She rolled her eyes. "If you understand the phenomenon of love scientifically, it's all glandular reactions related to primal survival instincts."

"Hmm. Well, my glands aren't spitting out a whole lot of sisterly love chemicals at the moment."

Her bright, cold smile returned. "I really don't care."

Sadly, I realized that was true.

An electronic door whooshed open and a small Asian man bounced into the room. He was obviously very happy. "Oh, Glory is here! Glory is finally here. I am so excited."

Erica stood to greet him and perform introductions. "Dr. Oshiro, Glory Templeton."

He extended his hand to shake mine, but I did not return the courtesy. His smile faltered slightly. "Ah, well, yes I heard about your little friend. These things happen."

I stared at him in stony silence and fought back the renewed desire to cry.

"Have you explained things to her yet?" Oshiro asked Erica.

"No sir, I was waiting for you."

He nodded enthusiastically. "Good. Well, there's no

time like the present." A burst of silly laughter exploded from him and he sat down at the head of the table.

"Perhaps it would be wise to find out what she already knows?" Erica suggested.

He nodded. "Good idea."

"So, Glory, you knew how to find me," Erica said. "What else do you know about this place and our work here?"

I chose my words carefully, so I wouldn't do anything to further endanger my friends and helpers. "Kaia—the woman you murdered—was a psychic. She saw a vision of you greeting us above ground at this location, so she brought me here. That's all I know."

Erica's eyes narrowed. "I don't believe that's all you know."

I shrugged. "I don't give a damn what you believe. I asked her to help me find you because our mother is falling apart and I hoped you would come home and help her. Kaia told me last summer she had a psychic hit that you weren't dead. She is...was...an excellent clairvoyant." My arm swept the lab. "Mom's done research into psychic development and it's not incompatible with science."

"True, true," Oshiro said.

"So, maybe you should tell *me* about this place and the work you do here," I said to him, a hint of challenge in my voice.

"Of course, of course," he said. "You're central to the experiment we've put together. We've just been waiting for the timing to come together." His grin widened—he looked like a lunatic. To add to the effect, he raked his fingers through his silver hair and it stood at attention. "Ack, there's so much to tell you."

I fought overpowering weariness. "I'm very drained. Could we just cut to the chase?"

"I don't imagine you've heard about quantum entanglement theory?" he asked.

I shot a cool glance at Erica. "Actually, yes I have."

"Oh, splendid." He frowned at Erica. "And you told me she was simpleminded."

I stifled my irritation, although my fingers tap-danced on the tabletop with impatience.

He noticed my fingers. "Yes, well, to the point. Your consciousness has experienced an intense quantum entanglement with a woman from the 19th century because of your romantic entanglement with a man from the 19th century who loved you both. Therefore, we believe you and this woman are actually now one and the same, which could allow us to send you back in time. We intend to try."

My fingers froze as I recalled Professor Greenberg's lecture about quantum entanglement: *Two particles, once connected, sometimes will act together and become a system. They behave like one object, but remain two separate objects. This connection appears to work outside of the known laws of time or space. Indeed, it appears to transcend time and space.*

Oshiro could only be referring to Zane's wife, Hope.

He looked at my fingers again. "Ah, so you have an idea who I'm taking about."

I tried to keep my voice calm. "Why would you think that?"

Erica leaned across the table and assessed me with curious eyes. "You aren't so simple, are you?"

I leaned across to meet her. "Never have been. Never will be."

"Oh girls, let's not get testy here. Our agenda is one we can all agree on."

"I doubt that," I said.

Dr. Oshiro pushed a button that opened a panel on the table, and then proceeded to manipulate levers and switches. The room darkened and a small holographic image appeared in the center of the table. It was Zane.

"Zane Dillon has the virus we've labeled VZD-1876. He came to our attention when he was hospitalized in 2007 in Texas and had blood drawn at an emergency room. Long story short, we discovered that what for centuries has been known as vampirism is a blood-borne virus that provides the carrier extreme strength and vitality, heightened sensory skills, stunning recuperative powers, and virtual immortality. We dove into the study of it in order to develop a new type of super soldier. Zane and his family believe we're trying to find a cure—of course knowing how to cure the virus would be necessary so we could turn it on and off—but primarily we're trying to learn how to manufacture it."

I quickly stuck my hands in my lap to hide their trembling. Several times Zane had mentioned the scientists he knew. All this time had he been referring to my own sister and her group?

The doctor flipped another switch and the holographic image shifted to one of Zane and me kissing on the balcony of Evan's penthouse. "We know you two fell in love. We know from our interviews with him that he believes you are also his wife, Hope, from the 19th century. We have extrapolated that there has been a temporal anomaly and you are indeed both Hope and Glory."

The lights came back on.

Erica said, "Dr. Oshiro is not involved in the viral experimentation. His special area of research is time travel."

"Time isn't linear," Oshiro said, bouncing in his seat like a jumping bean. "We aren't sure which came first in this scenario, but it's clear that since there is an entanglement of consciousness between the three of you, you would be the perfect subject to test the experiment."

"Experiment?" I managed to say.

"We have successfully sent others back in time, but they can only travel within their own lifetimes...just like on that TV show *Quantum Leap*. There is no experience of previous consciousness to allow them to travel further back. You, on the other hand, have an entanglement with the 19th century and theoretically should be able to transport all the way back there." He yanked on his hair again. "Isn't it exciting?"

I shook my head. "Why should I want to participate in your experiment?"

Erica sat back in her chair and gave me a Cheshire cat grin. "Wouldn't you like an opportunity to prevent Zane from being infected in the first place? He hates what he is and his life as a vampire has been pure hell. Since you love him, wouldn't you want to change that?"

Yes! I thought. Calmly, I asked, "But if I do that, then how would you discover your superman virus?"

The lights dimmed again and a holographic image of Zane's cousin Bo hovered above the middle of the table. "Patient Zero in this cluster," Oshiro said. "If you go back and successfully change history in reference to Zane, we'll still have our virus. And we'll have another weapon at our disposal in building the New World Order. We'll know that the past can be successfully changed.

The subjects of our short-term time travel experiments have been unable to change events in their own lives. This is an entirely different scenario and the power it could provide us, well, is thrilling to contemplate."

"But Zane already believes I was Hope, which means I've already been in the past, doesn't it? And he's still a vampire."

Oshiro shook his head wildly. "That's the paradox. We haven't sent you yet, but you've been there. So, if we send you now will events be changeable? Oh, it's all so exciting."

"There are many paradoxes involved with time travel. Time is a mysterious thing," Erica said, her voice thick with condescension. "You couldn't possibly understand."

Actually, I understood all too well. My mind chewed on the possibility—however remote it might be—that I could save Zane from ever becoming a vampire. It would mean I wouldn't have met him in this timeline, but I loved him enough that if it could prevent all his suffering I would do it. However, I still didn't understand. "I'm confused about Hope. Is she someone I'm supposed to possess like a spirit would?"

"He said you smelled exactly the same," Erica said.

Oshiro jumped to his feet in excitement. "Each person's DNA and body chemistry is unique. It would have a unique smell—a vampire's sense of smell is even more acute than a dog's. You and Hope, somehow in the temporal mechanics of the universe, were the same person."

"But he said we didn't look alike," I said.

Oshiro threw up his hands. "Another paradox. Perhaps it's like the symbiont concept of *Star Trek* lore. Two disparate beings merge to become one unique individual."

"But Hope—"

Erica interrupted me. "Her looks would be genetically programmed by her parents, her personality would be a product of her environment, but once the two of you merge you become an individual that is neither Hope nor Glory, but Hope/Glory, with the memories of both intact."

"This is our best guess," Oshiro said. "Isn't it magnificent?"

There was a long silence while I processed. "If I do this, can I—Glory—ever come back?"

Oshiro's manic swing took an instant downturn. He put on a sad face and stuck out his lower lip. "We don't know. We do know from past experiments in short term time travel that you will bounce around a bit within the span of Hope's lifetime—as mentioned, time is not linear. And based on the projections we've been able to make, it's possible you'll return when she dies. However, we don't know for sure because this is a first for us." He grinned. "But won't it be wonderful to find out?"

I looked at Erica. "What if I don't want to do this?"

She sniggered. "Actually, you don't have a choice."

I met her steel-eyed stare. "I never thought I'd say this to you who, until today, I have always loved. But bring it on, bitch."

* * *

The three of us stood together in front of the time portal—it looked like nothing more than a wall of shimmering light.

"Einstein said that time is a river of light," Oshiro said, and then he gave me a fierce shove. I felt like Alice stumbling through the looking glass.

CHAPTER ELEVEN

Kaia stood up, walked away from her body sprawled on the hard red ground at The Time Vortex, and didn't look back. White Bear, in his spirit guide guise, was there to greet her. He extended a paw and she grasped it with a sense of deep gratitude. The universe, at times, seemed like a place of utter isolation—alone in thoughts and feelings, the old refrain was "we're born alone, live alone, and die alone." However, a lifetime as a witch had taught Kaia otherwise. No one was isolated—everything was interconnected.

And there was always someone to greet the dead and help them move on.

I'm not moving on, Kaia's mind told White Bear.

Your parents are waiting. His furry arm swept the horizon where a bright light rose invitingly.

I'm not moving on, Kaia insisted, sensing his disappointment.

Then what can I do to help? he asked.

Watch my back?

Always have, always will.

Kaia looked down at herself. During her life, she had traveled enough in the astral plane to understand that her morphic field would maintain the same image on this plane of existence as it had in the physical world. Her energy body was clothed in multi-colored, shimmering light that resembled a long, flowing robe. She took a moment to assess her emotions and was surprised there was no grief. Instead, she experienced a strong sense of purpose. Her mind was in charge, which was a relief because she couldn't afford to get all sentimental and soppy—she had work to do.

It's different from what I expected.

White Bear cocked his head.

I've been here before when I've helped animals cross over, but I was more emotional then.

It's because you were still attached to your body, and the body is an emotional hormone factory. He pointed to what looked like an energetic umbilical cord floating away from her without tether. The silver cord usually connected the energy body to the physical form. The cord's light was fading.

She looked into his bright eyes. *Any advice?*

He smiled. *A prediction perhaps.*

She waited.

I don't think any of what lies ahead will be as you expect it to be. With that thought shared, he disappeared.

Now, Kaia was alone. However, she reminded herself that it was her choice. She looked around and found herself surrounded by mist. This was the in-between where thoughts and intention controlled reality. The instant the thought crossed her mind that she should tell Rory she was dead, she was at the girl's side. Rory and Evan were together in Kaia's cottage packing for their trip to Union.

The psychic link between the two was effortless. Rory gasped and then said to Evan, "It's over. Kaia's gone."

A wail escaped him, which Kaia heard, felt, and saw as an explosion of colors and muddied textures. She threw up shields to block him—she could not allow his grief to affect her. Kaia noticed Annie staring straight at her invisible form, so paused only to say goodbye—adding a stern admonition for her to be a good mountain lion—before willing herself to Union. Kaia had never been to Glory's home before, but she thought of Hallelujah and, in a flash, was there. Australian Shepherds were psychic and the two of them had previously forged a strong bond, so they connected immediately.

Hallelujah looked up at her and smiled.

Kaia returned her smile and sent the thought, *Don't be afraid, but I'm going to be hanging around for a while.*

Hallelujah snorted and her mind asked something along the lines of, *What? Do I look scared?*

Kaia had always loved Hallelujah's tough-girl attitude.

Hallelujah lay next to a picnic table in the shade of a giant cottonwood tree. Dominic sat at the table with a beautiful young woman whom Kaia instantly knew was the angel Glory called Rebekah.

Rebekah noticed Kaia's presence and nodded to her. "Dominic, there's a spirit here. It's Kaia and her body has died."

Dominic looked around with a wild expression, but his gaze went right through her. Tears filled his eyes. "Oh Kaia." His grief was thick, and Kaia remembered White Bear's comment about emotions, hormones, and the human body. It occurred to her that being new to human form, Dominic was going to have a big learning curve when it came to dealing with those glands.

Tell him that it's okay and it was my choice, Kaia's mind told Rebekah. *And tell him the last time I saw Glory she was okay.*

Rebekah conveyed the messages.

I've come to vanquish Nyx.

"Good," Rebekah said aloud, likely for Dominic's benefit. "Someone has to vanquish Nyx."

Kaia knew that Rebekah was the mothering angel to Micah and about the pain she had endured at his falling. Actually, Kaia knew a great deal more from the time when Micah possessed her and they shared consciousness.

Rebekah apparently read Kaia's thoughts. "Yes, Micah." She shook her head. "In our world, angels can do battle with demons who are directly attacking our charges, but what Nyx is doing is more subtle and we can't interfere."

But I can vanquish her, Kaia said.

"Yes, you can, and I understand your desire to because of what she did to your parents...."

Kaia heard an unspoken "but," so she waited.

Rebekah stood and moved to Hallelujah, knelt, and stroked her. Kaia felt Rebekah's stormy emotions calm the longer the petting continued. The witch found it interesting to get inside a high angel's consciousness. It was more human than she expected.

"Micah had just fallen when Nyx set her sights on him," Rebekah said. "You were the link that brought them together. Micah possessed you to hurt Dominic, and then when the Starlight coven invoked Nyx to shock you out of the possession it brought Micah and Nyx together. Now she has targeted three specific humans: Glory's mother and two best friends, Jesse and Carmela. Nyx is winning. Taking her out isn't necessarily going to bring any of those souls back into the light. There are other demons. Evil is everywhere."

Kaia was confused. *Are you asking me not to vanquish*

Nyx?

Rebekah looked up at her with an expression full of pleading and anguish. "I'm asking if you will try to bring Micah back into the light before you attempt the vanquish. If you vanquish Nyx, another demon will move in to replace her in his life. If you fail to vanquish her, nothing with Micah will change. You have a unique bond with him that might allow you a way to connect in a manner none of us have been able to."

Kaia's mind rebelled. This wasn't why she stayed behind—she had a very specific agenda and didn't want to allow herself to be sidetracked. However, she did feel compassion for Micah. *Damn.* Rory had cautioned her about caring for the enemy and here she was actually considering trying to save Micah's soul.

* * *

Being a witch wasn't easy—with power came responsibility. Kaia perched in a tree overlooking the farm that the demons had stolen and thought about her life—what it had been and what she now faced.

According to her beliefs, she wasn't born a witch by chance, but by choice. Tradition held that it was likely she had been born into a witch family before and would be again. Once a witch, always a witch, and she would want it no other way. Even the between-lives place of rest and renewal—what her people called the Summerland, the dimension of light she had earlier walked away from—was populated by similar souls. She hoped when she completed her work here that she would finally find respite in Summerland. Then, after a period of rest and renewal, she would be ready to return to the world and resume her work as a witch. Of course, none of this would happen if Nyx or Micah destroyed her soul.

A witch's loyalty was to the Mother Goddess, whose body was the Earth and whose children were the lives nourished by Her body and spirit. A witch honored the Mother and served Her creation. To that end, Kaia had trained to slay demons. Saving them was not part of the job description.

Kaia knew Micah intimately. The direct approach wouldn't work because he didn't want to be saved. When Micah had possessed her, she experienced the part of him who loved too much and cared too deeply. She remembered how he had to rearrange time in order to help a child die every few seconds and cross them over into the light. He treated each individual child with enormous care and compassion. Kaia couldn't wrap her mind around the sheer numbers of children under five years old who died every day—his mind had told her something like thirty thousand. His anguish at knowing their suffering, and his anger at the masses of humanity for their apparent lack of caring and action, is what sent him over the edge. Micah had done terrible things since his fall, and Kaia knew that karma would demand a reckoning. However, she also remembered that a part of him hated what he became. Evil was often the path of least resistance, but it was always possible to reverse direction.

Kaia thought about how the forces of evil worked relentlessly to increase their ranks. Rebekah said that Glory's two best friends were also under Nyx's influence. Kaia had seen wonderful photos of Jesse and Carmela. She captured their images in her mind and let them guide her.

* * *

Kaia found Jesse in his parents' office at school, lounging in a chair with crossed arms and a sullen expression. His parents sat on an adjacent couch with their young daughter between them. Kaia could hear all their thoughts and feel their emotions. She sat on the floor between them, watched, and listened.

"We are very disturbed by the fact your new friends made your sister cry in art class," Cosmic said. The man wore blue jeans and a tie-dyed shirt with matching headband. Kaia wondered if this school was some kind of alternative educational facility until her mind delved deeper and she understood the situation.

Jesse shrugged and glared at his sister, who shuddered and buried her face in her mother's belly. "Little Belle Starr is just a big baby."

Sunshine patted her daughter's head. "No, she's not. Four years old is a big girl and she's very mature for her age." Sunshine's tie-dye was more eye watering than Cosmic's tie-dye. The matching headbands were an interesting touch, Kaia thought.

"We raised both of our children to be mature for their ages," Cosmic said.

Jesse smirked and he thought about how their parents didn't raise them at all, but just expected them to emerge from the womb as miniature adults.

"There's a time and a place for bloody corpses, dead baby birds, and images of dying children. Art class isn't one of them," Sunshine said. "We want only happy art in our classroom."

"Life isn't happy, Ma," Jesse said.

Sunshine adjusted her headband and grimaced. "Of

course it is. Happiness is a choice. And surrounding ourselves with unhappy things will only inspire negative energies."

"We've raised you and Belle Starr to be happy individuals," Cosmic said.

No, Jesse thought again, *you didn't raise us at all. You made us raise ourselves.*

Sunshine's fluttering hands swept up and down in front of Jesse. "And what's happened to the whole James Dean rebel without a cause look? It was your special signature. We raised you to be unique."

Kaia did remember that in Glory's photo Jesse looked like the rebellious young actor from the 1950's. She thought it was fun. Now Jesse just wore Levis and a nondescript sweatshirt.

"There are better ways of being unique than dressing from another era," Jesse said pointedly.

"Such as?" Cosmic asked, oblivious to the scorn in Jesse's voice.

"I've decided to embrace my dark side. My sinful nature. Evil," Jesse said. "It's...." He paused while struggling to put it into words. "It's empowering. You always wanted me to empower myself."

Sunshine pulled off her headband, stared at it for a long moment, then put it back on. "Sin doesn't exist. It is simply *self-inflicted nonsense*."

"And we've told you all your life there's no such thing as evil," Cosmic said. "Where are you getting these crazy ideas?"

Belle Starr raised her head from her mother's stomach and pointed at Jesse. "Eyes. Bad evil eyes."

Sunshine slapped Belle Starr's mouth. "I've told you before that this new monosyllabic speech you're using is ridiculous. You're not a child anymore."

Belle Starr rubbed her mouth and blinked back tears.

"She was traumatized by the great tragedy," Jesse said with frustration. "Give her a break. It's post traumatic stress, or something. And, *yes*, she is a child."

"Evil eyes," Belle Starr mumbled.

Both Sunshine and Cosmic leaned forward to examine Jesse's eyes. Kaia did too and saw the simmering evil.

"Well, they look like druggie eyes to me," Cosmic said. "Have you been doing drugs?"

"What if I have been?" Jesse asked.

Cosmic said, "Your mother and I did our share of drugs in our day. We discovered that they did us more harm than good so we stopped—"

"Except for the pot and the wine you still manage to enjoy," Jesse said, interrupting.

"You can't really call those drugs any more than coffee or tea," Sunshine said, her tone clearly daring anyone to disagree with her logic.

"So, if you want to experiment with drugs, we certainly won't stop you," Cosmic said. "You're a man and need to make adult choices about how you are going to live your life. We trust that you'll know what you can safely handle."

Jesse stared at them for a long time before shaking his head. Kaia could feel his disgust. She could feel his need for guidance. He wanted them to care enough to give him direction. There had to be more in life than the pursuit of happiness. The stunning Gypsy girl who called herself Nyx was exciting, and daring, and lived for something other than herself. She had a cause. Her cause was evil and it thrilled him. As he had surrendered to it, he felt the rush of something more powerful than himself rising up within to possess him. It was strong and would take care of him. No one else seemed interested in the job, and even though his parents had been telling him for seventeen years that he was a strong man, he knew at his core that he was a confused kid. It scared him to have to count on himself alone.

Kaia tried to think of something she could do to help him.

"Well, I'm glad we had this little talk," Cosmic said.

Sunshine nodded enthusiastically. "Me, too." She pushed Belle Starr away and shoved her toward Jesse.

"Take care of your sister. We've got to set up for tonight's art festival."

Belle Starr recoiled from Jesse. "No." She felt his evil and it terrified her. Kaia could see it; why couldn't her parents?

Jesse grabbed his sister's hand and yanked. "Don't be such a baby, Belle. Remember, you're a little adult."

"She's very mature," Sunshine said, nodding with enthusiasm. "Go on now. Have a wonderful day!"

Wow, Kaia thought. What kind of parents were these kooks?

Lazy ones, said a voice that sounded like White Bear.

Then Kaia heard Jesse say something that frightened her. As he yanked his sister out the door he muttered, "You know, Belle, you'd be better off dead than raised by those useless dicks."

"Evil eyes," Belle Starr replied as she held his hand and trotted, struggling to keep up with him. "Scary. Bad."

* * *

Kaia found Carmela in the gym. She also discovered

many ghosts milling about. After a few minutes of psychic examination, she realized this room had been used as a morgue during the pandemic. Immediately, Kaia began multi-tasking—directing souls into the light while trying to follow what was going on with Carmela and a beautiful young woman named TNT.

"We shouldn't be in here, baby doll," TNT said. "The room was sealed for a reason. They've had this closed up since the great tragedy."

Carmela sat at the bottom of the bleachers and looked around with a lost expression. "Mom and my baby brother died here. Little Emilio hadn't even been baptized yet. Father Hans said he can't get into Heaven now."

"I swear Father Hans deserves a special place in Hell," TNT said. "I'd be happy to kick his ass all the way there myself and personally deliver him into Satan's hands. I wish they hadn't transferred Father Michael. He was a good priest." TNT sat down and slipped a comforting arm around Carmela's shoulders. "Do you want to say a prayer for your family? I'll say it with you. Our Father who art in Heaven—"

"Stop it. There's no God and no Heaven, and even if there were I'm damned because I'm gay and so please just stop it."

Kaia tuned into Carmela's mind and witnessed the condemnation her Catholic priest had cursed her with and felt the betrayal and loss of faith—a faith she needed now more than ever.

"Nyx says that God is cruel and unjust and not worth loving anymore anyway," Carmela said. "It's true."

"No, I disagree," TNT said. "That Gypsy girl is getting into your head and you need to push her out. She's bad news."

"Her potions make me feel better," Carmela said.

"Her potions are poison. They're stealing your soul."

Carmela shrugged. "My soul's damned anyway."

"It certainly is," Micah said to Carmela.

At the sound of Micah's familiar voice, Kaia stepped behind a tall stack of boxes to help shield her presence.

"Doesn't it give you a sense of freedom?" Micah asked Carmela. "I mean, no more struggle to be perfect for an invisible God who never gets His own hands dirty dealing with all the tragedy that befalls this world."

"He sends His angels to help us," TNT said.

Micah's cackle filled the gymnasium, bouncing off the high ceiling and cavernous depths, then echoing back onto itself and seeming to go on forever. "That He does. That's how He manages to avoid the day-to-day horror here. Quite an efficient system He's got." Micah's voice fell and he whispered, "Yeah, real smart guy, God is."

A door opened and slammed shut. Kaia peeked out from her hiding place and saw Jesse and Belle Starr.

"Well, well, what have we here?" Jesse asked. "Two scrumptious women who really need to have a good time with some men so they know what they're missing. Don't you think, Micah? Why don't we show them what sex with men is like. Then they won't be all Sappho anymore."

Kaia could see the demonic fire flash in his eyes. The demonic force inside Jesse was gaining power.

Jesse pushed little Belle Starr toward the stack of boxes where Kaia hid. "Go sit behind there and give us men some time alone with the girls. Don't want you making a fuss and ruining it for us."

Kaia looked at Micah and noticed his hesitation. He kept glancing at Belle Starr as she scampered to the boxes, grateful to hide from scary, bad, evil eyes. Was there something in Micah that actually still cared about little children?

When Belle Starr ducked behind the boxes she looked straight at Kaia and her mouth opened to form a large O. Belle Starr hadn't noticed Kaia in her parents' office, but the veil between the worlds was thinner here due to all the paranormal activity. Kaia raised a finger to her lips in a classic shush gesture, and the little girl nodded solemnly. Kaia could feel the terror Belle Starr had for Jesse and the gratitude that she wasn't alone in her hiding place.

"Don't you come any closer, Jesse," TNT said.

Kaia peeked out to see TNT standing protectively in front of Carmela, brandishing a baseball bat.

Jesse's wicked laugh didn't come close to Micah's practiced cackle, but it did successfully convey sinister intent. "Or what? You'll hit me with that? I doubt even you've got the balls."

"Don't make me do it," TNT said, her voice trembling.

Jesse didn't hesitate for a moment in his advance on the women. Demons don't have a fear gene.

As Jesse reached out to grab her, TNT swung the bat at his head and there was an ear-splitting crack. Jesse howled and TNT raised the bat higher.

"Get out of here now, or I will kill you Jesse James."

Jesse grasped his head, blood trickling through fingers. The demonic force that had been possessing Jesse to transition him from human to demon, temporarily fled the pain. Left on his own, fear mingled with agony, and Jesse stumbled toward the door and crashed through it.

TNT took two steps forward and raised the bat

menacingly in Micah's direction.

Micah, who hadn't moved from where he had been standing, shrugged. "It wasn't me who wanted some." Casually, he turned and left the gym.

It was then that Carmela screamed, dissolving into delayed hysterics.

Still shaking, TNT sat down next to her and clutched the bat to her chest.

Belle Starr left her hiding place and walked straight to Carmela. She took Carmela's face in her hands and bent forward to cover it with abundant kisses. She paused every few seconds and said, "Love, love." Within minutes, Belle Starr's gentle gesture drove away the tears.

As Kaia watched the magic Belle Starr possessed, she realized if the child had power to put out fires, she also had enough to thaw a frozen heart.

"Please tell me you're done with Nyx and her followers now," TNT said.

"Yes, I am." Carmela looked at her. "We need to go tell my dad what happened. I don't want you to get in trouble."

TNT nodded, released her death grip on the bat, and it fell to the floor with a loud thud. The two girls held hands and headed for the door.

TNT looked over her shoulder at Belle Starr. "You want to come with us?"

Belle Starr looked at Kaia, who smiled and shook her head.

Belle Star looked at TNT, smiled, and shook her head.

A moment later Kaia and Belle Starr were alone, except for lingering ghosts.

Belle Starr sat down on the bottom bleacher and Kaia

sat next to her.

"You look funny," Belle Starr said.

Kaia found that she could actually speak to the child in voice instead of just thoughts. "I'm a spirit."

"Like an angel?" the child asked.

Kaia thought about it. She didn't want to lie, but figured it wasn't a good idea to reveal herself a witch, what with all the harm *Grimm's Fairy Tales* had done for witchdom. So she simply said, "Kinda like."

"There are bad things here," Belle Starr said.

"Yes, there are. I could use your help in fixing one very bad thing."

Belle Starr looked up at Kaia with an amazed expression. "Me help angels?"

"Do you know that boy, Micah, with the face tattoos?"

Belle Starr squeaked. "He scares me."

"Do you think you could be brave enough to kiss his face?"

Belle Starr's squeak turned into something more intense. "No."

"God really needs you to do it."

"God?" Her obvious confusion told Kaia that God wasn't taught in Belle Starr's home. What term would wacky New Age hippies use? "Great Spirit?"

Belle Starr blinked.

"Universal lifeforce? Cosmic consciousness? Higher power?"

"Oh." Belle Starr nodded. One of them had apparently sounded familiar.

"Can you be a little angel and smother Micah's face with kisses and say, 'love, love?'"

Belle Starr thought about it. "Will it make the scary stuff go away?"

"Some of it. Yes, I think so."

"Do I have to kiss the things on his face?"

"Especially those."

Belle Starr thrust out her chin and suddenly seemed to radiate courage. Kaia cocked her head, wondering if White Bear was close and rendering assistance. However, she couldn't be sure. Metaphysically speaking, this was a very busy place.

"Okay," Belle Starr said at last. "Angel God love."

* * *

They found Micah sitting on a bench outside the school, near the Blood Mother River. He was watching the wild water with an expression of profound distress.

Kaia walked to a nearby tree and hid behind it. Belle Starr gave her a look of longing, and it was evident that the fear was creeping back in.

Kaia smiled at her and sent her all the strength she could muster.

Slowly, Belle Starr walked to Micah. By the time she arrived at the bench she was shaking and crying.

Kaia felt a pang of guilt. Perhaps she had pushed the child too hard.

Belle Starr moaned, grasped his face with both hands and covered it in sweet kisses, all the while whispering, "Love, love."

Micah seemed too stunned to resist.

When she was done, she took a step back and stared at him. Then she rubbed her face and nose with the sleeve of her blouse.

Micah reached out and wiped away a single teardrop she had missed. "You're *so* scared. How come you kissed me if you're that scared?"

"Love," Belle Starr whispered.

Doubt crossed Micah's face. "Who told you to kiss me?"

Kaia tensed. *Please don't say an angel.*

Belle Starr pursed her lips while she considered. Finally, she said, "God."

Micah gasped. "God?"

Belle Starr nodded solemnly.

Micah looked up, then reached out and put his arms around her, drawing her close.

"Thank you," he whispered.

"Good?" Belle Starr asked.

A sob escaped the depths of Micah's soul, and Kaia could feel him struggle for words. After a long time he simply said, "Good."

CHAPTER TWELVE

Bright lights and loud music filled the air and I struggled to get my bearings. I found myself waltzing with Zane on a crowded dance floor in the ballroom of a palatial Southern mansion. I had experienced this exact scenario once before in a dream that seemed terribly lifelike. In a flash, I now realized that was because it had really happened in another place, another time.

The time portal had worked. When I, as Glory, had told Zane about my dream, he confirmed that this was the night in 1875 when he was introduced to seventeen-year-old Hope Hawthorne.

I was keenly aware of my identity as Glory, but was also conscious of another mind and heart, both of which were quite in charge of the body we possessed. Quickly deciding not to interfere with the girl I understood to be Hope, it seemed more prudent to simply observe for a while. Even so, it was confusing because the consciousness that shared this body was the "I of awareness" Professor Greenberg had demonstrated to us in class. There was a Glory and a Hope, but only one I.

Zane completely enthralled me. Dressed differently from the other men who wore proper high society fashion, his fancy cowboy clothes undoubtedly passed as formal wear on the cattle ranch he represented, but the fine Victorian gentlemen sneered. However, the ladies didn't sneer. The ruggedly handsome cowboy with the piercing blue eyes and brilliant smile had their complete attention. Much to my parents' dismay, he had taken a fancy to me.

He whirled me around the dance floor, and under his mastery I felt as if I was floating. The hoop skirt of my long taffeta gown kept us a respectable distance apart, but that didn't matter because the connection between us was as powerful as it had been instant. I knew that nothing, or no one, would ever be able to sever that bond.

"Hope. You are my hope," he said.

"In what way am I your hope, Mr. Zane Dillon?" I asked. My voice was different—it held a thick Southern drawl and my tone was snotty. *Oh dear. What kind of girl was I?*

"I've met all the available women in Denver and found none who inspired my heart. I had given up hope of finding a bride, and now I've met you."

I giggled. *Oh dear, Hope was a giggler.* "Why that is the most presumptuous thing I've heard all evening, sir." For all the disdain Hope tried to inject into her voice, I did find myself leaning closer into him. His wild scent of leather and sage filled me to overflowing.

"Your eyes are beautiful. Like brilliant sapphires," Zane whispered.

"And how does a hick cowboy from the Colorado Territory know what sapphires look like?" *Did I say that? How incredibly rude of me. Who is Hope?* I glanced around at the opulence and remembered Erica's comments about personality being a product of environment.

"Well, I see a sapphire necklace around your pretty little neck right now, Miss Hope."

Oh. I wondered what color my hair was. "And my

hair? What does my hair remind you of?" I had seen a tintype photo of Hope, but it was old and poor quality.

"The mane on my favorite horse."

Well, that didn't help me very much. I wondered where the nearest mirror was. "That's not a very romantic thing to say to a girl," I said.

"I did say she was my favorite." His eyes twinkled mischievously.

"And why is that Mr. Zane?"

"She was wild. I broke her myself."

Hmm. Well he could be offensive too. I tossed my head that had hair of some mysterious horsey color. "What a thing to say to a lady."

He smiled slow and sexy. "Well, Miss Hope, a wild horse is free, and there's much to be said for runnin' with the herd. But she has no one to touch her, or pamper her, or love her. She has to surrender to someone in order to enjoy the true riches life has to offer."

Oh, man that is so hot! "Did someone say something about it being hot in here?" I asked, a bit confused.

His smile widened. "Why? Are you feeling flushed?"

This two personalities sharing one body thing was going to take some finesse on my end. I didn't want to drive Hope insane. I wondered if, over time, we'd integrate more. However, if I allowed that to happen entirely I might lose my focus. She was just going to have to deal with me. From what I could tell so far, she was feisty enough to cope with the unexpected. Both of me sighed.

"So, do you think you could tame me?" I asked.

He leaned forward and whispered in my ear. "Oh, I know I could. And I know you'd like it."

I melted while Hope giggled.

A man tapped Zane on the shoulder and indicated he wanted to cut in. Per proper custom, Zane surrendered me to—*eww*—a man who reeked of booze, sour body odor, and French cologne. "Monsieur Lucien Moreau, I was really rather enjoying dancing with that cowboy," I said.

"Ah," the French-accented voice said, "but you are promised to me. Do not forget that."

I squirmed to try to escape the clutches of his sweaty palms. "I am not, sir, promised to *anyone*. I don't care what kind of business partnership you and my father have arranged; I am no part of the bargain."

He smirked. "Oh, I wouldn't be too sure of that *ma chérie. Je t'aime.*"

"Oh, you do *not* love me. You only love yourself."

His eyes narrowed. "Well, I'm sure that cowboy you were just clinging to—rather improperly, I might add—would call you a feisty filly. I, on the other hand, call you mine."

Rage caused me to actually see red—which was a first in my own experience. I shoved Lucien away and stalked off in an apparently well-practiced huff. Glancing back over my shoulder I saw Zane watching me—so I winked at him. Then I stuck out my tongue at Lucien. Damn, but I was immature. However, I had to give my Hope-self an A for *chutzpa*.

As I stormed through the room, I saw myself in a mirror and froze. Wow, I was a knockout. My hair was flaxen, my eyes were indeed sapphire blue, and my face would be considered pretty in any century. However, I was pleased to note that my figure was lush. I had always liked having breasts and hips and a slightly round belly. It felt sexy. I smiled and spied a photographer who had his camera set up nearby taking tintype photos for party guests. I knew from my experience in photography he could take a picture of me and process it in minutes. I hopped up onto the vacant stool and smiled my most delightful Hope/Glory smile.

Fifteen minutes later, I tracked down Zane and gave him the tintype. "So you can find me again, in case I get lost in the herd."

"Oh, I've already got my brand on you," he said. "You just don't know it yet."

A few feet away Lucien visibly seethed.

I grew horribly dizzy and time shifted.

* * *

"I have not built up a multi-million dollar steamship company to allow my only child to traipse off to the wilderness and be a rancher's wife," my father said. Uncharacteristically, his voice held anger, and it frightened me.

"I'm sorry, sir, but what does one have to do with the other?" Zane asked, quite reasonably I thought.

"She is destined for a life of luxury. My grandchildren will have all the advantages that life can offer."

"With Monsieur Lucien Moreau as her husband?" Zane asked.

"Well, he does bring a lot to the table. He's quite high in society and wealthy in his own right," my father said.

"But I don't love him," I protested. "He's gross."

Mother's eyebrows kissed. "Gross? What do you mean? He's not thick or coarse."

Hmm. Our minds had blended. I needed to think 19th century. "He is disgusting."

"And this man who wears Levis and has cow pies on

his boots is not?" Mother asked with dramatic flourish.

"Zane is who I love. If you won't let me marry him, I'll...I'll run away with him."

"No, you won't," Zane, Father, and Mother said in unison.

We all looked at Zane with surprise.

"I'll not steal your daughter. I am askin' for her hand in marriage. I will beg for her. I will fight for her. I will do whatever I must. But I will be honorable."

Mother sat down with a sigh. I sensed his response softened her. "Mr. Dillon, you have no idea how spoiled our daughter is. She cannot conceive what will be required of her as a rancher's wife. Work is not even a word in her vocabulary. You both would be miserable. Please, *please* trust me on this."

I was offended, but practical too. Glory and Hope were unique personalities. We each had our strengths and our weaknesses.

"My sister, Trinity, is marrying soon and will be moving to her husband's ranch in Cheyenne, so I've arranged to have a housemaid to help me," Zane said. "The preacher at my church has found a young lady who graciously agreed to come into my employ. She'll be able to help Hope with the work. She'll be live-in help. My parents are dead, sir, but they left us a fine ranch that we've built into something good. It would be a simple life for Hope and our children, but a real decent one."

"You've only known each other a week," Mother said. I could hear a hint of surrender in her voice.

"But love—"

"Bah on love," Father said, interrupting Zane. "Love is overrated. You must be practical in life."

Mother turned her face away and hung her head.

Father, who wasn't entirely without heart, noticed and appeared properly chagrined. "I didn't mean...."

The world began to swim once again.

* * *

My father's office was down by the wharfs. Lucien and several other investors were there for a meeting with Father about the shipping line, and Zane was planning to stop by to finalize his plans to import four Angus bulls from Scotland for breeding stock. Once the arrangements were completed, Zane would be returning to Denver without me. He had been unable to convince my parents to allow us to marry. In despair, I followed Zane and planned to burst in at the last minute and grovel. I wasn't too proud to beg—not when it came to Zane. I had fallen in love with him all over again. The Zane I knew in the 21st century carried such profound inner wounds that I had never seen the humor and charm he possessed before he became a vampire. I couldn't let him get away from me again.

I sneaked in the back door and hid in the hallway between Father's private office and the meeting room where Lucien and five other men sat. The men sipped on brandy, went over financial records, and their voices carried more loudly than I expect they realized. Where I positioned myself allowed me to hear conversations in both rooms.

I heard money changing hands and a contract being signed in Father's office, but what caught my attention was Lucien's voice when I heard him bring up my name.

"Ah, that Hope is a cherry just ripe for popping. I can't wait to screw that impudent little bitch into submission."

The men chuckled lasciviously. I had never been more humiliated in my life. Why didn't any one of those so-called gentlemen stand up for my honor?

"And I'll teach her not to talk back. That's what the back of my hand is for—at least in my country. That's what marriage is for. Well, that and to seal business deals."

Raucous laughter spilled from the room and more lewd comments followed.

I was about to rush into the room and stand up for my own honor when Zane stormed past me—my father close on his heels. I peeked around the filing cabinet and watched as Zane beat Lucien into submission. "And that's what the fist is for—at least in my country," Zane said.

Zane panted, Lucien groaned, the other men in the room had the decency to look embarrassed, and my father granted Zane and me permission to marry.

* * *

White satin, lace, and a crown of flowers fade into darkness as the black velvet night rises to embrace us. I become lost in the song of flesh and desire, my heart beating like hoof beats—no longer running away to freedom, but racing home for arms to hold me, hands to stroke me, and whispers meant only for my ears.

"I love you," he says.

"Polish those words with your tongue," I tell him. "Make them last longer than the stars and shine brighter than the moon."

"I love you," he repeats, polishing the words that will

be mine forever.
I become lost again in the exploration of secret mountains and valleys. Passion flames forth and our dreams are made holy with sacred kisses.

* * *

Our Denver wedding reception was a homecoming in more ways than one. Familiar faces filled the ranch house and I struggled to navigate the sea of emotions that rose up to swallow me.

Last summer in the 21st century, I had met Zane's vampire family. I adored his sister, Trinity, whom I now realized I resembled. We were both blue-eyed blondes. Her fiancé, Caleb, was her husband when I met them. His teenage cousin Leah hated me when we first met because Zane obviously liked me—and boy did she hate me now that he had married me. If her hands had the daggers her eyes held, I'd be dead meat. The one who inspired true terror for me, however, was Caleb's brother Bo. Within the year, Bo would be turned by a vampire and end up turning the rest of the family by force. How was I going to be able to stop it? Interestingly enough, the man had an aura of nastiness about him now, even before the transformation. No wonder he couldn't handle the bloodlust that ultimately overtook him.

Those were the old faces, the ones I as Glory already knew.

I also met Caleb's and Bo's parents, a kindly couple who would soon be dead at Bo's hands. I felt terrible sadness at witnessing their sweet, joyful natures and knowing their own son would be the one to kill them. The family minister, Preacher Stewart, and the ranch foreman,

Rusty, were also guests at the reception.

Then there was Sasha—the newly hired live-in help.

"I wondered where you were," I whispered to her as soon as we were alone.

"Oh, I've been with you since you came through the time warp," she said. "You're never alone; no human ever is. Please don't ever forget that." She paused. "So, are you in love with Zane?"

I smiled. "Oh yes."

"Hope's in love with Zane," she sang in her silly singsong voice. She was still so young.

"Can you help me stop what's going to happen?" I asked.

"No. I'm so sorry."

"Can I stop it?"

"I honestly don't know."

"But you told me you were here with me before."

"Time is a mysterious thing," she said, echoing Erica.

It made absolutely no sense to me at all. And it made me mad.

* * *

Zane and I danced at a barn dance. The fiddlers played a lively tune and we two-stepped around the wooden floor, our embrace intimate. When the music finally stopped, Zane slid his hand down to my big belly and said, "Hope. This child is now our hope."

No! Where did all the time go? I wanted to experience every single precious second with Zane.

We sat down together on a wooden bench and he went to fetch us glasses of cold lemonade. I rubbed my belly and tried to come to terms with a life growing inside me.

Besides the obvious changes in my body, there was a sweet sense of another soul sharing my awareness. Professor Greenberg would call the baby "consciousness" and my womb "the point of convergence on its spacetime travels." Me? A rush of love simply called the baby "mine."

Zane returned with our drinks. "I have to leave at dawn for Cheyenne," he told me. "I got a message today from Trinity. Caleb and his parents are all real sick with fever and she's got some young heifers that the bull got with—now they're calving and some have died. She needs my help to pull the calves or more'll die. She said she's startin' to feel sickly too. I'm not sure exactly how long I'll be gone." He patted my belly. "But we've got time."

I remembered that Zane was turned into a vampire by Bo at the Cheyenne ranch. "Is Bo going to be there?"

"That's the problem. He's on a trip to San Francisco. He should be back soon, but Trinity doesn't know when."

My stomach turned over and I felt as if I was going to throw up. Bo was turned into a vampire by a prostitute when he was on a trip to San Francisco. He came back to the ranch, killed his parents, and turned everyone else. Then he burned down the house to hide his crime, and they were all believed lost in the fire. "Don't go," I begged.

"I've gotta go. My sister needs me."

Panic surged. "Zane, this isn't going to make any sense to you but something really bad is going to happen if you go to Cheyenne right now. You can't go!"

Heads turned to look at us.

I was trembling so hard I had to set down the lemonade.

"What are you talking about, darlin'?"

I thought about it. He was a product of the 19th century, and time travel and vampires were beyond his ability to comprehend. However, he was very religious. "An angel came to me and told me that something horrible would happen to you if you went to Cheyenne right now."

His face paled.

"I'm serious. I swear to God." It was the truth. The angel was sitting across the room from us right now watching me with concern.

He shook his head. "I don't know what to say. Even if the...angel...was right, I have an obligation to my sister. I have to do the right thing."

Tears exploded from me like a geyser at Yellowstone. "Please don't go." I felt the baby kick and grabbed my belly.

People moved closer and regarded us nervously.

"Is everything okay?" Preacher Stewart asked.

Sasha stayed right where she was, still as a statue. I knew she couldn't interfere.

Zane's hand flew to my stomach and his eyes searched mine. "Are you okay?"

"No. No, I'm not. Please don't go."

"Is the baby okay?" he asked.

I thought of lying, of trying to keep him here on the pretext that I was about to miscarry. However, I remembered something Kaia said to me on our drive from Crestone to The Time Vortex. She said that when people lied they separated themselves from creation, because creation was based on truth. She said that no lie was ever worth alienating oneself from the universe and no good could ever come of it. She said that everyone knew this fact in his or her soul, which is why conscience always resisted speaking an untruth. Kaia's entire speech uncoiled in my brain like a snake that had been patiently waiting for the opportune moment to strike. I looked at Sasha, who regarded me with infinite compassion.

"An angel told me that if you go something horrible will happen," I repeated. "If you love me, if you love our child, you'll stay."

"I do love you and our baby, Hope. So much. But I'm a man of honor and must help where the need is greatest, and that's at my sister's ranch. Her family and animals could die. She can't handle it alone and there's no one else she can turn to."

"Let me go with you then," I begged. Maybe I could do something to forestall the tragedy.

He shook his head. "I'll not put you and our baby at risk. There's bad fever there. No."

And so I could not change history.

* * *

I know when the nightmare begins—I feel it in my soul. Fear, betrayal, blood transformed. Blood lust and madness. Dark wings flutter in the crimson night.

I send forth waves of love that I hope you can feel. Forever, Hope will love you. I pray your faith will break through to God and grace will descend to end your anguish.

Unbearable loss. Unbearable sorrow.

I am alone with my heartbeats and those of our child. The world is forever changed...

* * *

In the 21st century, Zane had told me that he never returned to Hope after he was turned, but that he did always keep an eye on her from a distance. I could feel him. I spent hours, months, years looking for him. There were times I wondered if Glory had been real, or if it all was a dream. I felt myself going mad.

"She's going mad," my father whispered to Mother as regular as clockwork. "She keeps calling for Zane. She swears he's always close. What can we do?"

My son Jeremiah and I lived with them now. I had sold the ranch and returned home. 21st century death records had given me the exact date of Hope's death, and I even visited her grave once. I needed to have Jeremiah close to family who would care for him after I was gone. For those few precious years, I loved our son with as much passion as any mother in the history of time had loved a child.

"And I hear her talking to an angel she calls Sasha," Father said. "She yells at this angel for abandoning her."

I had not seen Sasha since I left Denver. Had she ever really existed?

"Hope's a great mother," my mother would always reply to my father. "Let's just let her be."

For the most part, they just let me be.

"You look like your daddy," I told Jeremiah. "You're so handsome."

"Yes, I am." Even though he was only six, he was a self-assured kid. It figured, given his parentage.

We were in our favorite park, flying his kite. It delighted him and I delighted in his joy. His favorite kite was one that looked like a horse with a flaxen mane.

I sat on my regular bench and watched him as he raced down the wide expanse of grass and made his horse fly.

Behind me, I heard a familiar voice—one that I had been blessed to have not heard for a long time. He was talking to friends and sounded, as always before, quite drunk.

"Have you seen those young girls who opened the boarding house down by the docks?" Lucien Moreau asked.

"A *boarding* house for sailors? Right," another man said. "It's obvious they're strumpets and it's a whorehouse."

"I wonder," Lucien said. "I took my horny ass and a pocketful of gold down there one night looking for a good time, and that little Spanish one who calls herself Jinx drove me out of there with a bullwhip."

"Hah!" his friend said. "You were obviously just not her type. Besides, where did you get gold? You've been broke as a wagon wheel since Hawthorne kicked you out of the partnership after you insulted his daughter."

Lucien growled. "I'll get even with that bitch yet."

"Rumor has it that the Jinx girl looks like portraits of the infamous Spanish pirate, Donna Diabla. Maybe she's a distant relative," one of the men said. "Would explain the wildness."

"Let me try that so-called boarding house next," another man said. "I hear there's a China girl, and a colored girl there too. And I've got *real* gold."

"Yeah, in your teeth," Lucien said, then hawked up a mouthful of phlegm and spat it in the wind, which carried a disgusting gob of it to me.

I didn't realize they were so close and wanted to get out of there before Lucien noticed me. Quietly, I made haste to Jeremiah and made promises of chocolate, peppermints, and finally ice cream if he would leave without fuss. The ice cream convinced him.

Ice cream. Perhaps Sasha's promise to never leave me alone was true and she really wasn't just a figment of my imagination after all.

* * *

It didn't take much inquiry along the wharves to find out where a bevy of young girls ran a boarding house for sailors. I practically ran to it and was breathless when Jinx opened the door.

Oh thank God, it was the Jinx I knew—the leader of the 21st century Goth Girls all-girl gang of vampires.

I could barely speak, but managed to blurt out, "I have to talk to you, Jinx."

She gave me a cool look. "Do I know you?"

"We know each other, but it's real hard to explain. Please let me come in. There's not much time and there's so much I have to say."

"Why isn't there much time?" asked the beautiful teenage vampire to whom time meant nothing.

"I'm going to die."

She raised an eyebrow, stepped aside, and let me inside.

The Jinx I had known before was a sultry Latina with caramel skin, full lips, and dark almond-shaped eyes. Her long, flowing hair had been dyed flaming red and she dressed in the style of modern Goths: ruby lips, black eye makeup, body glitter. The curve of her left breast had a tattoo that said FEARLESS. She was wild and sexy and had the self-confidence I only dreamed of having.

This Jinx wore no makeup but was even more beautiful—with lustrous skin and thick black eyelashes framing flashing eyes. Long black hair was pulled away from her face and fell in a cascade of ringlets down her back. An antique gold barrette nestled in her hair and matching hoops dangled from her ears. Her low-cut dress showed a hint of a tattoo by her breast, but it looked to be a symbol of some kind—converted later into the F in fearless. Pirates of earlier centuries were famous for their Polynesian tattoos. I had never asked her how many centuries she had been a vampire.

As was the case in the 21st century, I felt quite plain and uninteresting in comparison.

I stepped into a parlor filled with cozy Victorian-style furniture, chintz curtains, and an Oriental rug covering a pinewood floor. The air smelled of spiced oil from kerosene lamps.

"Would you like a cup of tea?" she asked.

"Tea would be nice. Thank you."

She gestured for me to sit in one of the plush chairs, disappeared for a few minutes, and returned with three girls whom I also knew from the 21st century. The British girl named Jezebel carried in a tea service on a large silver tray. She set it down on the coffee table and served me tea in a flowery china cup.

"Thank you, Jezebel," I said pointedly.

She gave me a curious look and took a seat with the other women, who sat side-by-side on a sofa across from me.

I took a sip of the steaming, flavorful brew and arranged my thoughts. "Are we alone?" I asked.

Jinx nodded and continued to regard me with a cool expression.

I gestured to the black girl on one end of the sofa. "I know you as Jasmine." I looked at the Asian girl on the other end. "I know you as Jade."

"Well, you've got the names right." Jinx crossed her arms and the others followed her lead.

"I know you're vampires. We've met before, but—and this is going to be hard to believe but just remember that the existence of vampires is hard to believe too—it was in the future."

All four girls wore the expressions I expected they might upon hearing my revelation.

"In the 21st century science has found a way to move through time, and I came back to keep a man named Zane Dillon from being turned into a vampire. I was unsuccessful."

They regarded me in silence.

"I met you in the future here in Savannah. You saved me from an evil vampire named Bo, and then you helped me save my mother's life. Jezebel, I know that Jinx rescued you the night before you were to be hanged as a witch in England. Jinx helped Jade escape from a life of forced prostitution in San Francisco during the gold rush. She freed Jasmine from slavery on a cotton plantation near here. I know you're all good and kind and I need your help now."

Jinx uncrossed her arms and leaned forward. "What do you know about Bo?"

Ah, they had heard about Bo already. I knew he had done horrible things to many people after being turned. "Bo is related to Zane by marriage. Bo killed his parents and forcibly turned the remaining family members. He's an awful, horrible creature."

Arms uncrossed, expressions changed, the atmosphere grew less chilly.

"In the 21st century my name was Glory Templeton. In this century I'm Hope Hawthorne Dillon. After my husband, Zane, was turned, I returned from our home out West to my parents' home here. I know I'm going to die next week. I know the exact date." Despite all my efforts to remain brave, a moan managed to escape. "I don't know how, but I do know when."

"What do you want from us?" Jinx asked in a surprisingly kind voice. "I can turn you, if you like. Then nothing can harm you."

A shot of adrenaline surged through my body like lightning. That was something I had never considered asking. If I let her turn me into a vampire, I could remain with Zane forever. Why hadn't I thought of that before? My mind raced and my body trembled. Dr. Oshiro had said that I might not be able to return. Was this the answer? The teacup danced in its saucer, and I struggled to set it down before it spilled. "Um, well, that wasn't what I came to ask."

Jinx cocked her head. "What did you come to ask?"

I took a few deep breaths and it was a while before I could answer. Tears fought for freedom. My thoughts tumbled drunkenly. Finally, I said, "In the timeline I know, my husband goes through hell trying to adjust to the harsh realities of the vampiric life—especially to the loneliness. He eventually comes to love you, Jinx. You're good for him. I need to ask you to find him and help him adjust. And I need you to make him love you sooner than he originally did so he doesn't suffer as badly this time."

Surprise appeared in all the faces staring at me.

I dug in my pocket for a letter I had written and handed it to Jinx. "And this is vitally important. I need you to read this letter and follow the instructions when the time comes. It's all spelled out. It won't make any sense to you now, but it will in the 21st century. I need your word of honor that you'll do what it asks."

Jinx shook her head. "How can I make a promise like that when, as you say, it'll make no sense to me now?"

My eyes captured hers. "You have to trust me, just like I trust you."

Jinx's eyes narrowed and I could see her sharp mind working. Then she folded the letter and tucked it into the bodice of her dress, deep inside her cleavage. "You have my word." She shrugged and added, "It's the least I can do for a woman who just gave me her husband."

As I watched the letter disappear, anxiety filled me. "You can't lose that letter. It's a matter of life and death."

Her sudden smile was dazzling. "I'll stash it with my hidden treasure of pirated gold. It'll stay safe forever."

"So, you were Donna Diabla?"

She threw her head back and laughed. "You bet your sweet booty. Doubloons enough to last a thousand years. Longer as our investments mature."

I managed a weak smile.

Compassion washed over Jinx's face. "Do you want me to turn you?" she asked again.

I jumped to my feet and paced wildly. "Oh God, oh God, *yes* I want you to turn me. I don't know if I've ever wanted anything more. I love Zane more than life itself. But we have a son. I would have to leave him and I can't abandon him—I can't imagine how that would affect him."

Jinx shrugged. "I could turn him too."

I stopped and stared at her. "But he would remain six years old forever, wouldn't he?"

"Yes."

My mind fought the crazy thoughts. "That would be horrible to do to him. No. I couldn't. Absolutely not."

The simmering tears won and spilled out in shuddering sobs. "I have to die next Saturday. It's the right thing to do."

Jinx cocked her head again. "Will you be able to return to the future?"

"I...don't...know," I managed to spit out, the words angry, hot, and desperate. "But people there need me, and if there's even a ghost of a chance, I have to try." Despair and terror filled me and I froze, unable to move, unable to speak.

Jinx stood and slowly walked to me, then enfolded me in gentle embrace. Her lips moved to my ear and she whispered, "I have never met anyone as brave as you. It's an honor to help you any way I can."

* * *

I feel you in the shadows, reaching out to me with your heart—a song on the threshold of hearing.

Alone. Ashamed of what you've become.

Hell opens up. Claws reach out to claim you, but you fight to hold on.

Lifeforce fading. Fire in your veins—love is what remains.

* * *

Saturday arrived and I didn't know what to do, except live as normal a day as possible. The park was Jeremiah's favorite place and the horse kite his favorite toy, so after giving him a treat of ice cream, we walked hand-in-hand to the sprawling park. I drank in his beauty and sweetness, filling my heart with the nectar that was my son. Soon, if I was lucky and became Glory again instead of disappearing into whatever mysterious oblivion death might be, my memories would be all that was left of him.

Horses drew carriages around the park, filled with lovers enjoying a lazy, romantic afternoon. Some would stop in the shade of a sheltering tree, spread colorful blankets, and share picnic baskets. Oh, how I envied them.

As usual, I could sense Zane's presence somewhere nearby. I felt his eyes and the longing of his desperate heart. His superior eyesight allowed him to see us, but even though I carried opera glasses, I never even got a glimpse of him.

All day I had also sensed another hidden presence. I had a feeling Jinx was following me, probably to see if I was really going to die as I predicted, or if I was just the crazy woman rumormongers in Savannah accused me of being. I was certain she investigated me because Jinx was intelligent and cautious. The secrets she had to protect were huge.

I prayed to the God and angel who had abandoned me to allow me to face my end with courage and grace.

Taking my usual seat on the wooden park bench, I watched Jeremiah race out into the distance with his kite dancing high in the wind. Joy like sunshine made his face glow, and delighted giggles carried like music to my ears.

"So, here sits the bitch who ruined my life." Lucien's voice was behind me.

I stiffened but did not look around. "You did that to yourself, Monsieur."

He moved to sit next to me, the sour reek of alcohol poisoning the sweet summer air. He pointed a trembling finger toward Jeremiah. "I see the little devil your brief marriage spawned."

"You see devils in angels because you belong to Satan."

Lucien's harsh laugh sent a shiver of fear through me. "Love him, do you? Just like you loved that disgusting, dirty cowboy?"

"Yes."

"I should kill you for what you did to me."

So, is this how it happens? Do I run? Do I fight back? Can I escape what is fated? I haven't been able to change anything I came to change.

Lucien stood and moved to stand behind me. I held my breath, paralyzed with uncertainty.

"But I think I will kill you slowly. Suffering is so much more satisfying to witness."

I leaned over and picked up a substantial rock, determined to fight back. It was worth a try.

Then his stink faded and I wondered if he had retreated. I turned and saw him mounting a nearby carriage. He saluted me and a wicked cackle filled the air—I had heard a similar cackle before; it was the utterance of pure evil. He lifted the buggy whip and a series of sharp cracks sent the horse into frantic motion. Then a shriek of the wild erupted from Lucien's dark spirit.

Horror flooded me as I saw where he was headed. "No!" I jumped to my feet and tried to outrun the carriage that was descending on my son. "Run Jeremiah! Get out of the way!"

People stood and watched, everyone frozen in place by the incomprehensible event they were witnessing.

My feet pounded the earth, my eyes went blind with terror, my lungs ripped into a thousand pieces of sharp glass.

I could hear the horse panting from exertion and Lucien screeching with delight. That's when I saw Zane, a distant dot on the far edge of the park racing toward us. My eyes could not discern the face, but my heart knew. Then, out of the corner of my eye, I saw another figure practically flying from the horizon to the point of convergence. It was Jinx. All three of us raced to save an innocent child—two supernatural beings with heightened powers of sight and speed, and one mother fueled by the invincible power of a magical umbilical chord that forever bound two souls.

By seconds, my body was the first to connect with Jeremiah. I shoved him out of harm's way as the horse trampled me to the ground. The carriage rolled over me before tipping on its side, trapping Lucien beneath.

The pain was beyond bearing, and in the human body's innate wisdom, shock urgently set in to offer me mercy. I heard Jeremiah's screams and the beating of my heart as it pumped blood onto the earth. My frantic eyes scanned for my son and I saw him in Jinx's arms, her hands forcing his face away from the sight of me.

Out of nowhere, Jezebel, Jade, and Jasmine moved in to surround me and provide a shield from the eyes of curious bystanders.

Then, through the fading light of my vision, I looked up to see Zane kneeling over me, his face awash in tears.

"I know what Bo did," I whispered.

He tried to speak but couldn't.

"Drink my blood. I don't need it anymore."

Anguish radiated from his soul so pure.

I reached up and pulled his head down to me—not to my face, but to my gushing neck. "Please?" I begged. "I want to give you strength. You must endure."

Sobbing, he buried his face in my neck and drank.

I stood up and looked at Hope dead in Zane's arms. I watched Jade trying to urge him to leave before more people arrived. I saw my sobbing son clutched protectively in Jinx's arms. I noticed Lucien's broken neck and unseeing eyes. Then Sasha's compassionate face appeared.

"It's almost time to go now, Glory. Hope's job is done."

The world spun turbulently on its axis and I experienced one last time shift.

*　　*　　*

We make love high on a cliff under the sky bright with a pregnant moon and shooting stars. I cling to you with desperation, knowing our time is almost over. You whisper words to me I cannot hear over the pounding of my blood.

Except for one. You call me Glory.

A shooting star falls from the heavens and fills my body with light.

CHAPTER THIRTEEN

Kaia and I were sharing a fierce hug in my car at The Time Vortex—scared witless about what was about to happen—when we both gasped.

"What happened?" Kaia asked, pulling away from me.

"I remember everything," I said, as the events with Kaia's shooting, Wonderland, and the 1800s came crashing into my consciousness.

"Me too," Kaia said, glancing down at her chest.

I looked at my watch. Jinx must have done what I asked her to do.

I felt the vibration in my body before hearing the sound. I glanced out the window and saw a familiar helicopter descending.

"How could this be?" Kaia asked.

"It's one of those time travel anomaly thingys that I'm too simpleminded to understand," I said, swinging the car door open. "Quick, we've only got a few minutes before Erica and her guards come out of their rabbit hole."

We jumped out of the car, and keeping our heads low, raced to where the helicopter landed. The rotor blades kicked up a red storm of sand, but I held my breath and ran as fast as I could.

The Blackhawk HH-60M helicopter that last summer had helped me rescue a team of friendly scientists from certain death arrived just in time to save Kaia from hers. As Kaia and I climbed up through the open door, we were greeted by the spunky Army National Guard pilot named Cookie who had once offered to help me if I was ever again in trouble.

"Well, if it ain't Sweet-cheeks, just like Wild-child promised," Cookie said.

I glanced at a seat behind her and saw Jinx, who in any century was certainly a wild child. Laughing and crying at the same time, I couldn't manage to spit out more than a hoarse, "Get us out of here, Cookie."

"You got it. I live for adventure." Cookie wasted no time getting the helicopter airborne.

I glanced down and saw the boulder slide open and Erica emerge. She looked up at me with utter fury.

"Hah, you bitch," I whispered. "I changed the timeline. What are you and your time wizards going to do about that?" After my well-deserved moment of gloat, I climbed into a seat next to Jinx and threw my arms around her. "Thank you. Oh thank you more than you'll ever know."

"It's the least I could do for the woman who gave me her husband," Jinx whispered.

I pulled back and looked into her eyes. "Did you...were you able to help him adjust better this time?"

She nodded. "When I told him you had given us your blessing, he didn't wait over a hundred years to allow himself to love again."

The news was a two-edged sword to my heart.

"Can you tell me what's going on?" Kaia asked, then she glanced at Cookie as if to ask, *Is it okay to talk in front of her?*

"Yes," I said. "And Cookie is someone we can trust to keep our secrets."

"You betcha, Sweet-cheeks. I never told nobody about

nothing that happened last time. Hell, they wouldn't of believed me nohow."

"The Time Vortex was what we thought," I told Kaia. "The scientists sent me back to 1876 where I became Hope, married Zane, and had a baby. I tried to keep Zane safe from Bo, but couldn't. Before I died, I found Jinx and gave her a letter with Cookie's phone number and the time and coordinates to pick us up here. I hoped it would prevent everything from happening like it did."

Cookie turned around, looked at me, and whistled. "Hot diggity dog."

Jinx said, "Your letter told me to remind Cookie she offered to help you if you ever needed it again. She didn't hesitate for a second."

"My word counts for everything," Cookie said. "Even if it makes no sense to me at all. Hell, last time didn't either, but we stopped the pan-plague. What did we stop this time?"

"Kaia's death," I said.

Cookie looked at Kaia. "Cutie-pie here?"

I nodded. Tears of relief raced down my cheeks.

"But it didn't stop it from happening," Kaia said. "It all happened and we both remember."

"Time is a mysterious thing," Jinx said, flashing her beautiful, timeless smile.

"We got trouble." Cookie pointed to two black helicopters headed our way.

"If we remember everything that happened, it's possible that Erica will too," I said. "They aren't going to want us to get away."

"You think they'd actually shoot us down?" Kaia asked.

"After what I saw underground, I have no doubt." I

hadn't thought this through very well. In trying to save Kaia, and possibly myself, I may have doomed us all. Even Jinx could die if the crash were spectacular enough. I moaned. What had I been thinking?

"Can you outrun them?" Jinx asked Cookie.

"Not likely," she said.

The helicopter's radio screeched and then voices came over the air. "Unidentified Blackhawk helicopter flying one mile east of the Mogollon Rim, in the name of the US government, we order you to land immediately."

Cookie chuckled. "Well, now that's the most unofficial order I ever got. Who the hell are those yo-yos?"

"The shadow government," I said.

She turned to look at me with narrow eyes. "Oh, *them*."

I guess I wasn't the only one familiar with conspiracy theories that weren't so theoretical.

Cookie whistled again. "Well, if I put her down, I get the feeling we're doomed. If I keep her up, they'll likely put us down. I could shoot at 'em, but it is two against one. We're deep inside a pretty grim pickle jar here girls." She looked at me and I could see the fear. "You don't happen to have one of them angels around like who saved the day last time, do ya?"

"Oh yes. Yes, I just might." I closed my eyes and prayed as hard as I could.

A screech of static came over the radio. "Unidentified Blackhawk helicopter, I repeat...what the hell? Who the hell are you?" the voice on the radio asked.

"I'm an angel and I'm here to tell you that God wants you to stop chasing that helicopter," Sasha's voice said.

I grinned and pumped my fist in the air.

The pilot from the other helicopter came over the radio. "Ah, Bob, what was that I just heard?"

"Well, there's sort of this, um, see there's a girl here. And Steve, she's, well, she's real bright."

"Cut the crap, Bob, we've gotta job to do and—" The voice cut off suddenly, but a ferocious growl could be heard, and then a man yelled.

"Steve?" Bob asked.

"A bear. A big, white bear just...happened," Steve said.

Bob's voice came back sounding stronger. "Okay, this has got to be some sort of Project Blue Beam technology experiment, or something. They shoulda told us they'd be running tests. The bear ain't real, the girl ain't real."

"No, I'm very real," Sasha said.

"*Ow.*" Bob shrieked. "She bit me."

"I eat a lot of ice cream. Calcium builds strong teeth," Sasha said sweetly.

"She's getting brighter and brighter!" Bob shouted.

I glanced out the window and could see the brilliant light inside the other helicopter.

"I can get so bright you'll pass out," Sasha said. "Then you'll crash and die. God doesn't want you to die, but it's your choice."

"What's the bear doing?" Bob asked, his voice sounding strangled.

"Ah, well, he's sort of smiling at me," Steve said.

"Go ahead, Steve. Make my day," a growly voice said.

"Project Blue Beam?" Steve asked, his voice laced with hope.

"Oh, to *hell* with this," Bob said. "I'm turning back."

"Me too," Steve said. "And we'll never talk about this again."

"Roger that," Bob said. "Out."

I watched as the black helicopters turned around.

When we all had laughed ourselves silly, I thought to ask, "What's a Project Blue Beam?"

Cookie groaned. "Oh, Sweet-cheeks, that's top secret government stuff I've heard about that I don't *even* wanna talk about. It's a bit on the dark side...if you git my drift. Gotta bad feeling about what it might be used for someday."

After everything I had learned, nothing would surprise me.

"Where to now, girls?" Cookie asked.

"We should go to Moonstone," Kaia said. "Get Evan and Rory. Evan can drive us all to Union."

"I've already sent my gang ahead to Union to wait for us," Jinx said.

I nodded, and Kaia gave Cookie directions to her covenstead.

"My son?" I asked Jinx. "He was okay?"

"You sacrificed your life to save his and were his hero. His entire life was devoted to living up to your noble example and making you proud of him," Jinx said.

I thought about what the alternative would have been if I had accepted Jinx's offer and abandoned him instead. I choked back tears. "Zane?"

"He never got over loving Hope, and he never will."

Hope would never get over loving him either.

* * *

Cookie set the helicopter down in a clearing above the river. Members of the Moonstone coven raced up the hill to greet us.

Cookie turned off the engine, opened the doors, and we all climbed out.

Evan swept Kaia into his arms. "How could this be?" Rory pulled Evan away from Kaia and inserted herself between them. She laid her palm flat on Kaia's chest. "You died, but then everything changed."

"You don't remember that I stopped by to let you know I was dead?" Kaia asked.

Rory shook her head.

Kaia looked at me. "Jinx remembers, you remember, I remember. So those of us actively involved in the alternate timeline know what happened." She looked at Jinx. "Does Zane remember?"

Jinx nodded. "He remembers everything."

I considered the possibilities. "I wonder what, if anything, Erica and her people remember? It's possible that all they know is what Zane has told them."

"Zane?" Evan asked.

"Zane's been working with the New World Order scientists since 2007 when they found out his secret from a random blood test," I said.

"They enlisted his aid by stringing him along about possibly being able to find a cure for vampirism," Jinx said. "He's not involved in anything else they're doing."

Brennan arrived at the top of the hill. "Oh, girls. What an unexpected blessing that you survived. Did you find Glory's sister?"

"It's a long, *long* story." I grasped Cookie's hand. "Brennan, this is Cookie. She helped us last summer. She saved us again today."

Brennan gave her a slight bow of respect. "Please join us for some refreshment before you continue on your journey."

Cookie's face was strained and she looked tired. "I'd sure like to start with a visit to the little girl's room. Or a nice private bush."

Brennan laughed. "We've got indoor plumbing." She took charge of Cookie while the rest of us walked in a tight group behind them.

Sasha joined us and I greeted her with a high-five.

"That was epic work up there," I said to her.

"I'm learning," Sasha said.

"What now?" Evan asked.

"I wasn't able to vanquish Nyx," Kaia said. "Glory's mother and friend Jesse are still under her influence, but I think Carmela has freed herself."

I was encouraged. "Really?"

"There's a lot I haven't had time to tell you, but if everything that I remember actually happened, then yes," Kaia said. "And it's possible...." She faltered and looked at Rory with a guilt-plastered face.

"Spit it out, girl," Rory said.

"Micah might have had a change of heart."

Rory shook her head. "Thought we had a talk about feeling sorry for demons."

I was surprised to see Kaia's sheepishness. "Yeah, well, fail."

Rory grunted.

I found it amusing that a twelve-year-old girl held such power to intimidate Kaia and figured it had something to do with the intensity of the younger witch's self-confidence. Evan and I looked at each other over the tops of their heads and shared winks.

"Thank you for whatever you did to help Carmela," I told Kaia.

"I didn't do a thing. It was Jesse. He was going to rape

her. It revealed the evil side of Nyx and her followers that she had refused to acknowledge before."

I was horrified. "Jesse?"

"It was the evil in him," Kaia said. "He's pretty much totally surrendered to it."

"But why? He's always been such a great guy." *That's why I love him.*

"We all walk the line. Every single one of us teeters on the edge between good and evil. Every choice we make is a step in either direction and it really doesn't take a whole lot of missteps to fall." Kaia paused as she obviously struggled to put her thoughts into words. "Kids need someone stronger than they are to give them direction and to lean on until they discover their own strength. Mr. and Mrs. Hippie-Dick James have made both Jesse and his little sister raise themselves, providing only airy-fairy platitudes and zero grounding. Nyx gave Jesse power and he grasped onto it like a life-preserver thrown to a drowning man."

"What can I do?" I asked, then turned on Sasha in fury. "Why can't Jesse's guardian angel manifest to him and give him a strong arm to lean on?"

Sasha shook her head. "Revealing ourselves like we've done to you is almost never done. I don't know why it's permitted in some cases but not others."

"After what I saw, it might be too late anyway," Kaia said.

"No." I refused to accept that. "We need to get back to Union as soon as possible. Every minute counts."

Kaia nodded. "And what about your mother? What are you going to tell her about Erica?"

Confusion overwhelmed me. "Is it better to let Mom believe Erica's dead or tell her she's alive, but evil?"

"I don't know," Kaia said, "but we've got to get your mother out from under Nyx's influence before it's too late for her."

Rory cocked her head. "If Carmela left Nyx's fold after witnessing the evil there, perhaps we need to make sure your mom also sees the evil."

I glanced at my watch. "If we leave now we'll make it back in time for the Blood Mother River Festival."

"I'll ask the coven to pack us a lunch for the road," Kaia said. "Who's in?"

Within fifteen minutes, we had said our goodbyes to Cookie, turned Annie over to Brennan's care, and were all packed into Evan's BMW. Even Rory chose to join us. As I glanced around the car, I had a flashback to last summer when this same group of amazing souls had helped me save my mother. It was *déjà vu* all over again, except this time the stakes were much higher. Souls trumped bodies every time.

* * *

It would have been an extremely cramped ride except that Sasha didn't really seem to take up the space she appeared to. I guessed it was an angel thing.

"Why did you abandon me those last five years when I was Hope?" I asked her.

"I didn't. Not for one second."

"But—"

"It was a test of faith."

I waited, but Sasha didn't seem inclined to explain.

"However, there are some things you do need to know," Sasha said.

I looked at her and was surprised to see fire in her

eyes.

"If you had lied to Zane in order to keep him from going to help his sister, it would have ruined the trust he had in you. It would have eventually killed the love you two shared."

"But at least he wouldn't have been turned."

Her eyes flashed. "The fever that was at the Cheyenne ranch was typhoid. Everyone on that ranch and anyone who visited it would have died. Bo turning those people actually saved their lives."

I struggled to assimilate what she was telling me. "They might have died, but at least wouldn't be vampires."

"But maybe there really is a cure on the horizon. Maybe God can write straight with crooked lines. Maybe there's much more going on in this world than any of us can possibly understand."

I felt Jinx stir next me and looked at her. "Would you take a cure if there was one?"

Jinx shook her head. "I like what I am. I've done good things with what I am."

That was true. She had used her strength of body and character to save lives.

"You know Zane better now than I do. With everything that has changed, does he still want a cure?"

She nodded. "He's desperate for it."

I thought about Zane. If he were human, would I, Glory, want to be with him or was that the Hope in me? It appeared there might be some very difficult decisions ahead.

Kaia and I spent most of the drive to Union sharing what had happened to each of us in the alternate timelines, however every time I glanced at Rory I noticed that she was staring at me with a strange expression.

"What?" I finally asked her.

"I don't know. But there's something."

"What?" I repeated.

"Something's different with you. Different in a huge way. You've changed."

I nodded. "Of course I have."

Rory shook her head. "No, it's not the obvious. Give me time. I'll figure it out."

Her tone was ominous. I wasn't sure that I wanted to know what she seemed poised to uncover.

I dozed for a while and when we pulled up to my house, I awoke to an instant panic attack. In one reality I had been gone a day. In another reality, I had been gone almost seven years. It felt foreign to be here again—as if I were a long, lost stranger returning home. Sasha took my hand and helped me out of the car, an act of kindness my rubber legs appreciated.

I saw Dominic step off the porch of the guesthouse and noticed Hallie racing to greet me, but when my mother walked out the back door of our house, my heart did a somersault and I ran to her.

"Oh, you're back," she said right before I slammed into her and knocked away her breath. I wrapped her in my arms and clung to her like the last leaf on a winter tree.

She stiffened. "Are you okay?"

Please put your arms around me too. Hold me.

"I was just going over to join Nyx and her friends. We're all headed to the festival."

I held on tighter—the wild winter wind of my imagination was threatening to rip me from the tree branch and abandon me to the sky. *Please love me again.*

"I love you, Mom," I whispered.

Slowly, tentatively, my mother slipped her arms around me. "Why, I love you too." Her tone suggested surprise, as if she had forgotten until now.

Tears rose like spring sap returning the gift of life. "Please, Mom, I know you've got to go, but could we spend a few minutes together first?" *Please don't look at your watch with impatience.*

Her soft fingers brushed away my tears. "Sure, let's go inside."

A bud of hope burst open my heart. "Can we go up to the attic? I want to show you something."

She went rigid again and pulled her arm from around my shoulders. "Do we have to?"

Don't leave me again. "No, but it would mean a lot to me if we could."

She stood in the middle of the kitchen, fluttering like a bewildered butterfly.

"Tell you what, Mom. Just stay here. Fix us some tea. I'll run and get the thing I want to show you." I took off before she could respond. *Please be there when I get back.* I pounded up the attic stairs, grabbed Dad's sketchpad, and ran back to the kitchen—so relieved to find her making us a pot of tea.

I sat at the kitchen table, trying to catch my breath, and waited while she swilled out the white orchid teapot that had once belonged to her mother. She opened the cupboard above the stove and stared at the large variety of teas, her expression vacant.

"We haven't had jasmine tea in years," I said. "It used to be our Sunday morning ritual—just you and me. We'd have jasmine tea and blueberry scones and share girl talk."

A pained expression crossed her face. "I don't have any scones. Your dad used to bake those."

"Just the tea, Mom. The tea would be so perfect."

In slow motion, my mother reached for the purple tin of Twinings jasmine green tea leaves. She filled the ceramic tea ball half full, dropped it into the warmed pot, and drowned it in boiling water. She put the pot in the middle of the table on a tea cozy and finished setting the table with matching tea cups, a small creamer filled with milk, and the honey pot. I grabbed pretty cloth napkins and teaspoons and waited for her to sit down next to me.

The scent of jasmine flowers rising in the steam evoked wonderful memories for me. I hoped that maybe they would do the same for her.

After a few minutes, I poured us each a cup of tea. There was so much I wanted to say, but had no idea where to begin. I had been married, had a child, and died protecting that child. I was a woman now and shared a bond with her that was new and terribly intimate. I also felt I understood her better than I ever had before. How could I possibly let her know all that?

"I had a...dream, Mom." I stopped to evaluate the fact that I had just lied and struggled to fix it. "In this, um, dreamlike event, I dreamt I had a baby and the experience was very complex and deep. It gave me a hint of what it must be like for you—being a mother. Loving like only a mother could love."

She gave me a sharp look of assessment. "Are you trying to tell me you're pregnant?"

Oh, dear. I laughed. "No, nothing like that. I'm just trying to tell you that I'm becoming a woman and am gaining a better understanding of what that means. I feel closer to you than I ever have."

She crossed her arms and her eyes narrowed. "What sudden understanding have you gained?"

I struggled to put it in words. "When a baby grows inside you from a tiny little egg and shares your body for all those many months, there's a connection that's forever. The umbilical cord is never really cut—it can't be. It remains as love, and sacrifice, and pain. It endures forever, no matter what and is beyond magical. It is miraculous."

Mom cocked her head. "You got all that from a dream?"

"It was a very complicated dream," I said.

She took a sip of tea. "Dreams are mysterious things."

I grabbed Dad's sketchpad off the edge of the table and opened it to the piece of art he had titled, FIRST DATE. "I had my first date last week. It was with Dominic. I came to tell you, but you were really upset and so I didn't. Afterwards I found this in the attic. The weird thing is that this is exactly how I looked—the clothes I wore, and even the rose in my hair that scratched my face and made it bleed." I lifted up Dad's art so she could see it better. "How could this be, Mom?"

Mom reached out with trembling hands and took the sketchpad. "Oh, I remember this. Your dad said he had a—" she looked up at me with startled eyes. "A dream."

I smiled. "I guess dreams really are mysterious things."

She closed her eyes for a moment. "I remember last week. Yes, you were wearing these clothes." She looked at me. "Are you sure you hadn't seen this before that?"

"I only saw it by accident when Hallie knocked it to the floor right before Dominic picked me up. That day I didn't even know what to wear for the date—I called

Carmela for last minute advice. Then Dominic showed up with a rose, and when he slipped it behind my ear, it scratched me. Just like this shows."

"Your dad loved you so much, Glory. Maybe he had a precognitive event. Maybe that's what your baby dream was too. My scientific research, and personal experience, has convinced me that psychic phenomenon is real."

The air was thick with words unspoken about Dad, Erica, and Nyx.

I reached out and grasped her hand. "Mom, no matter what happens we have each other. We'll always have our love for each other."

Surprisingly, she squeezed my hand and said, "Yes, Glory, we'll always have that."

*   *   *

I was disappointed that Mom didn't ask me any details about my first date, or where I had been the past twenty-four hours, and why I had returned with so many houseguests. I was worried when she declined an invitation to go to the festival with me instead of Nyx, but I was grateful for what we had shared. It was progress.

After Mom headed over to Nyx's, I shared passionate, kiss-filled reunions with Dominic and Hallie. It seemed a tie as to who was most excited to see me. Hallie cornered me first.

"Hallie, I've only been gone a day," I said when her enthusiastic squealing, graceful midair pirouettes, and sloppy kisses failed to wind down.

Kaia managed to distract Hallie long enough to have a brief psychic conversation with her. "Well, to Hallelujah it seemed like seven years."

I was flabbergasted. "How could that be?"

"Animals live in an entirely different reality than we do," Kaia said. "I haven't quite figured it all out yet."

When Hallie eventually allowed me to slip into Dominic's arms, it was truly like I had finally come home. His body, breath, scent, voice—it was all so right. Totally right. We kissed until our friends drifted away from either boredom or disgust, then we simply stood holding each other.

"Do you know what happened?" I mustered the courage to ask.

"Sasha told me."

"Are you okay? I mean, I married another man and had his baby. Are you upset?" I was surprised to discover that our empathic connection had weakened since he became human, and I couldn't get a read on his emotions.

"I'm very proud of you—the way you lived and died was extraordinary."

I waited for more, but he had nothing else to say about it.

The Goth Girls arrived in their sleek black Jaguar XF, signaling it was time to head to Union High's Fall Equinox Celebration. There might not be a traditional offering of the fruits of the fall harvest planned for this event, but it was where everyone in town would gather today. Kaia and Rory were in psychic agreement that something significant would happen at the festival. Me? I didn't need to be psychic to know the conflict between good and evil was coming to a head. Nyx had lost Carmela, and I didn't believe she would stand for any more losses. I was relieved that so many of my own tried-and-true team of light warriors would be by my side. Once again we stood together to fight the good fight.

Hallie, Sasha, and I climbed into Dominic's truck and we led the way to the festival, followed by Kaia and Rory in Evan's BMW, and the Goth Girls in their very cool batmobile.

When we arrived at the school, it appeared as if the entire population of Union and even some surrounding towns had shown up. Overwhelmed by the crowd, we split up and headed in all different directions to scope out the situation. I ended up walking with Kaia.

It was late afternoon and the sun rode low in the sky, already dipping below the tree line of woods that backed to the river. A bonfire had been set alight in an officially sanctioned fire pit on the riverside greenway that bordered school property. Nearby was a booth for the local Wiccan coven, the SISTERS OF AVALON. The booth overflowed with young women who were drenched in black: black clothes, black hair, black makeup, black nail polish. A lot of silver occult jewelry glittered in the firelight, and happy smiles covered faces.

"At dusk we're going to burn the Wicker Man in the fire pit," one perky witch whose nametag identified her as RAVEN told us. "Be sure to join us. We call this sabbat Mabon, and we burn the Wicker Man to honor the sacrifice of the Green Man at harvest time."

I expected Kaia to roll her eyes with disgust at these novice witches, but she surprised me by greeting the coveners respectfully. "Bright blessings be on you and your coven."

Raven handed her a flier. "Please consider joining our group. We're always looking for new members."

Kaia folded the flier and tucked it into her pocket. "Thanks for the invitation, but I have my own. However, I'd advise you to screen new members carefully. There are some dark spirits about."

Raven looked startled, but then pointed to a familiar figure crouched in the bushes next to the booth. "Does that belong to one of them?"

Nyx's evil puppy glared at us with glowing eyes.

Kaia nodded. "Her name is Hex. Just be careful. And don't try to pet her. She's not a nice puppy."

Raven looked at Hex, who sneered, revealing a whole lot of needlelike teeth.

"Can you make it go away?" Raven asked.

Kaia stared at Hex for a few minutes, who responded by standing up with hackles raised.

"She doesn't seem open to friendly persuasion," Kaia said.

Raven's expression toward Kaia changed. "You're a real witch, aren't you?"

Kaia gave Raven a warm smile. "So are you; don't let naysayers tell you differently. Some of us are born to it, others just play with it—often getting themselves in deep trouble—and still others choose it as a serious path and become damn good witches. I sense you're on the right path. What you put into it is what you'll get out of it."

Raven handed Kaia a necklace from her displayed collection. Its medallion said, ALWAYS PRACTICE SAFE HEX. "This seems an appropriate gift today, given our unexpected company. Please do me the honor of accepting it."

Kaia slipped it on and thanked her. "May the High Gods protect and keep you."

"And you too," Raven said.

As we walked away, I asked Kaia, "So, you really think she's going to become a witch with real power and not just a *Charmed* wanna be?"

"From the natural power I sense in her, I have no doubt."

The next booth we came to had a sign that said, HIGAN: REMEMBRANCE OF THE DEAD. Kenny Nakamura and his grandparents, Takao and Mai, sat together beneath a large, colorful umbrella. When we approached, Kenny stood and introduced me to his family.

"This is Glory Templeton. She's the one who arranged for us to get food."

Takao and Mai rose from their seats and both offered me respectful bows.

Flustered, I bowed back.

"We are honored to finally meet you," Takao said. "Thank you for your kind and gracious assistance."

"It was my pleasure to help, sir." I gestured toward Kaia. "This is my friend, Kaia Moonstone."

The Nakamura family greeted her respectfully.

Kaia said, "*Hajimemashite.*"

I wasn't sure what she said, but the Nakmamuras gave her a couple of extra bows and seemed delighted.

After the formalities, Kenny explained the sign over their booth. "*Higan* is a Buddhist equinox celebration for remembering the dead. My grandparents made special incense they're giving away as gifts to anyone who wants it." He handed each of us a small tin foil packet. "Traditionally, you would leave the incense, along with flowers and food, at the graves of your loved ones."

I accepted it gratefully. "Oh, thank you. This is so kind. I plan to visit my father's grave soon and know he'll appreciate it." As Kenny had specifically said it was a gift, it wouldn't be proper for me to offer to pay for it. However, I searched my pockets for some kind of gift to offer the Nakamuras in return. All I had was a big handful of individually wrapped peppermint candies. Respectfully, I offered it to them.

Kaia, who had nothing to offer, walked to the water's edge, picked a lovely wildflower, and handed it to Mai. She smiled shyly, and tucked it behind her ear.

After more bows and additional Japanese words I didn't understand, we moved on to the next booth.

Professor Greenberg sat under a sign that said, SPOOKY ACTION AT A DISTANCE. He was giving away tee shirts imprinted with the slogan Albert Einstein had coined to describe quantum entanglement.

I picked one up and looked at it. "Have you had many takers, Professor?" I was still unsure of where he fit into the great big complicated puzzle that was my lives.

He smiled. "Some."

"I would think you'd have set up something more interesting for people to see on the subject," I said, a hint of challenge in my voice. "A science project about string theory, time travel vortexes, or even Schrodinger's cat who is both dead and alive at the same time." *Kinda like me.*

Without saying a word, he reached into his briefcase, removed an old, yellowed newspaper, and handed it to me. It was an edition of *The Rocky Mountain News* from 1875. Midway down the front page was a story about the wedding reception for local rancher Zane Dillon. The photograph of Zane and Hope had an unexpected face in the background—Sasha. Caught on film, her angelic countenance was bright and clear, even after all these many years.

Startled, I looked up into the professor's twinkling eyes.

"I'd most definitely call that spooky action at a

distance," he said.

Kaia looked over my shoulder and said, "Oops."

The professor leaned forward and whispered to us, "Not all scientists work for the New World Order. My team is doing everything we can to stop them from executing their plans. An FYI you need to tuck away for future reference."

I couldn't speak, but merely nodded. Handing him back his newspaper article, I snatched a tee shirt for posterity and moved on.

The next booth we came to, further up the hill, was Nyx's. Her banner said, GYPSY MEDIUM – TALKS TO THE DEAD. I noticed my mom sitting with Nyx, but she barely glanced in my direction. Micah stood nearby and studiously avoided making eye contact with either Kaia or me. A group of teenagers gathered around Nyx, presumably to have a chat with the dead.

Kaia and I walked past them all as quickly as possible.

The greenbelt rose up a gentle hill where it connected with the long bridge that crossed the river. The art class had its display at one end of the bridge, and the rest of the bridge belonged to the music and dance department. Instead of melodious instruments playing autumnal music, the musicians were all percussionists beating out wild, tribal rhythms. Dancers tap-danced, Irish-stepped, and stomped their way back and forth across the bridge. It was rousing, evoking the heartbeat of the earth and the churning blood of the river. I glanced down over the low railing at the water. The river responded to the pulsing invocation and surged in the most spectacular manner I had ever witnessed. The water was crimson with passion and howled with savagery as it slammed into and around boulders. White sheets of foam reached up like spindly fingers to grasp the offerings it expected, but would not receive.

At the far end of the bridge, I saw the Goth Girls dancing like the wild women they were. I also saw Dominic, Rory, and Evan using my camera to take photos of the art exhibit—Evan was planning to report on the event for CNN online. None of them saw me, but Hallie sensed my attention and raced across the bridge toward me. I smiled—that was my girl.

The largest of all the booths was located where the greenbelt connected with the bridge. Big and sprawling, run by a half-dozen people, it belonged to JAMES FAMILY SUNSHINE FARMS. They were giving away fresh produce, homemade cheese, and their own organic ice cream. A huge crowd of people surrounded it. I wasn't surprised to see an angel in line at the ice cream stand.

Sasha winked at me and giggled.

"Do you think angels have addiction anonymous groups?" I asked Kaia.

"Do you think angels get fat?" Kaia asked me.

We were both pondering those seriously cosmic questions when a disturbance broke out at the far end of the booth. Past the mass of people, I saw Sunshine, Cosmic, Jesse, Belle Starr, Principal Sanchez, and a uniformed policewoman. Blood smeared Jesse's sweatshirt and glistened in his hair. I pushed my way through the crowd toward them.

"I want that girl Tina Nancy Turner—she calls herself TNT—arrested for attempted murder!" Sunshine shouted. "She hit my son in the head with a baseball bat!"

"Where's a doctor?" Cosmic asked. "Is there a doctor in the crowd? We need a doctor now."

"Dammit Jesse, sit down." Sunshine gave him a rough

shove into a chair and then hovered over him protectively.

Her bizarre bipolar demonstration of maternal concern startled me.

Principal Sanchez wrung his hands, his fingers entwining themselves with each other like panic-stricken snakes. "Jesse refused to see a doctor. TNT and my daughter came to me immediately after the incident and said they were protecting themselves. They said Jesse was going to rape them."

"Rape?" Sunshine asked. "Utter and complete nonsense. Jesse would never rape anyone. I raised him to have respect for women." She hit him upside the head for emphasis.

I winced with him as she struck his wound and tried to move in closer, but Cosmic blocked my advance. However, even from a distance I could smell the sour cloud of wine that hovered around Sunshine. Jesse had told me she drank, but this was the first time I saw it affect her behavior.

Officer Jenkins gave Sunshine James a disproving look, adjusted her hat, and said, "I believe this is something we need to take downtown. The boy should see a doctor, the girls have to make formal statements, and I want to bring Child Protective Services into this. We also need to find out if there were any witnesses."

"I saw," Belle Starr said.

"What did you see?" Officer Jenkins asked.

"She didn't see anything," Sunshine said. "She's just a baby." Sunshine slapped Belle Starr's face. "Liar, liar, pants on fire."

Belle Starr's eyes reflected pain, but no tears fell from them. I wondered if her face was slapped often. I wondered if that was why she kissed other people's faces.

"Stop that," Micah said, elbowing his way to where the James family stood. "How dare you hit her for telling the truth."

Kaia backed away, disappearing into the crowd. "Belle Starr mustn't see me," I heard her whisper.

"Who the hell are you to tell us how to raise our family?" Cosmic asked Micah.

Micah knelt to try to embrace Belle Starr, but Jesse leapt from his chair, kicked him hard, and sent him flying.

Jesse pointed a trembling finger at Micah. "You hypocrite." His finger wagged at his parents. "You're all disgusting hypocrites." He snatched Belle Starr and threw her up over his shoulder. "I'll show you a sacrifice of fruits to the Blood Mother River that none of you will ever forget." He took off at a run, leaving a cackle in his wake.

I knew that cackle and in a flash understood exactly what he was going to do. "No! Stop him!" I took off after them. "Jinx! Sasha! Do something!"

Thrown over his shoulder like a sack of potatoes, Belle Starr looked up at me—her eyes wide with terror. Pathetically, she didn't utter a sound, she merely stuck her thumb in her mouth and sucked.

"Jesse!" I ran as fast as I once had in my effort to save another child. And like that time before, people stood frozen, unable to comprehend the horrible evil about to transpire. Even Officer Jenkins stood rooted in place, her face a mask of confusion.

My screams couldn't be heard above the cacophony of drums and dancers. The one eye I did manage to catch was Jinx's—perhaps it was her extraordinary sense of hearing or remarkable sight. However, like that time over a century earlier, she was too far away, even with her many superpowers.

I reached Jesse just as he raised Belle Starr high in the air and threw her over the railing into the raging waters below. He threw his head back and laughed, so he didn't see me shoot past him and jump in after her. A second later, another body hit the water behind me—I turned and saw it was Hallie. I only had time to utter a sorrowful moan before the water dragged all three of us under. When I came up the first time, I saw a flash of Micah hitting the water. He reached for Belle Starr, but the undertow sucked him down hard and fast.

I fought the Blood Mother's fierce arms and greedy fingers. I slammed into her rocky bones and inhaled her blood, thick with red silt dredged up from the river bottom. I reached out for Belle Starr when the river spit her up, only to have her swallowed again, replaced by a frantically paddling Hallie before the water pulled her away from me too. Micah's howls carried over the savage voice of the river as she fought to claim the sacrifices offered and he battled to reclaim them.

The afternoon light slipped into darkness while the violent undertow dragged us under repeatedly. I was relieved to see the Sisters of Avalon light the Wicker Man because the enormous burst of light thrown over the water's rough surface helped. But not enough. My head hit a rock way too hard, a wave of peacefulness washed over me, and I surrendered to the river. She had won.

* * *

I had died before, but this time it was different. I didn't see my dead body float downstream or see an otherworldly light. Instead, I stood on the water in the bright light of the Wicker Man as the witches' fire consumed Him. The image's face reflected the joy the God of the harvest experienced in fulfilling His purpose. In His annual journey of life, death, and rebirth, He died so others might live. My soul bowed to His courageous nature.

I felt a stirring by my side when Hallie pressed up against my right leg. I could actually hear her panting—well, it had been a mighty struggle. "You silly dog," I said. "Didn't you calculate the impossibility of the odds?" My words were cold, but my heart was as hot as the Wicker Man's. Oh, how I loved Hallie—I would have given my life ten times over in lieu of hers. Then a tiny hand grasped my left one and I squeezed it as hard as I could. However, I couldn't look down into Belle Starr's tragic eyes. "It'll be okay now," I said. "No one will ever hurt you again." I wondered just how much pain she had endured at the hands of those who had supposedly loved her. Anger consumed me.

"That's the anger that drove me insane," Micah said. He appeared between the Wicker Man and us.

"I can understand why," I said.

"The fact that you're still feeling such strong emotions tells me there's a spark of life left," Micah said. "You need to return to your body."

"I don't even know where it is."

"Follow me," he said.

"What about the girls?" I asked.

Micah didn't immediately answer.

"Tell me."

His voice was a monotone. "Hallelujah's silver energy cord is very faint. And I can't see Belle Starr's at all."

I finally looked down at the little girl at my side. There was fear in her eyes. *Emotion.* Good enough for me. "Get us there fast."

In the blink of an astral moment, the four of us were standing in a hidden cove downriver. My body, Belle Starr's body, and Hallie's body were on the ground side-by-side, each tended to by Goth Girls. I instantly understood they had dived into the river to save us, found us too late, and pulled us out of the water in this remote location. I looked at Micah, who stood on the edge of the clearing with Rebekah at his side. Then I noticed Sasha in the shadows.

"This wasn't supposed to happen," Sasha said.

That was the way of the battle between good and evil—an ever-shifting kaleidoscope of unforeseen surprises.

While the Goth Girls gave us each CPR, Rebekah said to Micah, "I've been granted permission to take you home. There'll be a reckoning, a need for atonement, but eventually you'll be restored to your former status."

"I'd like to wait," Micah said. "If Belle Starr...well, I'd like to take her into the light if her guardian will allow me to."

Rebekah cocked her head as if silently communing with others, then she nodded. "It would be a good thing for you to do."

"I'm so sorry for all I did—" Micah began.

"Not now," Rebekah said.

Jinx worked on me, Jezebel worked on Belle Starr, and Jade and Jasmine worked together on Hallie.

"I ain't never given a dog mouth-to-snout

resuscitation," Jasmine said. "No clue what the hell I'm doing."

Jasmine blew into Hallie's muzzle while Jade did compressions on her chest.

At my side, Hallie squealed, her butt wiggled, and soon her entire astral body was quivering. I followed her gaze and noticed a light emerging from the shadows next to Sasha. My father stepped out of it.

Hallie made a move to run for him, but Dad said, "Stay." He looked at me and said, "I'm not certain it's your time yet—either of you. But I wasn't going to let this opportunity pass to let you two know how much I love you and how proud I am. So proud."

If disembodied spirits could cry, I would be giving birth to an ocean. "Back at ya," was all I could manage to say.

"I think Glory took a breath," Jinx said, then delivered another blow to my chest. As she bent to fill my lungs with her breath again, I grew dizzy and everything started to fade.

"Hallie, stay with Belle Starr," I managed to command before I was sucked back into my body. I coughed and sputtered, and Jinx flipped me over onto to my side so I could vomit a copious amount of river water. I gasped and tried to take in air, but it was like trying to swallow a sword.

Jinx helped me sit up and pounded on my back until water escaped my lungs and air replaced it.

"I thought the dog took a breath, but something happened," Jade said.

"You need to call Hallelujah," Sasha said. "You told her to wait with the child."

I felt like an idiot. I had meant for her not to follow

Dad. "Hallie, come," I said, my voice a croak, but my intent strong.

A series of coughs, sneezes, snorts and gasps signaled Hallie's return.

Jade and Jasmine quickly took action to help Hallelujah clear her lungs.

"Why did the dog jump in after you?" Jade asked.

"To save me," I said. "She tends to do that."

By the light of the full moon, I could see well enough to know Belle Starr looked really, truly dead. I crawled closer to where Jezebel still resolutely performed the resuscitation dance. "Bring her back. Please bring her back," I begged.

Jezebel looked at me and shook her head. "She's dead, Glory."

Grief stabbed my heart and incoherent shrieks escaped me.

Despite her weakened condition, Hallie stumbled over to where I sat and collapsed in my lap, nuzzling me as best she could.

Trembling, Micah stepped forward. "I'll take her home."

I looked at him, I looked at Belle Starr, then I looked at Jinx. A conversation I had with her in another lifetime replayed in my mind. "Turn her, Jinx. She's not gone into the light yet. Turn her now."

"Wait a minute—" Micah started to say.

"Shut up. This doesn't concern you." I struggled to my knees. I thought about what Sasha had told me about the typhoid fever at the Cheyenne ranch, the possible future cure for vampirism, the horrible life this child had had, and how with life there was hope. "Turn her." My eyes bore into Jinx's soul and I saw the doubt transform into resolution.

Jinx went into action. "Girls, I'm going to need help. I need to give her a lot of blood."

I saw a flash of a razor blade, someone forced Belle Starr's mouth open, and another held her head tilted back. Jezebel made a deep cut into the main artery in Jinx's neck and blood pumped out fast—they directed it straight into Belle Starr's mouth, massaging her throat to help her swallow. It was a blur of action, but very deliberate action, and the results manifested quickly. Within minutes, Belle Starr gagged, choked, and spit up thick red river water mixed with blood. They gave her more blood, and soon Belle Starr was breathing and moaning.

When I heard the moans, fear inserted itself into my faith. "I didn't think about the horrors of being turned. Will she suffer?"

Jinx sat up and clamped a hand over her neck while her body quickly healed itself. "Through the centuries I've come up with herbs that make the transition easier. We'll start her on them right away." She nodded to Jasmine, who pulled a small liquid-filled vial out of her pocket. She opened up the tiny bottle and poured the contents into the child's mouth.

Miraculously, Belle Starr sat up and smiled at me. I threw my arms around her and hugged as tightly as I could.

Belle Starr sniffed me, disentangled herself, scooted over to Hallie, hugged and sniffed her, then moved to the Goth Girls, hugging and sniffing each of them as well. She crooked her finger at Micah and he bent down to receive her examination. Then she sat back on her heels and pursed her lips. "I have never felt more alive."

It was the most articulate thing I had ever heard her

say.

"I can hear things, and smell stuff, and see like never before." Belle Starr pointed to the Goth Girls. "I smell and know you drink blood." She gestured to Hallie. "I smell her fear because you drink blood." She reached out and touched Micah again. "Your smell is funny. It's like a flower that got burned." Then she returned her attention to me. "You smell sweet and I can hear that you have two heartbeats." She rearranged herself until she was lying flat on her stomach, pulled my tank top up, took my round belly in her hands and—as she was known to do with faces—smothered it with kisses. With a radiant smile, she looked up into my eyes and whispered, "In the beginning God created love and said, 'With love all things are possible.'"

CHAPTER FOURTEEN

"I saw my father again and all I could say was, 'back at ya.'" I was beside myself with myself. "What was I thinking?"

Dominic smiled at me. "You weren't thinking. He knew what you were feeling."

We slowly walked upriver to the festival site. Rory's psychic ability had led Dominic and Evan to the hidden cove. By the time they arrived, the vampires were gone, and Rebekah had taken Micah home. Sasha's healing abilities strengthened Hallie and me, although Hallie was playing it for all she was worth and insisted that Dominic carry her. Well, I decided as her contented sighs filled the night air, it had been a traumatic experience, and she did deserve special comforting.

"It was so courageous of you to risk your life to save the child," Evan said. "I'm sorry you failed."

I looked at Sasha. I hadn't decided how to handle the truth yet.

"Evan, I have to say something, but I need to know if you will keep it off the record. I realize you're officially here to cover the event and—"

"I've given this a lot of thought lately," he said, interrupting me. "I am first a warrior of light. Everything else I do...*everything*...is secondary to that. That is my sacred oath. I love a good news story, and I also want to tell the world the truths it needs to hear, but if you want me to maintain a confidence, I give you my word I will."

I believed him. "Belle Starr died, but the Goth Girls turned her into a vampire so she could live again."

There was a silent moment while everyone digested the news.

"I'll report that she died," Evan said. "It'll be presumed her body was lost in the river."

"A four-year-old with a gang of wild vampires? How's that going to work out?" Rory asked.

"Actually, Jinx told me she had always wanted to be a mother," I said. "She named her Joy. I think it'll be good for all of them—the gang will spoil her rotten." My voice fell to a whisper as I considered what the child needed most. "They'll love her."

I heard muffled voices yelling in the shadows.

"There are a lot of search parties out looking for you," Evan said.

We turned a bend in the river and I saw that the Wicker Man was still burning. It had been burning for so long—how could that be?

Rory read my mind. "Kaia and her new friend Raven have been feeding the fire with their magic. They wanted it to be a beacon."

"It worked," I said. I thought of magic and miracles. "It worked," I repeated.

As we approached the bridge all hell broke loose, and much of what happened next was a blur.

My mother alternated between hugging and kissing me, and raging about "how the Gypsy girl, Nyx, laughed when Jesse threw that poor child off the bridge." She finally saw the evil and it horrified her. Relief overwhelmed me.

Jesse, Nyx, and Hex had disappeared.

An EMS team tended to Sunshine and Cosmic James, who were both in shock. When I passed them, they wouldn't meet my eyes. I didn't expect them to thank me for risking my life for their daughter, but, well, I guess I hoped they would. It would prove to me that they weren't the heartless, self-involved creeps I had come to realize they were. I vowed that if a cure ever allowed Belle Starr to become human again, I would never let them retake custody of her. I'd go to court and prove they were unfit parents. I'd adopt her myself, if I could. I had enjoyed being a mother and was a pretty darn good one at that.

An emergency medical team insisted I submit to an exam, and when I climbed into the back of the ambulance, I thought of Belle Starr hearing two heartbeats. "Could you listen really hard to my heart with that stethoscope?" I asked the paramedic.

He nodded. "You having chest pains?"

I didn't know how to respond so explored the TV medical shows in my subconscious inventory. "I just want to be sure there's not a murmur, or something."

The stethoscope didn't reveal a second heartbeat, and after a thorough going-over the paramedics released me, but suggested I see my own doctor for a follow-up.

Before we left, I made them examine Hallie too. They released her after suggesting a follow-up visit to her vet.

Evan took a photograph of Hallie and me for the CNN website. I guess we were now heroes. "You'll inspire the nation," Evan assured us.

Hallie didn't seem impressed. Me? I just wanted to go home and sleep for a week.

Before we headed out, I wanted to go back to the place on the bridge where Jesse had thrown Belle Starr into the water. Mom, still too shaken to assimilate what had happened, sat down on a bench near the parking lot to wait. Hallie kept her company.

The rest of us stood together on the bridge, now quiet and vacant. Festive holiday lights along the railing, the full moon overhead, and the still raging flames of the Wicker Man lit up the night. From what I could see of the river, she had quieted down—apparently satisfied with sacrifices made. There had definitely been sacrifices tonight.

I thought of Belle Starr and Jesse, both losing their humanity in one fell swoop. Belle Starr would be a four-year-old vampire forever, unless science could intervene. And Jesse was now a demon. Whether that would be a forever thing, I couldn't possibly know. However, I did say a silent prayer for his soul.

After a few minutes, Sasha said, "I think that you really do need to see your own doctor as soon as possible to make sure nothing happened to Genesis during the drowning." Her gasp, and the now-familiar sound of her hand slapping her own mouth, told me she had blown it again.

In his best Sean Connery as James Bond voice, Dominic said, "Miss Moneypenny, whatever are we going to do with you?"

"Oh, no," Sasha mumbled, looking horrified.

Rory jumped up and down with excitement. "I knew it. I knew something big was different. You're pregnant."

I managed a nervous laugh. "I can't be. I'm a virgin."

Sasha groaned. "What is the last thing you remember after Hope died before you came back to your own body?"

It wasn't hard for me to remember. Indeed, it had been haunting me:

We make love high on a cliff under the sky bright with a pregnant moon and shooting stars. I cling to you with desperation, knowing our time is almost over. You whisper words to me I cannot hear over the pounding of my blood.
Except for one. You call me Glory.
A shooting star falls from the heavens and fills my body with light.

"It's Zane's?" I asked. "How could that be?"

"Vampires can't sire babies," Kaia said.

"Zane is the father," Sasha said.

I was stunned and confused. "So it's Zane's, but from when he was human? That would mean what I remember happened *when* exactly?"

There was a tap on my shoulder. Startled, I swung around, my fists clenched, poised to do battle with some new surprise.

It was Professor Greenberg. He held up a SPOOKY ACTION AT A DISTANCE tee shirt. "You dropped this earlier. Thought you might want it back."

I snatched it from his hands and glared at it, then at him. I had just had a bomb dropped on me and was interrupted by this inconsequential crap? Then I remembered what it was that Einstein labeled SPOOKY ACTION AT A DISTANCE. It was quantum entanglement. Well, Zane and I certainly appeared to be quantumly entangled all right.

"Einstein said, 'Time is a river.' As you discovered tonight, rivers hold many surprises." The professor reached out and touched my belly. "Don't let anyone know the truth of this baby's conception—especially your sister and the scientists she's affiliated with. Your child would become a lab experiment, and that's not what

Genesis is meant to be. She's meant to change the world." With that, he turned and disappeared into the shadows.

I remembered Belle Starr's final words to me.

In the beginning God created love and said, 'With love all things are possible.'

I fainted.

*   *   *

The full moon rode high in the sky. Beneath it stood two gangs facing each other—some showdowns happened at high noon, and for those of us with an otherworldly persuasion, we met at high midnight.

I faced Jesse, Hallelujah faced Hex, Professor Greenberg faced Erica, Jinx faced Bo, and Kaia faced two enemies: Nyx, and Galen—the witch hunter who had tried to kill her last summer. Each of us squared off with our respective enemies as bats flew overhead. In a classic Western movie, the bats would have been vultures waiting to devour the losers. And in a proper Western movie a final resolution would arrive in a hail of bullets. But in my horror movie, all that was aimed at the good guys were threats.

"Our time will come, my little spitfire demon hunter," Nyx said to Kaia.

"And so will ours, you wildcat witch," Galen said to Kaia. "I've been keeping the burning fires real hot for you."

"The New World Order will take over the planet," Erica told Professor Greenberg.

Hex hissed at Hallie and her needlelike teeth snapped viciously at the air.

"I always did want me a little vampire daughter," Bo said to Jinx.

"I'll sacrifice your baby too," Jesse said to me.

My own screams woke me up.

Dominic and Hallelujah sat next to me on my bed, and both instantly moved to offer comfort.

"Hush," Dominic said, pulling me up into his arms. Hallie stuck her cold, wet nose in my face and gave me a gentle kiss.

I looked out my window. It was morning.

"How long?" I managed to ask.

"You fainted on the bridge last night. We brought you home, your mother undressed and put you to bed, and you've been asleep since. You've been through a lot."

Dominic fluffed up my pillows, rearranging them so I could lean back in a sitting position. He offered me a glass of water, which I wasted no time emptying. After I handed it back to him, my hand flew to my belly.

"Genesis is a pretty name for a girl," I said. "Wish I'd thought of it."

Dominic chuckled. "Well, actually, you did. It's just that Sasha is the best bean-spilling angel in the known universe."

I searched his face. "How do you feel about this? I mean, how does it affect us?"

He reached out and caressed my cheek. "As far as I'm concerned, it doesn't change a thing. However, there still is the fact of Zane to consider. You have to make some important decisions."

I shrugged. "I doubt if I'll ever see Zane again."

"Think again. You've got company waiting for you downstairs."

My heart stopped for the second time in twenty-four

hours.

Dominic kissed my forehead. "Get dressed and go down when you're ready. I'll be outside if you need me." He looked at Hallie. "Hallelujah has never liked vampires, so I'll take her."

"Does Zane know about Genesis?" I asked.

"No. And given who else is downstairs, I'd think long and hard before telling him."

I came to some quick conclusions. "No, stay with me—both of you. Vampires can hear heartbeats. I want you two close to help camouflage Genesis."

Dominic looked relieved. "I was hoping you'd want me to stay."

"How do I handle this, Nicky?"

"Carefully."

* * *

I went into the bathroom, washed up, pulled a brush through my hair, swiped on some lip gloss, and changed into jeans and Professor Greenberg's tee shirt—it seemed an appropriate choice. I never wore perfume but realized that everything I could do to overwhelm Zane's senses would be wise, so spritzed myself with Mom's Chanel No.5.

Taking Dominic's hand and calling for Hallie to follow, we slowly walked downstairs together.

Everyone was in the living room: my mother, Zane, and the third person my intuition had told me to expect—Erica. I stopped at the foot of the stairs and stared at Zane. Tactfully, Dominic withdrew his hand from mine but stood protectively close. Hallie leaned up against Dominic. My heart beat so fast and hard it hurt.

Upon seeing me, Zane jumped from his chair to his feet and whipped off his cowboy hat, holding it in front of his chest like a shield. I understood the unconscious gesture and wished I had something to use as protection for my own heart. His smile was bright like lightning and it created an intense explosion of thunder in me that manifested as a downpour of tears. I put my hand over my mouth to try to quell the sobs, but it was hopeless. All the love, all the loss, all the longing and passion poured out of me so powerfully I wasn't sure if I could stand.

Concern crossed Zane's face. "You okay, darlin'? What can I do?"

Oh, his voice. My knees went rubber. I looked for the closest chair and made a dash for it. I held up my hand to him in a classic gesture of "stay back" and accepted a handful of Kleenex from Dominic, who then sat on the arm of my easy chair. Hallie took a position at my feet.

Zane awkwardly shifted from one foot to the other, looked at Dominic and Hallie, and sat back down. "I'm sorry I've upset you."

I cleared my throat and managed to say, "It's so amazingly good to see you again...I'm just totally overwhelmed." *Oh God, how I still love you. I didn't think I'd still love you this much.*

"Glory, your sister's alive," Mom said. "Why didn't you tell me you knew?" She was sitting on the couch with Erica, trembling with unbridled excitement.

Startled, I whipped around to face them. *She knows I knew. What's going on here?*

Erica's smile was cold. How was I supposed to handle this? I struggled to steal my mind away from my heart so I could think. What had she already told Mom? What did she, herself, know? I was flying blind here and decided to wing it.

"I just found out she was alive, Mom. I hadn't had time to tell you yet."

"Well, Erica's told me everything."

Everything? I doubted that.

"No wonder you were being so cagey about your special 'becoming a mother dream,'" Mom said. "I understand now. You were dealing with top-secret information. I'm so glad Erica decided to bring me in on the project so we can get it out in the open now." She pointed to Dominic. "But shouldn't he leave while we talk about this?"

Erica's eyes narrowed. "Zane has informed us that Dominic is Glory's guardian angel, so I presume he already knows all there is to know."

My mom's hand fluttered to her mouth. "Oh, angels too? Vampires and angels both? Oh, there is so much for me to learn." She giggled. She actually giggled.

"What has Erica told you, Mom? Please tell me what you know so that we can indeed get everything out in the open now."

Mom said, "After Erica was kidnapped she somehow ended up in the hands of a group of scientists working in an underground facility in Arizona, and—"

I interrupted. "Excuse me? It was these scientists who kidnapped you, Erica?" Of course I knew the truth, but was curious how she was playing it.

"I was so young I don't remember who kidnapped me," Erica said. "All I know is that I was abandoned in the desert and was nearly dead when these scientists found me and took me in. I imagine they decided to keep me rather than turn me into the authorities because of the top-secret nature of Wonderland. You've been there. You know what it is. If word leaked out, well...."

Ah, very clever. Now Mom would never know that it was the scientists themselves who kidnapped Erica.

"When you and your psychic friend came looking for me, I was able to put the pieces of my life puzzle back together again and so came looking for my family." She took Mom's hand and gave it an affectionate squeeze.

Mom blurted out, "Erica told me about Dr. Oshiro's time travel experiments, and how you agreed to be sent back to see if you could save your friend, Zane, from being turned into a vampire. She told me how you had failed, but that you had married Zane in that alternate reality and had a baby, and how you died so bravely protecting your child." She gave me a tender look. "I am so proud of you for that, Glory. You'll never know how much."

I shook my head in disbelief. "And none of this surprises you?"

"I'm a scientist and have been involved in classified work my entire career. I know there are other projects. I even heard rumors about Wonderland, but had no proof until now."

"Mother's a brilliant virologist," Erica said. "We've asked her to join our project and help us try to find a cure for vampirism. If anyone can do it, Mother certainly could."

I was speechless.

"And the time travel experiments appeal to me too," Mom said. "Maybe we can figure out a way to go back and prevent the pan-plague from happening in the first place. Oh, that would be so amazing. The guilt I feel...." Her voice drifted off miserably. After a few minutes of uncomfortable silence, she said, "And if we could do that, then your father would still be alive. Think about it."

It was all becoming clear. Should I tell her that Scorpio Pharmaceuticals was part of the Wonderland project and these same scientists had been behind the engineering of the pan-plague in the first place? Would she believe me? I had to give it a try. "Mom—"

"Excuse me, Glory, but may I have a private word with you?" Erica asked.

"After I tell Mom—"

"It would be prudent for us to talk *now*." Erica stood. "Let's go fix some refreshments for everyone."

Her expression told me that I needed to listen to her.

I stormed into the kitchen on her heels and slammed the door behind us. "What?" I demanded.

Erica rummaged about in the refrigerator, pulled out a pitcher of iced tea, and proceeded to set a tray with glasses, sugar, and lemon slices. "If you tell Mother about the Scorpio connection to Wonderland, or the fact that in one timeline I shot Kaia, we'll kill her. It's up to you, Glory. On the other hand, maybe she will come up with a cure for your beloved Zane's disease. What's the harm in her trying?" She said it all so matter-of-factly that I had no clue how to respond.

I looked into her soulless eyes and knew that she wouldn't hesitate for a second to murder our mother.

She picked up the tray and headed for the door. "Will you be a dear and open that?"

I opened it.

As she passed by me, she whispered, "And I also think you're holding some secrets related to the time travel experiment. Just a feeling I have. But you can believe me when I say that we will find out what they are."

I couldn't let her find out about Genesis. The results

would be catastrophic. What was I going to do?

She winked at me. "Isn't it going to be fun to be a family again?"

"Did Erica tell you the plan?" Mom asked me as soon as I sat back down.

Unable to speak, I shook my head.

She handed me a glass of tea. "I'm going to move to Wonderland immediately and begin work. You're almost eighteen and can take care of yourself. And you've got your guardian angel here—and I expect his family are angels too?—to help take care of you. There is significant money in the bank account for you to support yourself with while getting your career launched after graduation. I won't be in touch often, because of security protocols, but you'll be the first to know when I have a cure for your husband here and—"

"Zane was Hope's husband, not mine," I managed to say.

Zane cleared his throat. "I totally understand that, darlin'. If they find a cure for me I'll be back to try to win your heart in the here and now." He looked at Dominic. "In the meantime, I'd like to ask Dominic here to take care of you and make you happy. I know you love him too, and if he's the one you ultimately choose, I'll respect that. But if I am cured, I would be so honored to have you as my wife once again."

My tears returned and this time they wouldn't stop. The enormity of my sorrow, my longing, and my fear was beyond belief. I dropped my glass of iced tea on the floor and ran blindly from the house. I found Rory sitting behind the big old cottonwood tree.

I stumbled to the ground next to her. "What do you see for the future?" I managed to ask.

"The truth?"

"The truth."

"I see the dark powers who have killed bodies and stolen souls are now planning to undermine mankind's spirit. I see the religions of man imploding. The witch hunters are coming back in full force. The evil vampires are going to gain a leg up. Demons are going to have a field day. I see a powerful coven of evil witches. There are a lot of mighty big challenges ahead, sweetie."

"Do you see any hope?"

"I see you, Genesis, and all of us who fight the good fight making a difference."

"Will it be enough of a difference?"

"Only time will tell."

EPILOGUE

KAIA

Kaia was giving Annie a hunting lesson, but the teenage mountain lion insisted on being, well, teenagey. "Will you please stop being so rebellious? You don't know it all yet." Annie's thoughts were smug and decidedly know-it-all. Frustrated, Kaia plopped down on a boulder and absently twisted her wedding ring. "I miss Evan and staying behind to train you would be much more worthwhile if you would bloody well learn your lessons."

Annie proceeded to play with the delightful new toy she had found—a field mouse who loudly resented being a squeaky toy.

"Squeak!" said the mouse.

"Purrrrrr," said Annie.

The air pressure changed, a shimmer rode the wind, and someone sat down next to Kaia. She glanced up to see Davina.

"Oh." Kaia jumped to her feet so she could bow respectfully to the unexpected guest from the Caretakers.

Davina tossed her long, curly hair, grasped Kaia's arm and pulled her back down to the boulder. "Forget the royalty treatment. We're all in this together."

Kaia stared wide-eyed and open-mouthed at Davina. They had met before, but Kaia was always awestruck by her presence.

"To what do I owe the honor of your visit?" Kaia asked, her voice breathless and uncertain.

Davina pointed to Annie. "She's lost respect for you because your love for her has made you soft. There is sentimental love and there's serious love. You've gotten all soppy with her."

Kaia had no clue how to respond, so she did the wise thing and said nothing.

Davina stood and walked to Annie, who looked up and immediately stopped purring. The Caretaker glared at her. "You will never play with your food again. You will hunt only to eat and to feed your young. You will kill swiftly and with compassion. You will never, ever harm a human or a domestic pet unless you are protecting yourself or your young. And you will be grateful for what the earth provides you. Do you understand me?"

Annie's eyes widened, she blinked a couple times, looked away, and lowered her head.

Kaia almost burst out laughing as she sensed Annie try to figure out how to display humility.

Davina pointed at the cowering mouse. "Go home to your family. My blessings upon you for a long life free from becoming someone's lunch."

"Squeak!" the mouse said before scampering off.

Kaia had never felt such simple gratitude from a creature before as that mouse experienced at Davina's unexpected act of mercy.

Davina turned on her heel—hair and long, flowing gown both swirling in the air with great dramatic flourish—and sat back down next to Kaia. "There. Now you have no excuse not to be at your husband's side. Annie is ready to face the world without you."

"Thank you?" Kaia said. It came out as a question. Was this really why a Caretaker of the World had made a rare appearance?

"Your courage and willingness to sacrifice your life in the performance of your duty continues to impress us," Davina said.

"I have vowed to serve the light." Kaia's voice was calm, but inside she was jumping up and down, doing cartwheels, and generally beside herself with excitement.

"You promised your husband you would move into his home. We know you don't want to live in the city, but what's the real reason you're not yet honoring that commitment?"

Always tell the truth, Kaia reminded herself. "Fear," she admitted.

Davina's fire-filled eyes met Kaia's shame-filled ones. The Caretaker's arm swept the glorious beauty that surrounded them. "This has been a nurturing womb that helped make you what you are. You've drawn your courage from the known, the solid, and the undeniably true. However, it's time to be like Annie and strike out on your own."

Davina was right, of course, and Kaia was grateful for the reminder. She looked down at her feet while trying to think of a humble, articulate response. When she looked up, Davina was gone.

Kaia looked at Annie. "Well, she certainly told us, didn't she?"

Annie whined.

"Come on then. Time for me to pack. I'll let Brennan handle your transition back into the wild. Whole new worlds await us both."

* * *

GLORY

Hallie and I visited Dad's grave. The *Higan* incense I had received from the Nakamura family somehow survived drowning, and I opened the packet and sprinkled the aromatic powder on the ground in front of his gravestone. I also laid down a rose and a freshly baked blueberry scone—I had found all of Dad's recipes and was teaching myself to cook. I was now head of the household and wanted my daughter to eat well.

Hallie and I settled down together to talk to him.

"I'm sorry I said 'back at ya' when I could have said, well, a bunch of other more important things." I patted my growing belly. "You're going to be a grandfather to a girl named Genesis. I understand she has a special destiny."

"Like you," a familiar woman's voice said.

I looked up to see Davina. Unlike the last time I saw her, today she was dressed casually in jeans, a Saints baseball team cap, and a tee shirt. The shirt had a picture of Albert Einstein on it, along with his famous quotation, ONLY A LIFE LIVED FOR OTHERS IS A LIFE WORTHWHILE.

The first time we met was right here by my father's grave when she asked me to become a warrior of light in the battle of good versus evil. When I accepted, it was on the condition that Hallelujah be left out of it. "Hallie's still in the thick of things. I thought she wasn't part of the bargain," I said in greeting.

"Hallelujah isn't under any obligation to us, but she continues to make her choices. It's an issue of free will."

"Stupid brave dog almost died," I grumbled.

"She's an amazing soul."

"Did I do the right thing by asking Jinx to turn Belle Starr?" I was horribly conflicted about what I had done.

"We never know if our decisions are the correct ones—we only do the best we can. Time will tell."

"Yeah, time and I have some seriously unresolved issues, let me tell you." I was feeling mighty grumpy.

She laughed. "I like you, Glory. I really do."

I looked at her. "I'm so scared for my mom. Can you do anything to help protect her?"

Davina didn't respond. I hadn't really expected her to.

I sighed. "I realize things are going to be bad, and you can't tell me anything useful, so why are you here?" I hoped my peevishness was coming through loud and clear.

"I came to say that courage is more contagious than any virus ever unleashed upon mankind. Use that knowledge to help others face what is coming."

"Can you tell me anything about my baby?"

"Genesis will be the salvation of the future." With those words spoken, Davina disappeared.

I knelt on Mother Earth in that graveyard with Hallie, Genesis, and my dad. I thought about entangled lives, the mystery of Genesis's conception, the past, and the future.

It seemed to me that time wasn't, as Einstein said, a river. It seemed to me that time was alive—a creature with dreams and hopes and plans. I had danced in the arms of time in a way no one else in this world ever before had. I had changed time in a way no one in this world had ever been able to do. Time and I were definitely on intimate terms. And in that moment I could sense the future, and the future was holding its breath.

THE LEGEND OF GLORY

Glory: The first novel in the series introduces Glory and her courageous band of rebels as they race time in order to save billions of lives from a deadly pandemic plague.

Genesis, the thrilling conclusion to *The Legend of Glory* trilogy is forthcoming. Glory, Hallelujah, Dominic, and Sasha band together to protect baby Genesis from evil forces determined to destroy her. Meanwhile, Kaia pursues her quest to slay the demoness Nyx, despite the terrifying return of witch hunters and a mysterious coven of evil witches who try to claim Kaia as one of their own. Finally, the Goth Girls must do battle with evil vampire Bo, who has set his sights on the youngest and most innocent vampire of them all—Joy.

Both *Glory* and *Pretty Sacrifices* are available as audio books, narrated by talented New York actor Becca Ballenger. Becca's tour de force makes the novels come alive.

A prominent Hollywood producer has contracted with Devin O'Branagan to shop *The Legend of Glory* trilogy as a possible TV or film project.

Visit Devin's website at **www.DevinWrites.com** and sign up for her eNewsletter so you will be notified as soon as *Genesis* is released!

ALWAYS PRACTICE SAFE HEX

Devin's online gift shop has a custom-made necklace that reminds us all to Always Practice Safe Hex!

It may be found on the Gothic Jewelry page of her gift shop at **www.DevinsGiftShop.com**

While there, explore the other custom-made Gothic jewelry designed with the Goth Girls and Hope in mind.

AUTHOR'S NOTE
HALLELUJAH, MILTON, & HEX

Hallelujah the Australian Shepherd was inspired by my own late Aussie, Jazz, who was utterly fearless. However, Jazz was a brown-eyed girl and the character of Hallie has blue eyes, so when I was looking for a photograph to represent the character, I chose a gorgeous Aussie named Muse, who belongs to Shelly Hollen-Wood.

* * *

The Border Collie Milton is based on a real Border Collie named Milton Aldridge. Milton is just such a delightful real-life character that I wanted to immortalize him in one of my novels. Thank you, Molly Aldridge, for allowing me to include your very cool dog in *Pretty Sacrifices*!

* * *

I once held an infamous "Wicked Dog Contest," asking fans to submit photos of their scary-looking dogs. A red merle Australian Shepherd puppy named Cuddy won that contest and makes her evil debut in *Pretty Sacrifices*. Gaspar Toro and Alejandra Reyes own Cuddy, and she lives with them in Chile.

(I understand that she is really quite sweet...)

* * *

To see photos of these wonderful dogs please visit:

www.GloryLegend.com

AN EXCERPT FROM GLORY

My dad was dying and I didn't know what to do.

As I stood at the kitchen sink filling a pan with cold water, I looked out the window at the flurries of white fluff dancing in the wind. Cottonwood trees were shedding seeds of new life on our farm, while seeds of death swirled around the planet taking root and growing in every human host they could claim. And now the black seeds of the pandemic-plague had found fertile ground in Dad.

This morning at breakfast, he had been fine. He put on his chef's hat and baked tasty cinnamon rolls we shared with Mom before she left for work. He talked about the new painting he was working on—a portrait of our Australian Shepherd Hallie. He joked about what an uncooperative model she was, and then concerned his teasing might have hurt her feelings, fed her a warm, frosted roll as a peace offering.

Uncharacteristically, Mom didn't fuss over Hallie being fed from the table. Lately she had been moody and distant. I understood that her failure to create a successful vaccine for the pan-plague weighed heavily on her, but her gloominess made me so uncomfortable that I was relieved when she finally left.

Now I would give anything if she would only come home.

I fumbled in the pocket of my jeans, pulled out my cell phone, and hit redial for the umpteenth time. Mom's voice mail picked up again.

This is Dr. Kate Templeton of Scorpio Pharmaceuticals International. Please leave a message and I'll respond as promptly as possible.

Where was she? Why didn't she return my calls? Had she become sick too? The ambulance had refused to come for Dad—the 911 operator said the hospitals were overrun with pan-plague victims and had closed their doors. Mom was a scientist and would know what to do. I needed help. I couldn't handle this alone.

I didn't leave another message. I slipped the phone back into my pocket and returned to Dad's bedside with the water and a clean washcloth.

I dipped the cloth and wrung it out, then placed it on his forehead. He groaned and Hallie jumped onto the bed. She nosed him with worry and he managed a weak smile. "Glory, promise me you'll take care of Hallie. When I'm gone, she'll keep you safe."

Fear tried to steal my voice. "You're not going anywhere."

He became agitated. "Promise me."

"I promise I'll take care of Hallie."

"I'm not going to make it, honey. You need to know how much I love you."

I grabbed his hand and squeezed. "Please don't leave me, Dad." I couldn't imagine a world without him in it. If he died, how would I survive without his love?

He struggled to say something else, sighed, and then fell asleep so abruptly that—for a horrified moment—I thought he was gone. After what seemed like an eternity, I heard his raspy breath return and I, too, began to breathe again.

Hallie's sky-blue eyes met mine and she stretched out alongside him. Earlier, she had been the one who let me know that Dad was in trouble.

A well-trained farm dog, Hallie never barked unless she had good reason. I was fixing lunch when I heard her frantic alarm and raced outside to find her standing over Dad, who lay on his back floundering in a sea of cotton. His face was red as blood, his eyes wild as fire.

"Cotton to spin," he said, looking at a handful of the fluffy seeds. "Spinning, spinning. 'We come spinning out of nothingness, scattering stars like dust.'" It was a quote from his favorite poet, Rumi, and I gasped as I realized he was delirious with fever.

I knelt and pushed Hallie out of the way. "No, no, no." This couldn't be happening. Not Dad. My hand flew to his face and recoiled from its heat. I managed to rein in his eyes and held them. "I'll help you stand. We need to go inside."

"Kate? Oh you're so beautiful. Marry me."

Dad recently told me that I looked just like Mom did at seventeen.

I forced a smile and imagined myself as her. "Let's go inside and talk about it, Mark. You're going to have to convince me that I should marry a dreamer; I'm a very practical woman, you know." I took his arms, pulled him into a sitting position, and then supported him as he struggled to his feet.

"My dear Kate, 'in dreams and in love there are no impossibilities.'"

The only other time I ever heard him quote two epic poets back-to-back was one New Year's Eve when he had too much champagne. Now, it was as if he had drunk an entire bottle of it. He lurched and stumbled toward the house, his arm thrown around my shoulders. Hallie nipped at his legs, doing her best to herd him along.

We got him into bed just as he passed out.

Cases of the pandemic-plague manifested as sudden fever and delirium accompanied by dizziness and fainting. Severe tremors and excruciating pain followed. Next came moments of clarity sandwiched between slices of unconsciousness. Then the victim died. The span of time from first symptoms to final breath was brief.

I glanced at my watch. It had already been three hours. As I sat on the edge of the bed holding Dad's hand, his heat began to overwhelm me. I wrung out the washcloth and momentarily placed it on my own hot forehead. The summer air was oppressive and I stood to open the window, but halfway there the floor began to rise and fall beneath me. Confused, I looked around the room and saw that everything was spinning. Spinning, spinning. Claws of terror ripped into my stomach as I realized I had the virus too.

Somehow, through my disorientation, I managed to make it back to the bed and crawl in next to Dad and Hallie.

My thoughts were disjointed. *Couldn't be happening. So unfair. Too many lives cut short. This disease, death's servant, was an evil monster.*

If tears could slay the beast, then the torrent of mine would have blasted him out of existence.

I cried myself into a restless sleep filled with feverish dreams. In a particularly vivid one, Hallie appeared to me as a beautiful blue-eyed cowgirl. She threw her hands to her hips, gave me a disgusted look, and said, "Don't be such a wimp, Glory. It's time to cowboy up."

"Easy for a herding dog to say," my dreamself replied.

The field of dry grass where we stood erupted in flames and a howling wind whipped it into a firestorm.

My shrieks joined those of the wind.

www.GloryLegend.com

ACKNOWLEDGMENTS

Carol Cail is my angel. Her editing, support, and patience with me during the writing of this novel was extraordinary, and I am deeply grateful.

I must also thank my amazing beta readers: Julie Campbell, Jurlia DeKesthler, Krista Walsh, Diane Wallace, and Nicole Riviezzo.

For research about all things ranch-related, I always turn to Terry Martin.

My highly intelligent, wildly creative, and incredibly sexy writers' group is amazing. The members of my online writers' forum contributed a great deal to this project. For generously offering editorial advice and encouragement, I especially want to thank Sue Campbell, Sue Wentz, Tammy Crosby, and Sally A. Wolf.

Then there are my oh-so-special Facebook friends who share so much with me. I couldn't do what I do without you guys! Join us on Facebook at:

www.facebook.com/devin.obranagan

ABOUT THE AUTHOR

Bestselling author Devin O'Branagan writes novels about uncommon heroes. Her genres include young adult urban fantasy, paranormal romance, paranormal thrillers, and romantic comedy. Her books have been published by Simon & Schuster's Pocket Books, German publisher Heyne Verlag, Turkish publisher Dogan Egmont, and indie press Cornucopia Creations. They are available in paperback, eBook, and audio formats.

Visit her website at **www.DevinWrites.com**

Made in the USA
Columbia, SC
13 June 2017